MW01658380

## *"What kind of game are you playing, Joe?"*

"I'm not playing any game, Willie. And I'm not trying to do your job."

Willie looked at him, and Joe felt she was trying to read something in his face.

"Why did you come back? What are you trying to prove by taking over a two-bit newspaper in a two-bit town?"

She was so close he could feel her breath against his cheek, and suddenly he longed to feel her skin against his lips. He swallowed hard and took a deep breath.

"I told you. I've come home."

"Men like you don't come home, Joe." She looked at him as if daring him to contradict her.

"This one has." He brought his hand up and cupped it next to her cheek. "And whether you like it or not, I'm here to stay."

Dear Reader,

When two people fall in love, the world is suddenly new and exciting, and it's that same excitement we bring to you in Silhouette Intimate Moments. These are stories with scope, with grandeur. The characters lead the lives we all dream of, and everything they do reflects the wonder of being in love.

Longer and more sensuous than most romances, Silhouette Intimate Moments novels take you away from everyday life and let you share the magic of love. Adventure, glamour, drama, even suspense—these are the passwords that let you into a world where love has a power beyond the ordinary, where the best authors in the field today create stories of love and commitment that will stay with you always.

In coming months look for novels by your favorite authors: Maura Seger, Parris Afton Bonds, Linda Howard, and Nora Roberts, to name just a few. And whenever you buy books, look for all the Silhouette Intimate Moments, love stories *for* today's women *by* today's women.

Leslie J. Wainger
Senior Editor
Silhouette Books

**Susanna Christie**

# Close Encounter

Silhouette Intimate Moments
Published by Silhouette Books New York
**America's Publisher of Contemporary Romance**

SILHOUETTE BOOKS
300 East 42nd St., New York, N.Y. 10017



ISBN: 0-373-07203-1

First Silhouette Books printing August 1987



America's Publisher of Contemporary Romance

Printed in the U.S.A.

**Books by Susanna Christie**

Silhouette Intimate Moments

*The Find of a Lifetime* #143
*Eden's Temptation* #186
*Close Encounter* #203

---

## *SUSANNA CHRISTIE*

is a descendant of Mormon pioneers and resides in Utah, a state she loves. She has worked in Europe for the U.S. Army as an electronics technician and has also studied and lived in Spain. When not writing romances she works as an electronics technician and an engineering writer for a major corporation. Her writing is influenced by mystery and suspense writers, the supernatural and a vivid fantasy life.

# *Chapter 1*

Wilhelmina Callen tucked her buff-colored shirt into matching tan slacks, buckled the black leather belt and adjusted her holster to follow the gentle curve of her hip. She reached for her .38 police special, then slipped it into its case and snapped the strap over it. As she turned from the mirror, Willie noticed a smudge on her boot. Lifting her foot so it rested on the edge of her dressing-table chair, she brought back the boot's black sheen with the edge of an old T-shirt.

She twisted her dark-blond hair into a single braid as she absently looked out her bedroom window. She could tell that the day would be another scorcher. Already the heat was drying out her night-irrigated garden. The tomato leaves curled in the morning sun. Taking hold of her hair, she walked back to her dressing table and fastened it to the nape of her neck with a heavy silver barrette.

Tawny hazel eyes just a shade darker than her hair peered out from under the brim of her hat. Satisfied that she had tipped it to just the right angle, not too cocky but definitely self-assured, she gave herself a final inspection, then walked out her front door.

Her Jeep Cherokee was parked on the gravel drive next to her house, and she frowned as she noticed that yesterday's late-August thunderstorm had left pale-red sand caked inside the Jeep's wheel wells. She got in and made a mental note to drive it through the car wash before lunch.

The morning DJ on Cisco's only radio station played a snappy country-and-western tune, and Willie hummed along as she drove the two-and-a-half miles to work. Her neighbor, owner of the town's auto parts store, passed and she honked. She wondered if he'd had any more trouble with his son since the boy had lost his license the preceding month on a DWI. As she pulled into her usual parking place in front of the courthouse, she decided to stop by the parts store on her way home and have a chat with him.

Willie walked past the stairway on the first floor. The second floor was the county courthouse; the basement, the county jail. She walked down the hall, then turned right. Hannah Hubbard, the mayor's older sister and her day dispatcher, greeted her.

"Good morning, Willie. Carl's already in. That boy must be turning over a new leaf." Hannah chuckled, sorting through papers on her desk. "There's no messages, but LeRoy picked up Buck Zimmer on a drunk-and-disorderly last night. I already called his wife. She says he can rot in jail for all she—"

"Thanks, Hannah," Willie interrupted her, grinning. "I'll have Carl take care it." She walked into her office before Hannah could say anything else.

Carl, one of her deputies, was on time for a change and already going through the week's batch of bulletins from Denver.

"Morning, Sheriff." Carl looked up and paused, waiting for the full effect of his punctuality to sink in.

"Morning, Carl."

Willie smiled and walked over to her desk. She took off her hat and hung it on the rack. Out of the corner of her eye she saw Carl shrug and return to sorting out bulletins. Wes

Grayden, another deputy, walked in and stopped when he saw Carl.

"What's the matter, Carl? Did your new bride kick you out of the house this morning? Is the honeymoon over so soon?"

"No way." The younger man shook his head and grinned. For a moment, Willie swore that he looked as if he should still be in high school. In fact, both her deputies looked as if they could be playing hooky from the starting lineup of San Juan High's fighting Wildcats.

Wes sat down at his desk and flipped open the Monday-morning edition of the county's only newspaper, the bi-weekly *San Juan Independent*. Willie looked over the previous night's log sheet. She had just read the 1:00 a.m. log entry when Wes let out a low whistle. She looked up in time to catch the glance he threw at Carl. It was the kind of look she was used to, the one that said, "Wait till Willie hears about this."

Wes had tilted his chair back and covered his face with the paper. Willie waited. When Wes whistled under his breath again, she put the logbook down. "Okay, Wes, what is it this time? Did Virgil Jones take out another full-page ad promising to bring law and order to San Juan County if he's elected sheriff? Or did Joe Kelly put a picture of another forty-pound turkey on the front page?"

Wes dropped the paper and sent another significant glance in Carl's direction.

"What's the earth-shattering news?" she repeated.

"You're not going to like this, Willie." He folded the paper in half and handed it to her as if it were an old drunk's coat.

"I'm sure I can handle anything Mr. Kelly can print."

She opened the paper and put it on her desk. It took a moment for the headline to sink in, but when it did, it was her turn to mutter under her breath.

"'UFO Sighted in San Juan County?'" Willie read. "What does he think he's publishing . . . *The National Ex-*

*posé*? This is a small-town paper, not a national scandal sheet." She looked at Carl, and he shrugged again.

"I told you you wouldn't like it, boss." Wes tried to look serious, but she detected some amusement in his eyes. "Didn't you tell us last week that you had all the UFO business straightened out with Joe?" He glanced at Carl, then back at Willie. "At least he didn't mention anything about the election."

"I can just see it now." Carl smirked. "The two sheriff candidates squaring off in a debate over how to handle UFOs."

"I don't think it's funny." She knew they could both tell her blood pressure was rising. "But if Kelly keeps this up, that's exactly what might happen."

Willie scanned the rest of the front page. Most of it was devoted to a detailed account of the sighting by a farmer and his wife of "mysterious bright lights" the week before. A man who wished to remain anonymous claimed he saw a spaceship land. The article stated several times that these were not the first occurrences in San Juan County of so-called close encounters. During the past six months, more than half a dozen citizens had sighted "strange and unexplained phenomena." There was even a picture of the farmers, Jake and Ina Hauser, pointing to the "exact spot" where they had seen a beam of bright light come from an "irregularly shaped spaceship."

Willie put her fist down on the paper, right on the shot of Jake and Ina. She took several deep breaths, willing herself not to lose control. Then she stood, put on her hat and walked across the room. Her hand was on the door when the phone rang.

"It's for you, Willie." Wes put his hand over the mouthpiece. "Hannah says it's Mrs. Wiemer."

Willie stifled the groan she felt rising from her throat. Mrs. Wiemer was probably the wealthiest woman in town. She was also the craziest, thought Willie as she remembered the countless calls of the past. The woman had done everything from complain about noisy schoolchildren who dared to pass her front gate and disturb her nap to call to alert Willie that Mrs. Wiemer was being followed by secret agents intent on kidnaping her. She'd wanted Willie to provide an around-the-clock escort. Willie could just imagine what the *Independent*'s headline had done to Lucy.

"Tell her I'm out." Willie started to leave.

"She says she just heard you. She says she wants to talk to you."

Willie walked over and took the phone out of Wes's hand. It was his turn to shrug.

"Mrs. Wiemer, this is Sheriff Callen. What can I do for you?"

Willie was silent as the elderly woman spoke for several minutes. Finally Willie interrupted her. "I know you're concerned. We appreciate that. But it's our opinion that the newspaper accounts have been highly exaggerated. Apparently Mr. Kelly values sensationalism more than journalistic responsibility." She paused as Mrs. Wiemer responded. "Yes, I agree that his brother, Paul, would have never given it the front page. It's hardly news. People will think they see—"

She fiddled with the telephone cord as the woman droned on. Finally Willie was able to break in again. "My deputies and I are prepared for any event, even an alien invasion. Wes will fill you in on the details, but I have to go. I have urgent business."

She handed the phone to a grimacing Wes. Carl was chuckling to himself as she walked out of her office, the newspaper rolled under her arm.

Willie straightened her hat and strode across Center Street to the office of the *San Juan Independent* and Joe Kelly.

"Good morning, Sheriff," called Debbie, the young secretary at the front desk. "Can I—"

Willie only nodded and walked past the counter to Joe's office, which was partitioned off from the rest of the room. The familiar smell of paper and ink filled her nostrils. When she opened the door marked Editor, for a moment she expected to see her friend Paul Kelly sitting at his rolltop desk. Instead, she saw his older brother, Joe, his back to the door.

"Just put those proofs on the table, Debbie. I'll get to them before lunch." He didn't turn, and Willie studied him. His back was wider and much more powerful-looking than his younger brother's had been. But that wasn't surprising, since he'd been a big football star, the only young jock from Cisco, Colorado, ever to make it all the way to the pros. His hair hung over the back of his collar, and Willie knew he would have several days' growth of beard darkening his chin. Again she fought back the fierce desire to see Paul sitting in Joe's place. Trying to quell the what-ifs and why-nots, Willie cleared her throat.

"What is it, Debbie? I'm busy right now. Just write it down and we'll talk about it later."

"I'm not Debbie, and I don't care if you're busy. I want to talk to you."

Joe whirled around in his chair. When he saw Willie, the surprise in his pale-blue eyes turned to a smile beneath his heavy black brows. "Sheriff Wilhelmina Callen. I wondered how long it would take you to call on me. I had no idea that reading my paper was so high on the list of your morning priorities. I'm flattered."

"Don't be." Willie walked over to his desk and flung down the paper in front of him. "I thought we'd had a little talk about this."

"We did."

"Then why did you print this story?"

"It's news. I run a newspaper."

"If you want to print news like this, you can go to New York or L.A. I'm sure one of those national scandal sheets could use a talented, experienced journalist like you."

"Look, Willie, I didn't promise I wasn't going to write about it. I just told you I wouldn't try to sensationalize it."

"What do you call this?" She pointed to the bold headline. "I would say that proclaiming 'UFO Sighted in San Juan County' is pretty sensational."

"I put a question mark after it," he said, pointing to it. "It's not a statement but a supposition. Just because you don't believe in UFOs doesn't mean there aren't plenty of people around here who do."

"That's just the point, Joe. People around here believe this stuff. They'll read this, and pretty soon the whole county will be seeing mysterious lights and strange spaceships. A few will even think they see little green men."

"You ought to talk to Jake and Ina. They were pretty sure about what they saw. I didn't make this up. I've had ten calls in the last month on this. I think it's news."

"Well, I've had one call this morning on this. It was a concerned citizen who was scared to death."

The smile left Joe's face. "Who called? I'd like to talk to whoever it is. It wasn't my intention to get anyone upset over this."

"A citizen." Willie folded her arms across her chest. "If you can have anonymous sources, so can I." Again she pointed to the newspaper story.

"This is different. A newspaperman is allowed to keep his sources confidential. I just want to explain that we have no proof that the lights those people saw in Spanish Valley are UFOs. I thought I pointed out in my article that there was probably a logical explanation for all this." As Joe talked, his full lips parted to expose even, sinfully white teeth. He must have realized that Willie wasn't going to reveal her citizen if he didn't reveal his source. "You've got me, Willie."

Willie didn't smile. The dark, devilish face that had managed to charm a whole nation wouldn't succeed with her, she told herself.

"Okay. I'll tell you who saw the spaceship land if you'll tell me who called."

"You mean alleged spaceship. Even you don't believe—"

"Alleged spaceship," Joe agreed.

"It's a deal." Willie paused as she looked into his clear, pale eyes. "You go first."

She could tell Joe was going to protest but then changed his mind.

"It was Matt Bishop, the guy who has one of the turkey farms up in Spanish Valley."

"Yes, I know Matt." Willie sat down in the chair next to Joe's desk. "He's the last person I would've expected this from. The man's as sober as a judge. I don't think I've seen him smile in thirty years."

"That's why I felt so compelled to print his story. I knew he wasn't just making it up as some sort of joke. Jake and Ina Hauser seem to be pretty steady, too."

"But that's beside the point. A story like this is just too disrupting. It's too..." She waved her hand, searching for the word.

"Controversial? Especially when the sheriff happens to be up for reelection?"

"That's not the point and you know it." It took Willie a great deal of effort, but she managed to keep a pleasant note in her voice. "If Virgil Jones wants to make this a campaign issue, let him. Personally I think he'll be laughed out of San Juan County."

"It would certainly be more interesting than the current budget 'controversy.'" He started to say more on that, but then he stopped. "Aren't you forgetting something, Willie?"

His eyes were bright, and the skin crinkled slightly at the corners. All those years of playing football had given his face a healthy, lived-in look, she thought, then said, "I don't know what you're talking about."

"The concerned citizen. The one who was scared to death of an alien invasion. You promised to tell me who it was."

"Oh." Willie smiled. "That was Mrs. Lucy Wiemer. She called just before I came over."

"Mrs. Wiemer!" Joe shook his head. "That woman calls us up two, sometimes three, times a day. She's bothered by everything."

Willie shrugged. "Well, it seems she's bothered by this, too."

Joe sighed and rubbed his hand over his stubbly jaw. "I promised Matt Bishop I'd keep the story anonymous. I told you because I thought someone was really upset. But Mrs. Wiemer? I can't believe I fell for it." He shook his head, but there was a gleam in his eye. "I don't suppose I can ask you to keep this whole thing confidential."

Willie smiled. "No."

Joe frowned.

"But it's unlikely I'll have to question Matt about any of this UFO business, because the only place it really exists is right here." She indicated the front page.

"I didn't make it up, Willie."

"But if you wouldn't write about it, the folks around here would forget it. You're just agitating the whole town by printing this kind of thing."

Willie looked into his pale, cool eyes and could feel her blood pressure rising again. He stared at her and absently ran his tongue across his bottom lip. Willie wondered why the man couldn't have stayed back east.

"Maybe this town could use a little stirring up, Sheriff." The words were spoken as a challenge, but there was only friendliness on his face.

"Stir things up? And I suppose you're just the person to do it." She leaned closer to him, so close she could smell the crisp, woodsy scent of the soap he must have showered with that morning. "I'll tell you one thing, Joe Kelly. Your brother, Paul, would never have given this kind of nonsense the front page!"

Willie regretted her words the moment she uttered them. Comparing Joe with his dead younger brother was something else she had promised herself she would never do, at least not out loud.

Joe was surprised by her comment. Then a slow smile crept across his lips. "So that's what this thing is all about. I wondered why you seemed mad at me the minute I came back to town. You're angry because I'm not Paul. You're furious because it was Paul who died and not his arrogant has-been of a brother." Joe sat down in his chair, and Willie took a seat across from him.

Since it wasn't true, she thought about denying it, but the moment passed. Instead, she sank back against her chair, "I'm sorry I said that. I had no right to." She looked around the office, and for the first time in weeks, her eyes stung at the thought of Paul. "Sometimes I still come in here and expect to see him. It's such a shock when..."

"When you find me in his chair?"

She looked at Joe and nodded, willing the tears to go away.

"You must have cared for him very much." He was stating it, not asking.

Willie shifted in her chair. "He was my best friend," she said quietly. "He helped me through a very difficult time."

Joe leaned back in his chair, and Willie knew he was somehow relieved. She sensed his gaze and empathized with Joe for what he had lost. Nervously he flipped a pencil end over end against the desktop, his huge hands balancing the slender piece of wood. Not once did he let his eyes leave her face.

"I remember the night he called to tell me they'd elected you sheriff." She noticed a thin scar that ran from his left cheekbone to his jawline, and it reddened slightly when he smiled. She wondered how he had gotten it, but she resisted the urge to ask. "He was so excited. I tried to imagine Irene Callen's little sister, Willie, as sheriff of San Juan County." He laughed. "I guess I'm still trying."

Willie looked at him. "It's no harder than trying to imagine Joe Kelly, famous quarterback, as owner and editor of a hick Colorado newspaper."

The memory of just how beautiful Irene had looked on Joe Kelly's arm flashed across Willie's mind. She'd been devastated as only a thirteen-year-old can be when Joe had left Irene behind and shattered her dreams of having a real, live hero in the family.

Another smile curled across his full lips, and the thin scar darkened. Willie noticed that his nose had some interesting bumps that she didn't remember having been there twenty years before. The marks the years had left on his face took away the pretty-boy look he'd had as a teenager. Willie realized for the first time that he probably carried some scars on the inside as well. She tried to look away but found herself intrigued.

"Listen, Joe, why don't we just call a truce? Obviously I can't tell you what to print in your newspaper. If you want to say that Martians are raising turkeys in Spanish Valley, I can't stop you."

"But you are going to try to appeal to my intelligence and sense of public responsibility and ask me to stop, aren't you?"

Willie smiled. "You took the words right out of my mouth." She stood. "I hope you can find it in yourself to think about the effect a paper like yours has on a community this size."

He walked with her to the outer office. "Did it ever occur to you that there just might be something to all this UFO business?"

Willie stopped and stared at him. "Are you serious? Don't tell me you actually believe in all this nonsense."

"I might." He put his hands into the pockets of his faded cords. "It's not impossible, you know."

"I didn't say it was impossible. I just think it's improbable and ridiculous."

She started walking toward the door. Debbie had turned around at her desk and was staring at them. Willie felt Joe's hand on her arm. It was the first time he'd touched her, and the gentle pressure alerted every nerve ending in her body.

"It could be actual UFO phenomena, or it could be something very earthbound. All I'm saying is that when so many people are sure they've seen something, somebody should listen."

Willie sensed for the first time that Joe just might be more serious about this UFO issue than she'd thought. "I'll listen, Joe, anytime you or anyone else wants to talk. That's part of my job."

"How about listening tonight, over dinner?"

It took Willie a moment to realize he was asking her for a date. She smirked. "It was very sly, the way you slipped that in. I guess that's why they called you Slippery Joe."

"I was only slippery with the opposing team." He grinned. "Well, how about it?"

Willie was about to say no when Wes, her deputy, walked in. He touched the brim of his hat as he walked past Debbie.

"We just got a call from Grady Wheeler up in Spanish Valley. He says something happened to his turkeys."

Willie and Joe turned toward him.

"What do you mean something happened to his turkeys? Did those wild dogs get into his flock again?" She shook her head and turned to Joe. "Now, that's something you can write about. All the people who've let their big dogs run loose and breed, then get into the farmers' livestock and—"

Wes interrupted her. "I don't think that's it, Sheriff. He didn't say it was dogs. Whatever happened, he sounded pretty upset."

"Then let's go." Willie started toward the door with Wes.

"Hey, wait for me!" Joe grabbed a camera from behind the counter and followed. "This sounds like a story. Mike's still in Phoenix, visiting his mother, and you know he's the only reporter I've got."

"I don't think you should go with us," Willie protested.

"Debbie needs the company car, and mine's getting a tune-up." He gave her his most endearing look. "I won't get in the way, and besides, it'll be something on the front page besides UFOs."

Willie shook her head.

"Look," he said, the charm suddenly gone. "I'm going to interview Grady Wheeler anyway. Wouldn't it be better if you were around? Then you couldn't accuse me of 'coloring' the facts just to make a headline."

Willie considered this. "You just convinced me." She turned to Wes. "You take the other car and bring some specimen bags and equipment. Wheeler may want some help in determining the cause of death." She walked out the door, Joe close behind her.

The ride to Spanish Valley was over fifteen miles, half of it on narrow two-lane blacktop. Like most of the ranchers in the valley, Grady Wheeler had been raising turkeys for all of his adult life. Certainly ever since Willie could remember. She had gone to high school with his kids and even dated one of his sons.

She turned off from the main road and onto a gravel drive that led to the Wheeler farm. She glanced at Joe and caught him looking at her. He didn't bother to turn away, and she put her eyes back to the road. Rock crunched under the tires, and Willie gripped the steering wheel more tightly.

"You like this, don't you?" Joe asked.

"What's that?"

"Being sheriff."

Willie turned to him briefly. "I guess I do."

"At first I thought you must have liked the power it gave you, but now I think it's something else."

"Oh? And just what do you think it is?"

"You really care about these people, don't you?"

Willie thought about it. No one had ever put it to her quite that way. "Yes, I do."

"I remember I couldn't wait to get out of this little nowhere town," Joe told her, turning his attention back to the road. "I'd wanted to be somewhere else since I was twelve years old. I wanted to be somebody."

"Well, you certainly got your wish."

"But the feeling never went away." He looked out the window and shifted the camera on his lap. "I still always wanted to be somewhere else. Until I came back here."

"Back to this little nowhere town," Willie said.

"I guess it was destined to be." He laughed suddenly.

Willie saw a slight crinkling at the corner of his eyes. She wondered if he was serious. It was hard to tell with Joe.

Grady Wheeler came out of his rambling stucco house as they pulled up in front. He walked toward them, and Willie could tell that the old man was upset. Only a wispy web of white hair covered his sunburned scalp, and he wiped his forehead with an old red bandanna, then tucked it inside his overalls.

"Morning, Willie, Joe." The old man nodded.

"Good morning, Mr. Wheeler." Willie paused and looked around his farm. It seemed quiet, too quiet. "Wes said something happened to your turkeys."

"I'll say something happened to 'em. Most of 'em up and died."

He walked toward a long, low building, and as they approached, Willie saw clumps of gray, white and brown feathers scattered across a huge pen. What remained of his flock was sheltered in a separate pen.

"Were those turkeys with the others?"

Wheeler shook his head. "No, I just brought 'em in from the range yesterday. Didn't get around to putting 'em with the others."

She leaned against the fence, and Joe stood next to her. He brought the camera up to his face, and Willie put her arm up to stop him. "Do you mind if Joe takes pictures?"

"Not if he thinks four hundred and fifty dead turkeys is news."

Joe took several shots and then all three of them walked inside the pen.

Willie noticed a faint, unfamiliar odor as she walked around. It wasn't the smell of dead animals but of something else, something metallic and almost bitter. As she heard Wes pull up, she waved for him to join them. Then she turned back to Mr. Wheeler.

"Did you call the vet?"

"Doc says he'll be out as soon as he can. I said there's no rush, since there's not much left to save."

She bent down to get a closer look at the lifeless birds. None of them had any marks on them.

"It doesn't look like any kind of animal got in here. What makes you think they just didn't get sick?"

"'Cause last night everything was fine. Not one of 'em was sick. You'd think I'd have had some sort of warning or something. Turkeys just don't keel over like this."

"It looks like you should have told the turkeys that," Joe said. Willie shot him a glare that told him to keep it to himself, but Wheeler only smiled.

"Guess you have a point there, son."

"Don't turkeys sometimes get spooked?" Wheeler and Joe looked at her. "I remember your son Leo used to tell me how sometimes a plane or even a hawk would fly overhead and the whole flock would run scared. They'd pile up against the fence and suffocate."

"I've seen 'em do that a couple of times. But then they'd be piled up against the fence, not scattered all over the yard, like this." Wheeler shook his head and looked at the birds.

Joe took a few more pictures and Willie walked around the yard. Wes put on some gloves and gingerly placed several of the turkeys in a large plastic bag.

"Be sure to get some of the feed." Willie pointed to the troughs. "Is that what they ate yesterday?"

Mr. Wheeler nodded. "I put it out myself around five o'clock. This is the time of year I start on heavy feeding, since there's only a couple of months left until I ship 'em out."

"Have you got any enemies, Mr. Wheeler? Anybody that would like to see this year's crop ruined?"

Wheeler scratched his head. "A man doesn't get to be sixty in a little town like Cisco without making someone mad. But nobody's ever tried anything like this." He chuckled. "Carl Johnson punched me out in the Wagon Wheel three years ago, but we was both drunk at the time. Besides, Carl's too dumb to figure out how to poison turkeys."

He paused for a minute and scratched his head. "Homer Beede and I went at it about a year ago. Matt Bishop and I fought him over water rights." He glanced at Willie. "But then you probably remember that." Willie nodded. "He's calmed down since we managed to settle it out of court. In fact, he's been right neighborly."

He shook his head and walked around the compound. Willie watched him as he wiped his forehead again, then slowly came back toward her.

"You know, this sounds crazy, but some mighty funny things've been happening around here."

"Funny things?" Willie looked at the old man.

"You know, those lights that Jake and Ina saw last week. People even say that Matt Bishop saw something."

Joe came closer. "Have you seen anything, Mr. Wheeler?" he asked.

Wheeler turned to Joe. "I can't say that I have, but I've been getting some pretty funny feelings lately."

"Like what?" Joe asked. Willie tried to give him another glare but he ignored her.

Wheeler shrugged. "I don't know. I've lived here all my life, and things just feel different somehow."

Joe and Willie exchanged looks.

"This sounds funny, but I think it might be those UFOs that're making me feel weird," Wheeler said.

"Are you saying you think they did this to your turkeys?" Joe asked.

Wheeler glanced at Joe and then at Willie. Then he turned around and studied his dead birds.

"Yeah...I wouldn't have put it that way before, but that could be it." He turned back to them. "I've been raising these birds for a long time, but I've never seen nothing like this. I think it was the aliens."

"Aliens, Mr. Wheeler?" Willie shook her head. She felt like sending Joe to join the turkeys. "Don't you think we should wait for the lab report before we make assumptions?" She fixed her eyes on Joe.

Joe shrugged. Willie noticed that at least he had the decency to look embarrassed.

Wheeler turned back to Joe. "Joe here believes me. I've read his stuff in the paper, and I think the boy's right on target."

He addressed Willie. "Don't you think we ought to alert somebody in the government...maybe the National Guard or the governor or somebody?"

"I'll take care of it, Mr. Wheeler." She turned toward Wes. "Take those samples in and we'll send them off on the afternoon flight north." Then she looked at Wheeler. "I'll call the vet and get his opinion. Do you need any help cleaning this up?"

"Some of the neighbors are coming over. I guess I'll just burn 'em out back." He looked over the landscape. "Nothing's ever happened like this before. I think it's those aliens. What do you think, Joe?"

Joe started to open his mouth, but Willie laid a hand on his arm. Under her fingers she could feel the muscles tense, then relax. Quickly she pulled her hand away. "I think Joe wants to wait for the lab report before he jumps to any conclusions." Joe nodded as Willie led him toward the car. "In fact, Mr. Wheeler, Joe Kelly and I plan on having an in-depth discussion of this case right now."

# Chapter 2

Willie climbed into the Cherokee and started the engine. Joe barely had time to close the door before she slipped it into reverse and backed down the gravel drive. When she reached the main road, she turned the vehicle around and headed back to Cisco. She didn't look at Joe; she just forced herself to count to ten. When she had finished, she still felt like calling him stupid and idiotic, so she started counting over again.

She was in the middle of her fourth slow count when Joe interrupted her. "Okay, go ahead and say it."

Willie was silent as she kept her eyes on the road.

"Look, Willie." She could feel the weight of his fingers as they rested on her arm. "I didn't mean to get Wheeler all shook up. The last things I had in mind when I came out here were aliens and UFOs."

She glanced at him. "I knew I shouldn't have brought you with me. I had a feeling you couldn't be trusted."

"What do you mean I can't be trusted?"

"I mean you can't be trusted to use any common sense."

"Wait a minute. I wasn't the one who started talking about the 'strange feeling' that Wheeler had. He brought that up all by himself."

"And you put the idea into his head that aliens were somehow responsible for what happened to his turkeys." Again she took her eyes off the road and looked at him. "I suppose in the next edition of that newspaper of yours we're going to read all about how aliens are coming from Mars or Venus or wherever and killing off all the turkeys in the county."

"Sure," he said, his arms folded tightly across his broad chest. "And I'm going to say that they drained every drop of blood from those stupid birds. It'll make a great story."

She gasped. "You wouldn't dare!" She turned to face him and realized he wasn't serious. Or at least she thought he wasn't serious.

"Of course I wouldn't print that. What kind of a person do think I am?"

Willie looked at him, her face full of warning.

"On second thought, don't tell me. I don't think my ego could take it." Joe stared at the winding road ahead. It followed a snaky path alongside the Dolores, a narrow band of green water peeking out from behind the tamarisk that covered its banks. The red rock cliffs above were bleached pink in the morning sun.

Willie had stopped counting to ten. Instead, she just kept both hands clenched around the steering wheel and her eyes on the road.

They were almost in town before Joe spoke again. "I'll make a deal with you, Willie."

"A deal?"

"I won't put any mention of aliens and turkeys on the same page."

Willie raised her eyebrows. "What happened to your motto of 'news is news'?"

"I mean I won't print anything about Wheeler's funny feelings and his theory about aliens. I'll just say that the death of his turkeys is under investigation. And I'll bury the story inside the paper with no pictures."

"No pictures?" Willie glanced at Joe and he nodded. "That's only what any intelligent newspaperman would do."

"I'll ignore that remark. I think Wheeler's ideas about aliens would make a very interesting human-interest story, if nothing else."

"So what's the deal, Joe?"

"If I take it easy on this story as a special favor to the sheriff of San Juan County, I want something in return."

"I knew it," Willie said under her breath. She turned from the Spanish Valley junction onto the highway that led into Cisco. "Just what is this special favor?"

"I want to know about the lab results on those dead birds as soon as possible." He paused. "And I want you to have dinner with me."

"The lab results are part of an official investigation, but I suppose it won't do any harm letting you know what they are. After I find out." She was silent for a moment, wondering whether he would let her forget about the second favor.

"And what about dinner?" he prompted her.

"Why do you want to go out with me? Every time we get together, we do nothing but argue. It's a great way to ruin an evening."

"I want to go out because we do argue. Obviously we're going to be seeing each other, whether you like it or not."

She pulled up in front of the courthouse and stopped. Then she sighed and leaned her head against the door. The thin scar on his cheek had darkened, and he wasn't smiling.

"I'm the owner of the county's only newspaper, and you're the sheriff. Half the news that's fit to print comes from your office. It would make things a lot easier if you got rid of that grudge against me that you're carrying around."

"I don't have a grudge against you." They were both still seated in the front seat of the Cherokee, and she twisted her body to face him. "See? We can't agree on anything."

Finally he smiled. "Whatever it is, we've got some unfinished business to settle."

She tapped her neatly clipped fingernails on the top of the gearshift. "What kind of unfinished business could we have? We haven't seen each other for the last twenty years."

"That's just it. We're still dealing with the Willie and Joe we used to know, instead of who we are right now. You're not a skinny little thirteen-year-old, and I'm not the high school football star who dated your older sister."

"You and Irene were engaged." Willie wanted to get the facts straight.

"Engaged? Who told you we were engaged?" He started to laugh, a look of surprise on his face.

"Irene, who else? She even showed me the ring you gave her. It wasn't a diamond ring, of course, but you told her it soon would be."

"I never said anything like that. It was just a cheap little ring I got one afternoon at the drugstore. It didn't mean anything. Irene knew that."

"She did?"

Joe sighed. "This is why we have to talk. I think you're more upset at me for leaving than Irene ever was."

"Is that why she cried every night for two weeks?" Willie knew she was dredging up the past, but she couldn't help it.

"She got married six months later. I think she had a swift recovery from any broken heart she suffered over me."

"That's irrelevant."

"Then why are you bringing it up?"

"You brought it up!" She turned away from him. "This is getting us nowhere."

"Then how about continuing the conversation tonight?" He got out. After he shut the door, he leaned in the open window. "I'll pick you up at eight."

"I'm busy tonight."

"Eight o'clock, Willie Callen. You were a terrible liar when you were thirteen, and you're not any better now." He smiled, then walked away.

Willie watched him as he crossed the street to his newspaper office. He was as tightly muscled as she remembered him twenty years before. And he still walked with the grace of a bobcat and the cockiness of a young rooster.

When Willie finally made the drive home, it was nearly seven. She passed the closed auto parts store and wondered where the day had gone. The turkey carcasses had been packed in dry ice and shipped up to Denver that afternoon. She'd delivered them to thc airport herself. When she'd called the vet, he'd told her he was puzzled. The turkeys looked healthy and didn't seem to have suffocated. He was just as eager as she was to get the lab results.

Mrs. Wiemer called back twice. She'd already heard about Wheeler's turkeys and wanted a detailed account of what the sheriff's office was doing to protect the citizens of San Juan County. Willie wasted almost half an hour giving it to her.

Two high school freshmen had downed several beers each during lunch. Willie and Carl had had to haul them out of biology class after they'd dared each other to swallow several of the frogs scheduled for dissection.

Once home, she stripped off her clothes and stood under a steaming shower. The heat filled up the small tiled enclosure and sank into her body, easing every tired muscle and nerve. Willie emptied her mind as she relaxed her body. The water turned from hot to warm to tepid, and she felt the tiny needles of liquid caress her body. Her hair fell around her head like a long silky cap, slick and shiny. She finally turned the water off, when it had gotten too cold to bear. She wrapped a huge towel around her body and wound a smaller one around her head like a turban. She made it to her bed and lay down, her body and mind finally free of the day. It was only a few moments before her eyes were closed and she was breathing deeply.

In her sleep she heard her name spoken softly. Then came the feeling, seconds before she woke, that she wasn't alone, which made her want to scream.

Her eyes opened, and she stared at the startled face of Joe Kelly.

"What are you doing here?" she demanded, sitting up. A feeling of dampness and then chill tingled across her bare skin and she glanced down just in time to see her towel fall away from her breast. With a swift movement of her hand she brought it back up, but not before she saw Joe's look of surprise turn to one of astonishment.

"What are you staring at?" she asked.

He smiled. "I could say 'nothing,' but that would be a lie."

He moved from the edge of her bed and backed toward the door.

"You're the first date I've ever had to wake up before we went out."

"Date?" Willie closed her eyes and groaned. "I forgot."

Joe chuckled. "Your front door was open and I thought you might be out back. I'll just wait in the living room until you get dressed." He walked into the hallway and disappeared.

"I never agreed to a date, you know," she called after him.

His head reappeared at the doorway. "I know. Like I said, I'll be waiting in the living room."

Willie waited a few seconds, then got up and shut her bedroom door. She sighed and leaned against it, the wood cool against her bare back. Joe had a way of getting what he wanted. She'd seen him use it with Irene, and he hadn't changed. She barely knew the man, and he'd already been in her bedroom. She stared at the brass bed that had been her grandmother's and tried to remember the last time she'd had a man to share it with. No one came to mind.

Willie walked over to her closet and pulled out a nearly new pair of jeans and a pale-pink blouse. With some pleasure she remembered that Joe had been wearing dress slacks and a tie under his blue cotton sweater. She would be definitely underdressed for what he had planned, and that suited her fine.

She twisted her damp hair in a thick braid and let it hang down her back. Her vanity urged her to put on some mascara and a touch of lipstick, but she resisted the temptation. It took her less than ten minutes to get herself ready. This was one occasion when she regretted her ability to make herself presentable in less time than it took most people to wake up. It was a habit she'd learned in the army. She considered sitting on the edge of her bed for ten minutes and making him wait. Instead, she cleared her throat and headed for the door. She might as well face him and get it over with, she thought.

Joe smiled when he saw her. Willie frowned slightly as he opened the front door. Obviously he wasn't going to comment on what she was wearing. Maybe his years in the city had made him too jaded to care what his "date" was wearing. But then she caught him glance down at the jeans hugging her body and realized that he definitely had noticed.

He opened the door of a late-model four-wheel-drive wagon. It had a bright-orange sun with boldface lettering on the door that said *San Juan Independent*. She looked back at him, her eyebrows slightly raised. She felt as if everyone who saw her in Joe's car would wonder about their relationship. It was something even she was beginning to think about.

He must have sensed her hesitation. "My car's still in the garage."

"You couldn't be more obvious, Joe." She got in, and he walked around to the other side and slid in next to her.

"Are you ashamed to be seen with me?" He said it with that half smile of his. She was beginning to recognize that it meant the other half was serious.

"No, I'm not ashamed to be seen with you. It's just that..." Willie deliberately let her voice trail off.

"It's just that you don't want to be seen with me." Joe finished the sentence for her as he started up the engine and backed out into the street.

"That's not it. I'm the sheriff, and you've got the only newspaper in the county. It's only natural that people will be curious about our relationship."

"So you're admitting that we do have a relationship. Progress is being made."

"I'm not admitting anything." Willie stared straight ahead.

"And what did they think about your relationship with my brother?"

"That was different. He'd been my friend for years." Willie glanced out the window as they drove down Main Street. "Where are we going?"

Joe looked at her as if he was going to say something about Paul, then changed his mind. "Have you eaten yet?"

Willie shook her head. She'd be glad when they got out of the confines of the front seat and had a table between them.

Joe drove right past the town's only really decent restaurant and finally pulled into Ned's Stop and Eat. Willie started to open the door when he leaned over and put his hand over hers.

"We'll just let the waitress come out and take our order. I thought that since you'd rather not be seen with me, it would be more discreet to eat in the car." He smiled and held on to her hand a little longer than necessary.

The faint fragrance of his after-shave made her catch her breath. It was tangy and reminded her of lemons. It blended with the smell of sage coming in the open window from the vacant lot behind the drive-in. She could feel the slight heat of his body as he leaned across her. Finally he withdrew his hand and settled in next to her, narrowing the gap between them.

"Do I make you nervous, Willie?"

"No."

He looked at her doubtfully, and finally she could feel herself relaxing. "Okay, it's another lie. Twenty years ago you made me nervous, and you make me nervous now."

Joe laughed and was about to say something when the waitress appeared at the window to take their order. They both ordered hamburgers and fries. Joe ordered a diet soda, and Willie smiled as she ordered an extra-thick shake.

When the girl had gone, Joe turned to Willie. "So, I make you nervous. Why should I make you nervous? I'm just a guy who grew up in your hometown and dated your big sister."

"And who made every sports page and personality magazine for almost ten years." Willie looked out the window. The sun had just disappeared behind the wall of red rock cliffs on the west side of town, streaking the sky with orange and lavender. "And you married that blond heiress—what's her name..." Willie deliberately paused a few moments. "Marissa Crandall?"

"Kendall. Her name was Melissa Kendall." Joe looked out the window, away from Willie. "But that wasn't the Joe you knew. That was an invention, a myth."

"Whatever happened to Melissa Kendall? If I remember right, she was rich and beautiful—everything a man could want." Willie smiled and tried to take some of the edge off her voice. "It wasn't a wise move to let her get away." Willie glanced over to try to gauge his reaction. But all she could see was the side of his face.

"I didn't let her get away," Joe said quietly. "Just for the record, it was Melissa who walked out."

Willie raised her eyebrows, and Joe turned to her. "You're wondering why a woman would leave the great Joe Kelly?"

It was the way he said it, rather than the words, that made Willie blush slightly. She knew she shouldn't have brought up his failed marriage.

"She left because I was no longer the great Joe Kelly but just another burned-out football player. Age and injuries finally caught up with me, and the photographers and reporters stopped coming around. I was yesterday's news, and so was Melissa. She went on to greener pastures." He sighed. "Look, to be honest, I wasn't an easy man to live with. For Joe Kelly, the party had finally ended."

Joe had made no attempt to hide the pain in his voice, and Willie looked down, suddenly feeling compelled to examine her hands, folded in her lap.

Silence filled the small space between them, and Willie didn't know what to do. She said the first thing that entered her mind to break the awkward silence.

"I'm sorry," she whispered. "I didn't know it was an unfriendly divorce."

"Is there ever a friendly one?"

The comment briefly brought back memories of Willie's divorce. She'd always told herself it had been one of the "friendly" ones. But somehow she knew Joe was right. There wasn't a painless way to end a marriage.

The food came and they ate in silence. When he'd almost finished his hamburger, Joe cleared his throat. "So tell me, what have you been doing for the past twenty years?"

Willie looked at him, then laughed. "Nothing quite as interesting as playing pro football and marrying heiresses."

Joe smiled. "I'd say you've had a pretty busy past. Paul told me you went to law school."

"I almost graduated," Willie said, trying to keep any regret out of her voice—and almost succeeding.

"What happened?"

"I got married. When I was divorced, I went into the army."

"You say that as if it's what every young woman does."

"More of them should. It was one of the smartest things I've ever done. It taught me that some things were more important than Willie Callen."

"What things?" Joe asked.

"The man or woman standing next to you. The community you live in. I was an M.P. for three years. I really learned what it meant to have to count on another human being, and I learned that I had to be responsible for someone besides myself." Willie glanced away. It was a lesson she wished she'd learned before she'd married Mac. Oh, well, she thought, all that was history now.

Sensing the change in her mood, Joe was quiet as he finished the rest of his food. Then he turned to her.

"Have any more leads come in on the Great Tragic Turkey Deaths?"

Willie had a mouthful of French fries, and she laughed, nearly choking. "Don't tell me that's what you're going to call it."

He looked at her sideways and grinned. "I can just see the headline now: 'Turkeys Drop Dead; Farmer Puzzled.'"

"I thought you said you were going to bury it in the middle of the paper."

"Don't worry. Even ex-football players keep their word."

The waitress came and took away the tray. Willie was acutely aware that Joe made no move to start the car. Instead, he slid closer to her, draping his arm over the back of her seat. Even though he kept it away from her neck, she knew it was there. For a brief moment she was an awkward, shy thirteen-year-old in the presence of the town's only star. Then the feeling evaporated like a popped bubble and she was Willie Callen, thirty-four-year-old sheriff, divorcée. This wasn't the first time a man had tried to put his arm around her. She laughed and turned to Joe.

"What's the joke?" His eyes crinkled, and she saw the two icy-blue pools turn warm.

"The only joke is on me, Joe Kelly." She swiveled toward him and leaned back against the door. "And to answer your earlier question, no, I don't have any more leads on the Tragic Turkey Deaths. The vet is as in the dark as we are."

"What do you think?"

"I'm no turkey expert, but I have a feeling they didn't die from natural causes." She shrugged. "We should get the results in sometime tomorrow afternoon. I told Denver it was a rush job."

Willie was aware that Joe hadn't taken his eyes off her the whole time she'd been talking. He didn't even seem to notice she'd stopped.

"I wasn't aware that turkeys could be such a fascinating subject," she said as she returned his stare.

"They're not. But you are."

Willie tried not to roll her eyes at his corny line. Did he think she was just another hick country girl waiting to be seduced by a sophisticated man from the city?

"I never noticed your eyes before. They remind me of the ones I once saw on a mountain lion I spotted up at Miner's Basin when I was a kid."

That was definitely not a corny line. "Thanks," Willie mumbled. "That's the first time I've been compared to an endangered species."

"She was a beautiful cat," Joe said softly. "Sleek and strong. I was up there hiking, and she came across my trail early in the evening. She looked right through me, like she knew every trick in the book."

"And what did you do?"

"I was hypnotized by her. I was afraid. I wanted to get out of her way, but I couldn't. I just stood and watched. I wanted her to go, but I wanted her to stay."

"A standoff?"

He shook his head. "No. Finally she grew bored with me and turned around. She left me. I was as insignificant as a speck in the middle of the road."

Willie tapped her fingers on the bottom of the open window. "So what's the point? You're afraid I'll get bored and leave you in the middle of the road?"

Joe smiled, his eyes cool now. "Let's just say I've seen the look of cold indifference in your eyes before."

Willie smiled. That look of cold indifference was probably hot anger. She could imagine feeling just about every emotion for Joe Kelly except indifference. She had no idea whether he'd just made up that little story to tell her something or he really meant she had the eyes of a cougar. She glanced at her watch.

"I have to work tomorrow. It was a great dinner but..."

"But you've got to get going. I know. So do I." He slid back behind the steering wheel and started the car. "Mike's still going to be out of town, and we have a paper to put out by Thursday. And I've still got to write up the Great Turkey Obituary."

Willie sighed as he pulled out of the drive-in. She hadn't expected him to give up that easily. But then maybe he figured she just wasn't worth the energy.

Joe drove back through town, his eyes never leaving the road. Willie suddenly felt like a bashful teenager again. By the time he pulled up in front of her house, the silence had become thick and uncomfortable. Willie almost jumped out of the car when it came to stop on her gravel drive.

"Hey," he called after her as he got out. "Aren't you going to invite me in?"

Willie stopped in her tracks. It was the last thing she expected to hear from him. "No," she answered, "I wasn't."

"In that case, I'll invite myself." He followed her into the house.

Willie felt herself becoming nervous all over again. Maybe if she ignored him he'd go away. She went into the kitchen and walked over to the sink, not bothering to turn on the light. She took a glass from the cupboard, turned on the faucet and filled the glass with water. What on earth was she going to do with him? She'd tell him to leave, she decided.

Swiftly she turned around, only to see his silhouette blocking the light from the living room.

"Do I still make you nervous, Willie?"

"Very. And right now I think you'd better go home. I'm tired, and I have to work tomorrow."

He walked toward her. Suddenly the room seemed quite small as her back pressed against the cold metal edge of the sink.

"Was it that remark about your eyes?" He was standing in front of her. Again she smelled the slight fragrance of lemons and spice. She could feel the heat of his body fill the room. "I meant it."

"You meant what?" she asked.

"That both you and the cougar have beautiful eyes." He slid his arm forward slightly and gripped the edge of the sink on her left. He brought his other hand up and brushed back a wisp of hair that had fallen across her forehead. "They're almost the same color as your hair."

Willie felt as if tiny birds had taken flight inside her, their wings fluttering against her skin.

"It's late, Joe," she managed to whisper, her eyes focused on the darkened planes of his face.

"No, it isn't. It's never too late."

Slowly he brought his face forward and pressed his mouth lightly against hers, his lips as light as dancing butterflies.

He was a fraction of an inch away from stroking her hair with his hand, when she heard the unmistakable sound of a man clearing his throat. It took her only a second to realize that the sound hadn't come from Joe. Apparently Joe had heard it, too.

Shadowed against the door was her third deputy, LeRoy. He was on the night shift this month and obviously embarrassed as he cleared his throat again.

"I didn't mean to barge in on you like this, Sheriff, but I tried to call before and got no answer. When I saw your lights on just now, I figured, well...I figured I'd just stop by and..."

"That's all right, LeRoy. Joe was just leaving." She was grateful that the light was off and LeRoy couldn't see the color washing over her cheeks. She moved away from the sink and away from the man who had only moments earlier stood in front of her. Moving to the center of the room, she became aware of the awkward silence filling the small space.

LeRoy seemed to be staring at his feet.

"LeRoy?" Willie said. "Was there a reason you wanted to stop by here? Something that couldn't wait until tomorrow?"

LeRoy was the oldest but the least experienced of her men. His head bobbed up.

"Yeah, Sheriff, there was something." He looked at her, then at Joe. "I was on my way out to the Bishop place. Matt called me. Seems something happened to some of his turkeys. I thought you might be interested, since he figured it might be the same thing that happened at the Wheeler place."

Willie glanced briefly at Joe, daring him to say something. He was quiet, and she turned to LeRoy.

"I'll ride out with you."

She was in the living room, relieved that Joe for once had responded to her obvious desire to do her job without him, when she realized that he was still behind her. She swung around. He was just about to open his mouth.

"Let me guess," she said. "You want to come along, too."

He grinned. "I couldn't have said it better myself." He turned to LeRoy. "And she tried to tell me we're not compatible. Why, the woman can practically read my mind."

Willie walked out the door toward her deputy's car. She realized that there was no point in arguing with Joe Kelly.

# Chapter 3

Willie sat in the front seat beside LeRoy. She was silent as Joe climbed in the back. All the way out to Spanish Valley she watched her deputy clutch the steering wheel and fidget with the radio. The air was thick with emotion, and she realized that the poor man had no way of knowing what had passed between her and Joe. For all LeRoy knew, he had just walked in on the hottest love affair in Cisco. If only he'd known that his interruption had, for the moment, spared Willie the uncomfortable task of setting Joe straight on a few things. Which she still intended to do, just as soon as she set herself straight.

Matt Bishop's place was two miles closer to town than Grady Wheeler's. The fact that they were neighbors made Bishop's call only a little less surprising than it usually would. But not much. Bishop raised turkeys, like Wheeler, and was about ten years older.

When Joe had told her earlier that Bishop had been the one who said he'd actually seen the "aliens," she was amazed. Bishop was known as a solid citizen—hardworking, no drinking and little play. She knew a man like Matt

Bishop just didn't report UFOs unless he'd actually seen one or he had gone a little crazy. Obviously it was the latter.

Joe was humming tunelessly and tapping his fingers against the metal of the open window when they pulled up to the Bishop place. A light was on in the farmhouse, but floodlights illuminated the poultry pens about two hundred yards to the north. Matt worked the place with his youngest son and occasional hired help. His wife had died nearly three years before, and Willie had heard rumors that Matt was having heart trouble.

Willie, LeRoy and Joe walked quickly to the turkey pens. Gratefully she noted that this time Joe didn't have his camera with him. All she needed was a countywide panic caused by photos of hundreds of dead turkeys. Half the farmers in the valley raised turkeys as their cash crop, and anything that threatened their livelihood would be cause for alarm. She wanted to keep things under control because she was sure there was a reasonable explanation for the whole thing.

Half the pens were covered to give the birds some shelter from the heat of the desert summer. As long as they were well-watered and out of the sun, the turkeys seemed to thrive. But the ones in Bishop's pens were definitely not thriving; they were dead. Heaps of feathers covered the yard. As at the Wheeler place, the birds seemed to have fallen in random piles. Joe walked up and looked into the pens. Some of the birds were still moving, but obviously would not be for long.

"I've never seen anything like this," LeRoy said.

"I have," Joe answered. "This morning at the Wheeler place."

Matt Bishop and his son, Ed, emerged from the barn. They stepped over dead turkeys as they strode toward Willie. The younger man, gazing down, focused on the birds. But Matt moved forward, his head erect.

He reached Willie, and she nodded in greeting. The old man eyed the trio from town and then inclined his head once in reply.

"I see you've had some bad luck with your turkeys, Mr. Bishop. It could be the same thing that happened to Grady Wheeler's flock earlier today," Willie said.

Slowly Matt moved his eyes from Willie to Joe and then to LeRoy. Ed shuffled nervously behind him. He finally spoke when his gaze returned to Willie. "You could be right, Sheriff."

He turned and gazed toward the dead birds. "I brought half my birds in this afternoon. After I heard what happened to Grady's birds, I thought I'd best keep an eye on 'em." He glanced around again. "They would've been better off out ranging like the rest of the flock." He regarded Willie. "Only real question is, what exactly did happen?" He paused and addressed Joe. "And who did it?"

"Don't you mean 'what' did it, Mr. Bishop?" Joe asked. "Willie and I think it might have been something in the feed."

"Or possibly some groundwater contaminant or disease." Willie wanted to tell Joe she could explain her own theories about the case. At least there hadn't been any mention of aliens and spaceships.

"I mean 'who' did it. That's if you can call something that comes in the night from some ungodly planet a who."

Oh, no, here it comes, thought Willie. "I'm sure there's a logical explanation for what happened here, Mr. Bishop."

"There's no logical explanation but the real one."

Willie realized he wouldn't back down. The man knew what he had seen—or at least he thought he knew.

"Why don't you tell Sheriff Callen exactly what you did see? Just like you told me out at Jake and Ina Hauser's place," Joe said.

For the first time, the old man glanced back at his son, and the boy nodded. "It's okay, Dad. I think Willie will listen."

"Of course I'll listen. That's my job." As soon as the phrase left her lips, she realized that they were the same words she'd used on Joe this morning.

Bishop paused, then gazed up at the night sky. Willie's eyes followed, as did those of the rest of the group. The moon was a tiny sliver almost hidden in the bright expanse of stars. The light-speckled canopy of darkness was bordered on two sides by sandstone cliffs. A dog's howl echoed across the valley, and for a moment Willie felt as if she were looking at a sky that could hide any secret.

"I first saw it last week," Bishop began. "I'd heard rumors that others up here had seen something, but I didn't pay it any mind. People are likely to say anything, long as it gets them in the paper." He glanced at Joe. "Least that's what I thought before last week. Then I saw it again last night."

"You saw something twice, Mr. Bishop?" Willie asked.

Solemnly he nodded. Willie sighed. It would have been much easier for her if the old man had been smiling. But he was serious. Dead serious.

"Last night I was up late. I'd been looking over some papers in the kitchen, but then I turned the light off and was just sitting there. Ed had gone into town and hadn't come back yet."

"I was over at MaryLou Potter's," Ed volunteered. "I sure was mad I'd missed it, though. It's not every day you get to see something like what Dad saw."

"Just let me tell the sheriff what I did see, son." Bishop's voice was gentle but commanding. Ed put his hands in his pockets and looked over at the stock pens.

"Like I said, I was in the kitchen when I heard this strange humming noise, same as the week before. It seemed to be coming from out back, behind the barn."

"Exactly what time was this?" Willie took a small notebook and pen from her hip pocket. Finally she had some facts to write down.

"I'd say it was at least one o'clock, no later than one-thirty."

The floodlights from the barn allowed her to make out what she was writing down.

"How long had you been sitting in the dark?"

He looked at her for a moment, then back at Ed. "I guess for about an hour, maybe more. I think I might have fallen asleep, because I remember being startled when I heard that noise."

"The humming sound?"

Bishop nodded.

"Then it was a loud sound? Something that would wake you?"

Bishop shook his head. "It wasn't loud at all. It was just different."

"Different?"

"I'm a farmer. Been one all my life. I have to know what's going on. If anything's different, I notice." He obviously could tell that Willie still wondered what he was getting at. "If the light changes, it might mean some turn in the weather. If there's some sort of different noise, it might mean the well pump's ready to go out or the incubator motors are down."

Willie got the picture. She looked over at Joe, who raised his eyebrows in an I-told-you-so gesture. Her deputy seemed to be mesmerized by the farmer's story.

"What did you do after you heard the noise?" Willie asked.

"I realized right away something was wrong. I got my flashlight and went outside. That's when I could tell where the noise was coming from."

"And where was that?" Joe broke in and motioned with his hand toward the house.

Bishop and his son turned around. "Just out back, between the barn and the house. 'Bout two hundred fifty yards to the south. In that little gully back there."

"I think it would be a good idea if you showed us exactly where."

Bishop nodded and turned to Ed. "Go get the flashlight."

Ed ran into the house. By the time they were behind the barn, he'd rejoined them. Ed and his father walked ahead with LeRoy, while Willie and Joe followed.

"See what I mean?" Joe whispered to her. "This guy's on the level."

"He heard a noise. Big deal," Willie whispered back. "He'd already read those crazy accounts in your paper and made it into a flying saucer."

Joe shook his head and chuckled under his breath. "Just wait. He hasn't gotten to the good part yet, and I bet the sighting he had last night was even better than the one he told me about."

Willie sighed and hurried toward the men in front of her. When they'd reached the shallow, wide gully, Bishop stopped and waited for Joe to catch up. He did, and with the flashlight's beam Matt pointed to a spot at the bottom of the gully.

"I walked outside my house and could tell where the noise was coming from. When I got beyond the barn I saw a bright light coming from the gully. I followed it out here and came to this spot."

Willie noticed LeRoy looking down at the ground. Then Bishop moved the beam of light to an area about one hundred and fifty yards down the gulch. Willie could smell the tangy aromas of sage and cedar on the dry night wind. And there was something else—the same vague odor she'd smelled at the Wheeler place. Again she heard a dog howl, and the beam of light started trembling. She looked at Matt Bishop and realized that the man must be almost seventy. Whatever he had seen out there last night had shaken him badly.

"When I saw it, I put out my light and got low on the ground. I didn't know what it was, but I knew it didn't belong behind my barn."

He drew the back of his shirtsleeve across his brow, and Willie saw that he was sweating. She wanted to get this over with so the man could get some rest. "Just what did you see, Mr. Bishop?" she asked him gently.

"I saw an object—a pretty big object—covered with bright lights. The lights were mostly in front, so they blinded me. I really couldn't tell the shape of it."

"And that's where the humming noise was coming from?" Joe probed.

Bishop nodded. "It was coming from there, all right. Then I noticed the things moving around in silvery suits."

"Things?" Willie wrote down "things in silvery suits" on her notepad and told herself she was just interviewing a witness. It shouldn't matter that the witness sounded off his rocker.

"I don't know what you call creatures from another world. It don't seem right to call 'em people."

"What did these 'things' look like?"

"They were big. Not a one of 'em under six foot. Everything was covered with these suits, including their heads. They had enormous heads, and they had some sort of case protecting it."

"They probably couldn't breathe our air," LeRoy offered, and Ed nodded in agreement. Willie looked sharply at LeRoy and then at Joe, daring them to open their mouths again. Bishop's gaze was focused on the spot where he'd seen the "aliens."

"What were the 'creatures' doing?" Willie asked.

"They were loading long cylinders of something onto their spaceship. The cylinders had hoses trailing off one end."

"And sure enough," Ed added, "when we came back the next day, we found footprints and deep gouges in the ground where they'd dragged those cylinders. They must have been heavy."

"How many things in silver suits were there?"

"I saw at least two. But then there must have been somebody left in the spaceship. I watched them for about five minutes. Then they just took off. Because of the lights, I never got a better look at the thing they were flying. And I didn't dare get any closer."

"Why didn't you contact me sooner?" Willie made her voice even but firm. "I think this should have been reported first to my office, rather than Mr. Kelly's."

The old man turned to her. "I didn't want to tell anybody. I thought I'd be the laughingstock of San Juan County. But the more I thought about it, the more I had to let somebody know besides Ed here. Then, when Jake Hauser told me what he'd seen, I remembered Joe had written those articles. I thought at least he wouldn't laugh at me."

"I'm not laughing at you, Matt," she told him.

He turned toward her, silent for a moment. "I appreciate that, Willie."

LeRoy drove Willie and Joe home. She could tell that LeRoy wanted to talk about what Bishop had seen, but somehow he had enough sense to follow Joe's lead and remain silent. She was tired, and she needed time to think. She mumbled vaguely to Joe as he got out of the car and only told LeRoy that she'd take care of the report on the Bishop case as soon as she got in to work the next day.

Joe Kelly was wide-awake. He rolled over, the twisted sheets taut against his sweat-soaked body. The luminous hands on his bedside clock told him that it was only five. He sighed and stretched, then folded his arms behind his head.

"Damn it," he muttered as the image of Wilhelmina Callen floated to the surface of his consciousness. It wasn't the first time it had appeared in the past several hours, but now he didn't try to dismiss it.

Her tawny-blond hair was loose, hanging down her back. Since she always had it tied up or tied back, he'd never seen her wear it like that, so the image was all the more fascinating. The night before, her hair had been damp and hidden underneath a turbaned towel when he'd found her asleep in bed. He told himself he hadn't meant to sneak up on her like that. But seeing her quiet and vulnerable had made it impossible for him to turn away. He was lucky she hadn't torn his head off when she'd woken up and found him staring at her. He sucked in his breath at the memory of her breasts.

He laughed. He realized that what he had was a simple case of lust. What made it even funnier was that the object of desire was the formerly skinny kid sister of an old girlfriend. But Willie was no longer skinny; she was beautiful. And she was the sheriff. The thought made him laugh again.

He swung his legs out from under the sheet and forced Willie's golden cat eyes and full lips from his mind. If he was going to get anywhere in this town, he had to put Willie Callen in her proper place: fully dressed in the tan uniform of the law. He pulled his pants on and tried to tell himself to forget about what her long, slender legs might look like underneath the twill trousers. He willed himself to stop thinking about the curve of her breasts and the way she smiled when she finally knew she could do nothing else.

Paul had often mentioned her in his letters. When Paul had come to Miami for a quick visit, Willie had seemed to pop up in conversation. Joe suddenly felt himself envying what must have been a wonderfully uncomplicated friendship. It was something he'd never had with a woman. Something he certainly couldn't have with Willie. His relationship with her was getting more tangled every day.

He didn't bother to turn on the light as he buttoned his shirt. A pale slice of dawn cut through the curtains of his bedroom. For a while it'd been Paul's bedroom, but twenty years before, it had been Joe's. As the older brother, Joe had always gotten the biggest and the best. Over the years he'd often wondered why Paul hadn't ended up hating him.

Instead, Joe had known only brotherly love from Paul. He'd always been aware that in Paul's eyes he could do no wrong. He stood up and faced a darkened mirror. He saw the outline of a man who could, indeed, do wrong.

Joe thought of his failed marriage and vanished career. During the past fifteen years, more money had gone through his hands than most men see in a lifetime, even several lifetimes. He'd managed to hold on to some, but not nearly as much as he should have. He shrugged his shoulders and moved forward, tucking his shirt into his jeans. The motion made him wince, and he stopped, again looking at his image in the mirror.

After years of depending on the strength of his body to earn his living, Joe was keenly attuned to every message it sent him. The silhouette he saw in the mirror was off balance. It was so slight that only he would notice it, but the awkward stance confirmed what his left knee was telling him. He grasped the edge of the bed and did several deep leg lunges. His knee protested with stabs of pain, but Joe persisted. When he stood up, the stiffness had lessened. Months ago he'd stopped cursing the weakness that had cut five years off a lucrative career. Now he only stared at the damaged leg with acceptance.

Acceptance. That was a word he'd used often in the past few months. Acceptance of pain, of loss. But Paul's death had been hardest of all to accept.

He moved to the window and looked at the silver predawn sky. Maybe that's what I'm doing here—chasing demons, learning to accept the past, he thought. When he'd moved back to Cisco after his brother's death, he'd taken over the newspaper and the family home that Paul had lived in for the previous ten years. He'd even taken over his brother's bedroom. At the time he'd told himself it was because it had been his own first and it had a beautiful view of the Blue Flint Mountains. Now he realized it was because it made him feel closer to Paul and made the loss easier to bear.

As he hunted under the bed for his boots, he thought of Willie. It was through Paul's eyes that he'd first seen the grown-up Willie. He'd always found Paul's stories interesting, but she was the last woman he would've expected to keep him up nights. The real Willie was strong-willed, even ornery. He realized that she didn't try to flatter his ego like all the other women he'd met in the past twenty years. Maybe that was part of her charm. But she had the very unfeminine occupation of county sheriff, he thought, pulling on his boots.

Downstairs, Joe made some fresh coffee and poured it into a thermos bottle. As long as he was up, he reflected, he might as well take a ride out to the Bishop place and see if he could find some hard evidence of aliens and spaceships. He laughed. Whatever the explanation, it was bound to make a good story.

As he screwed the top of the flask on he realized that his fascination with the sheriff was definitely peculiar. Cisco wasn't exactly crawling with beautiful single women, but there had to be some just as attractive and far more willing than Willie. He climbed into his newspaper's four-wheel-drive car and told himself that from now on, his thoughts about Willie would be strictly business.

He whistled along with the radio as he drove along the river road toward Spanish Valley. When he reached the turnoff to the Bishop place, he pulled off the road and parked. Grabbing his coffee and camera, he set out on foot, heading over the small hill toward the place Matt Bishop had pointed out the night before.

He reached the gully. To the south he saw the shiny metal roof of Bishop's barn. The deep ditch looked plain and dusty in the early-morning light. Just an ordinary irrigation ditch, now dry. Red rock cliffs rose up on one side of the valley and glowed orange. To the east were the blue-green peaks of the Blue Flint range. He looked at the mountains and realized that he'd come home. For years he'd been restless and attributed it to a fading career and an unfaithful wife. Now he knew it was because he had been out of place, lost. This morning he felt something he hadn't felt in a long time. He felt as if he belonged.

He sat on a little hill overlooking the gully and sipped his coffee. As he looked at the dry ditch a few yards away, he tried to put the events into perspective. It had been five days since Matt Bishop had first seen the "spaceship" land. It had rained since the sighting the night before last. The thirsty desert soil soaked up rain quickly, and he knew that the deep gouges in the ground that Bishop and his son had seen would be gone. Still, there might be some evidence of the things in silver suits.

Joe put his coffee down and stood. He had no doubt that Bishop had seen something, just as he had no doubt that what the man had seen wasn't a ship and a crew from outer space. But if there was one thing life had taught Joe Kelly, it was that he'd been wrong before, and as sure as the sun rose each morning, he could be wrong again.

He walked down into the gully and followed it for about fifty yards. He looked at each clump of sage and scrub oak, wondering what he hoped to find. A piece of the silver suits that the visitors had worn? Maybe a discarded cylinder? He didn't know, but he continued to look, carefully retracing his steps.

He had a hunch, he realized. He smiled at the word. It was something his father had always said a good newspaperman had. His father had been a good newspaperman. It didn't matter that it had been on some hick paper; he'd still been good. Joe wondered whether he himself would ever be as good and thought about his hunch that the turkey deaths and the UFO sightings were connected.

Turkeys, dumb as they were, didn't just die for no reason. And whether the deaths of Wheeler's and Bishop's turkeys were from natural causes or were linked to visitors who looked as if they came from another planet, Joe wanted to find out what had killed them. It would make a great story, he decided as he combed the area once more. It might even get picked up on the national wire services.

He saw something shiny and knelt down. It was a bottle cap, and as he stood up to toss it away, he caught a glimpse of movement on the ridge above him. He turned and saw Willie Callen coming toward him.

The shadow from her hat hid her eyes, but he saw that her mouth was unsmiling. He tried to think of something to change that when his glance fell on the rest of her body—on her hips, swaying slightly as she moved forward, on her long, well-curved thighs. Then he remembered his vow of that morning and tried to think of a valid explanation for his early-morning visit. Something that didn't have to do with spaceships or aliens.

# Chapter 4

Good morning, Sheriff,'' Joe said. He looked around, his head moving in a slow, elaborate gesture. ''Nice morning for a stroll.''

''What are you doing, Joe?'' Her voice was even and controlled. Too controlled, thought Joe.

''Would you believe I'm just taking in the beautiful view? We had nothing like this back in Miami. Just miles of sand and ocean and—''

''Cut it out, Joe. I know why you're here.'' She moved a step closer. He could see the pulse beat against the white column of her throat, and he caught a subtle whiff of a delicate floral scent. Sheriffs weren't supposed to smell like this, he thought. They weren't supposed to remind you of roses after a spring rain. They were supposed to be big and burly and tough. He stared at her.

Willie cleared her throat. ''Look, Joe. If I'm going to give you a bad time for being here, the least you can do is pay attention.''

He looked at her face and thought he saw a hint of a smile in her eyes.

"Sorry." He shrugged. "I was just thinking that it's no use making up some story about why I would get up at five o'clock in the morning to take a walk in some farmer's field. I'm here for the same reason you are. I wanted to see if there was any hard evidence to Bishop's story."

"Seems to me you should have thought about that before you printed it in your newspaper."

"Nobody had any dead turkeys when I printed my story. It was just a human-interest piece."

"And now what is it?"

"A case—a bona fide case—that needs to be solved."

Immediately he could sense the change in Willie. She tensed her body; her eyes lost their warmth.

"You're right, Joe. It's a case. My case. I'm the sheriff. This isn't Miami, and you're not the star of the show. You're just a newspaperman in a one-newspaper town. You print the news; you don't go out and make it."

"I'm just trying to find out what happened to that old man's turkeys." This was the first time he'd seen Willie angry, and there was something about her that demanded his full attention.

"You're trying to make a story. Linking livestock deaths and UFOs on the evidence we have now would be pure fiction. We don't know what Matt Bishop saw. But one thing is certain: it wasn't a UFO."

"What makes you so sure of that?" Joe knew the question was ridiculous; he just wanted to know why she was sure it wasn't.

"Because if there is intelligent life out there, why would they come to Colorado and kill turkeys? There's no motive."

"Motive?" The simplicity of her answer threw Joe off.

"Yes, motive. For every crime there's a motive. Even one involving extraterrestrials."

"I see." Joe looked down at the ground. He couldn't argue with her logic.

"No, you don't see." She brought her hands up and rested them against her slim hips. "What I'm telling you is I want you out of here and off this story. I'll solve the case, and then I promise you'll be the first newspaper reporter I'll call."

"You can't tell me what to do." Joe could feel the anger rising inside him.

"Yes, I can. I want you to leave it alone."

"And if I don't?"

"There are laws against tampering with evidence, against interfering with an investigation."

"You wouldn't dare." Joe knew she was bluffing. At least he hoped she was bluffing. "You're up for reelection in less than six weeks. You can't afford to alienate the owner of the county's only newspaper."

"Can't I?" She stepped closer, and he could see the embers in her golden eyes. Once again, he was reminded of that sleek female bobcat. "I'm interested in one thing. Solving the case. I'm not a politician. If you're going to use that newspaper of yours against me, then go ahead. I won't let your threats or anyone else's interfere with my job."

"Wait a minute." He forced his voice to soften. "I wasn't threatening you."

"That's what it sounded like to me."

He stepped closer. There was less than a foot between them, and Willie started to back up. He wrapped his hand around hers. He felt her muscles tighten as she tried to pull away. Reflexively he tightened his grip. "What are you afraid of, Willie Callen?"

"Let go of my hand," she whispered.

He let go, but she didn't move. He stood over her, and impulsively he took off her hat. When she looked up at him, her eyes hadn't softened.

"What kind of game are you playing, Joe? This isn't a football field. It's a real town. And these are real people, not just some reporter's fantasy in a magazine."

"I'm not playing any game, Willie. And I'm not trying to do your job."

Willie looked at him, and Joe felt she was trying to read something in his face.

"Why did you come back, Joe? What are you trying to prove by taking over a two-bit newspaper in a two-bit town?"

She was so close he could feel her breath against his cheek. The sun had risen a bit, and the wind was stirring the dust in the little gully. Her eyes glowed, and suddenly he longed to feel her golden skin against his lips. Instead he swallowed hard and took a deep breath. "I told you. I've come home."

"Men like you don't come home, Joe." She looked at him as if daring him to contradict her.

"This one has." He closed the gap between them with one subtle movement. Slowly his hand came up, and he cupped it next to her cheek and nestled it against her face. His voice was a husky whisper. "And whether you like it or not, I'm here to stay."

Deliberately he brought his arm against her back and eased her body toward his. He knew that if he had done it swiftly she would have found it easy to push him away. But he was slow, his eyes holding hers, and it seemed as if minutes passed before their bodies actually touched. Gently he brought his lips to hers, and with the slightest pressure he touched her.

Against his mouth he felt her resistance, and lessened it with delicate insistence. He could feel her thigh muscles relax, and her whole body seemed to melt into his. He knew he wanted her, and for a moment he felt his desire threatening to race out of control. He released her and stepped back, her back still cradled in his arm.

It was only a second before she recovered, easing away and taking her hat from his hand. She put it on her head and stepped back a few feet.

"You only proved one thing, Joe," she said, then turned and walked up the side of the gully.

"What's that, Willie?" he called after her.

She didn't stop until she had reached the top of the ridge. Then she looked down at him. "That you're one heck of a good kisser." She turned and was gone.

Willie started the engine on the Cherokee and backed up on the little dirt road. She had turned onto the main road before she let herself bring her hand up to her cheek. She swore she could still feel the heat of Joe's touch and then cursed under her breath.

If he'd grabbed her, she could've pushed him away. But he hadn't. His touch had felt like nothing she'd ever experienced. It was slow and soft and sure...very sure. He'd known exactly what she would do, how she would react. And Willie Callen had to admit that scared her.

The heat had left her cheeks by the time she pulled into her parking space in front of the courthouse.

"Good morning, Sheriff." Hannah smiled as Willie passed her cubicle. "Mrs. Wiemer's called already. Twice. I think it's about Matt Bishop's turkeys. Seems Grady Wheeler was over at the Wagon Wheel last night talking about how it was those aliens in the UFO. A couple of other people have called, too." She sifted through some papers and handed a bunch to Willie. "If you want my opinion, I think Grady's crazier than a bed—"

"Thanks, Hannah." Willie cut her off. It was only 7:00 a.m. How had Hannah found out Grady had been at the Wagon Wheel? That woman must have sources all over town, she mused.

Willie was wondering whether to waste her time now or later on Mrs. Wiemer, when the phone rang. Hannah settled the question for her by putting the woman's call through. Willie spent the next fifteen minutes trying to reassure Mrs. Wiemer that she and her deputies were doing all they could for both the citizens and the turkeys of San Juan

County. Willie listened patiently as Lucy explained her vision of the aliens and as she offered to lead the welcoming party for the visitors from outer space. Lucy, she told Willie, was sure that the aliens had already communicated with her and wanted to know if she could help Willie settle the matter of the dead turkeys. When Willie finally put the phone down, Carl had come in.

"LeRoy just told me about old man Bishop's turkeys. It's too bad. I just hope that whatever it is, it doesn't spread to the rest of the valley."

For most of the morning Willie tried to clear up a backlog of paperwork. The routine reports of fender benders and petty thefts weren't compelling enough to keep her mind from wandering back to Joe. Every time she thought she'd replaced his face with another fact on paper, those cool blue eyes were staring up at her from the forms on her desk. She could feel the callused hand against her cheek, the texture of his lips as they brushed against hers.

She was staring down at her desk when Carl spoke again. "It's a quarter to ten, Willie."

Willie looked up. "It is?"

Carl nodded, then smiled. "I guess you'll want me to go over to the grade school. Remember? It's safety week, and we promised to send someone over."

"No, I'll go." She grabbed her hat, grateful for the diversion. "You did it last time." She was out of the office before Carl could say another word.

It took a roomful of eager first-graders to finally drive Joe from her mind. It was nearly noon by the time she was finished and she headed for the school parking lot. Her steps slowed when she caught sight of an increasingly familiar form. It was Joe Kelly, and he was leaning against her car.

"What do you want?" she demanded.

"I just picked up my car from the garage. I drove past, saw your car parked here and decided to stop." He turned toward her and put his hand against the door, preventing her from getting in. "I thought you'd be pleased to see me."

"What makes you say that?"

"After the compliment you paid me this morning, I thought you'd let me take you to lunch."

"I said you could kiss. I didn't say I wanted to see you. Besides, it only proves what they say is true."

"And what's that?"

"That practice makes perfect." She removed his arm, opened the door and got inside. "Obviously, you've had a lot of practice. You don't need me." She put the key in the ignition.

Joe leaned in through the open window. "I suppose this means no to the lunch."

"It means no to the lunch."

He shrugged. "Then how about tonight? I've got two tickets to the dance at the Sportsman's Club. A lot of people will be there—a lot of voters."

"Thanks, but I've already bought my own ticket."

"So that's it." He smiled and looked around. It was noon, and a crowd of schoolchildren were racing out of the building for lunch.

Willie looked at him. "What do you mean, 'so that's it'?"

"I'm good enough to kiss in a gully but not good enough to take you to a dance."

She studied his face. It was a face that could get away with anything. Almost anything. But the light in his eyes and the darkening of the thin red line on his cheek gave him away. "You're the one who kissed me."

"You kissed back."

She was about to set him straight when she became aware that several pairs of inquisitive eyes were staring at them. Some of the first-graders who'd heard her talk about safety were listening to her now.

"I think we'd better discuss this later," she whispered as she smiled at the children through clenched teeth.

Joe glanced around at their audience, then turned back to Willie.

"This is something I want to settle now," he said calmly, in a voice that was sure to carry. "Did you or did you not kiss me back?"

At the mention of the word "kiss," two pink-cheeked little girls started to giggle. A freckle-faced boy rolled his eyes. Willie couldn't believe she was having this discussion in front of the kids.

"Okay, you win." She started up the car. "Pick me up at eight." She waved to the kids and slowly backed out of the parking lot. The look of satisfaction on Joe's face was unmistakable.

It was five-thirty and Willie still hadn't left the sheriff's office. She paced back and forth, until Wes finally said, "What's up, boss?" He smiled and eyed the clock. "I'll wait until LeRoy comes in. If the lab up in Denver hasn't called by now, they won't call until morning."

Willie nodded, perfectly willing to let her deputy think she was eager to hear about the lab results on some dead turkeys. In fact she was, but that wasn't what had her pacing the floor. It was the dance.

The dance wouldn't have been easy under any circumstances. It was an annual event sponsored by several civic groups. She'd gone for years, first with her husband and then as a single woman. Now she was going as the sheriff. This would be her fourth year. And it hadn't gotten any easier.

It was the kind of occasion that always gave her the most trouble. She couldn't very well wear her uniform to a dance. But even without it, no one was likely to forget that she was the sheriff. And something in the back of nearly everyone's mind, including hers, said that sheriffs didn't wear dresses. It had taken her a long time to decide that this sheriff did.

Now, just when she was getting used to the idea that she could occasionally recognize, even advertise, the fact that she was a woman, she had to face the prospect of going with Joe.

She glanced at her watch. In fifteen minutes her chances of getting something new to wear would be gone, because the only decent dress shop in town would be closed. She made her decision. She grabbed her hat and said good-night to Wes.

As Willie pulled up to the Cactus Flower, LaDonne Glover was putting the Closed sign in the door. When she saw Willie get out of her car, she waved and opened the door.

"Hi, Willie," LaDonne said as Willie stepped into her shop. "What can I do for you?"

Willie said nervously, "It's not too late to get something, is it?"

"So you're going to the dance tonight?" LaDonne grinned. "Come on in. I think I can find something you might like."

Willie and LaDonne had gone to school together, and though they hadn't been close, they'd known each other all their lives. LaDonne led her over to a rack near the back of the shop.

"These should be in your size." She looked at Willie, and her expression grew serious. "Do you want something really pretty, or are you going to settle for your usual sedate denim skirt?"

Willie looked at her. "So I'm that obvious, am I?"

LaDonne laughed. "I can't remember the last time you were in here—or the last time I saw you in a dress." She pulled several flowered skirts off the rack. "In fact, I think the last time was exactly a year ago, at the last dance."

Willie took the clothes, then started to look through the rack. She caught a glimpse of herself in the three-way mirror at the back of the shop. She stopped. It was an odd picture; a woman dressed in tailored slacks and a uniform top, a thick black leather belt defining her waist, a gun at her hip. Her hat hid her face, and she reached up to take it off. The flowered skirts lay draped over her arm like a limp bouquet.

LaDonne seemed to sense her unease. "Maybe this isn't your look," she said, and took the skirts from Willie and put them back on the rack. Then she took Willie's hat and set it on a chair. "You might as well make yourself comfortable. I have a feeling this is going to take a while."

It was almost seven by the time Willie parked in front of her house. She picked up the two hangers with clothes encased in long plastic bags and took them inside. LaDonne had finally found something, all right. And when Willie tore off the plastic and hung them from her closet door, she couldn't believe she'd just spent a good portion of her next paycheck on the two items she was looking at.

She reached out and stroked the skirt, the texture of the suede unbelievably smooth. It was the color of warm butter. When she'd tried it on, even she had to admit that the way it hugged her hips, then fell to a gentle fullness below her knees, was flattering. And the suede felt like heaven next to her skin. Willie remembered she had a pair of soft leather boots several shades darker than the skirt. LaDonne found a silk blouse in a paler shade of yellow, declaring it a perfect complement to the skirt. And LaDonne convinced Willie that both had been made for her. Willie experienced only a moment of doubt before she agreed.

She showered quickly. Willie wasn't about to let Joe catch her wrapped in a towel a second time. She let her hair fall into natural waves past her shoulders, then pinned it away from her face with several gold barrettes. As she put on earrings, she smiled, remembering Joe's story about the bobcat. Each earring was set with a large topaz.

She was in the bathroom putting the finishing touches on her makeup when she heard Joe's knock on the door. A swift glance in her mirror told her she had really stepped out of character this time. Looking at her reflection, she realized it was possible that even she might forget she was the sheriff.

Nothing she'd seen in the mirror, however, prepared her for the expression of surprise on Joe's face when he saw her. For a moment she thought something must be wrong—maybe LaDonne had been intent on making her look foolish, and she had willingly cooperated.

Joe did a double take, then looked at the outside of her house.

"You are the Willie Callen I kissed this morning, aren't you?"

"If you're going to keep bringing that up, you might as well turn around and go back home. I'm getting sick and tired of—"

He raised a hand. "Now I'm positive you're the same Willie Callen." He grinned. "I just had to make sure. Nobody can give me hell faster than you." He stepped inside and closed the door behind him. "Don't hold it against me, but I must admit you don't look like a sheriff. You're beautiful." She opened her mouth, and again he put up a hand before she could speak. "I meant that only as a compliment. You make a great-looking sheriff, too."

"Thank you," she said quietly. She stopped in front of the door. "To show you I'm taking this all in the right spirit, I'll even let you open the door."

With a flourish he did so, then stepped aside to let her go first. She even waited for him to open the door to his red Blazer. It was the first time she'd ridden with him in his own car. She somehow felt a little better knowing that the door didn't have *San Juan Independent* plastered all over it.

It was a short drive out to the south end of town and the Sportsman's Club, a rambling cinder block building whose owners had tried valiantly to disguise it as something else. Cisco's one attempt at big-city sophistication, it succeeded because most of the farmers in Cisco had no idea what big cities were like. The interior had been redone in soft hues of coral and green and the dance floor lit with recessed floor lights, which gave it a slight disco flavor. The overall effect made the country-and-western bands that played there seem vaguely out of place.

Willie found it hard to ignore the obvious interest she and Joe aroused as they entered together. Tom Hubbard, Hannah's brother and mayor of Cisco, was the first to greet them.

"Willie?" he said, all smiles. Then he looked approvingly at Joe. "So this is what our sheriff really looks like." He leaned forward and gave her a peck on the cheek and Joe a slap on the back.

Joe exchanged a few pleasantries, but Willie was stunned. As they walked away, he bent down. "What's wrong now?" Joe whispered in her ear. "We've been here only two minutes. What could I have possibly done wrong?"

"It wasn't you. It was the mayor."

Joe turned around and looked at the back of Tom Hubbard's plaid sport jacket. He was busy hovering over someone else. Joe turned back to Willie. "So what did he do?"

"He kissed me." She turned to him. "Didn't you see that?"

"So? He's kissing everybody tonight. The man's up for reelection."

"Well, so am I, and you don't see me going around kissing everyone in sight." Willie nodded to several other people as they made their way to a booth. "He's never done it before. Just because I put on a skirt doesn't mean that I'm some little sweetie every man can kiss."

Joe stopped and faced her. "Look, Willie, don't you think you're overreacting? You look great. Why don't you just forget your job for one night and enjoy yourself?"

Willie bit her lip. "Maybe you're right. It's just that I walk such a fine line. I've worked so hard on just the right image."

They sat down and each ordered a glass of white wine. After the waitress had gone, Joe looked at Willie.

"Your image looks just fine from here." He smiled, showing his even teeth against a clean-shaven face. She realized for the first time since he'd been back that his pretty-boy face had become quite handsome. A certain strength that had only been hinted at years ago was now clearly visible.

Self-consciously he brought a hand up to his face and rubbed it. "What's the matter? Did I miss a spot shaving?"

"No, you look just fine," she answered nervously. "I mean your face looks good." She laughed. "I was just wondering how you managed to keep all those teeth after being knocked around for the last twenty years."

Joe grinned. "The truth of the matter is I'd rather get hit anywhere but my face." Almost automatically he put his hand up to his cheek. With his finger he traced the outline of the scar that ran from cheekbone to jawline. "After I got this little souvenir in college—along with a broken nose—I decided I'd better watch it or I'd end up with a face I didn't recognize."

"Football's a rough sport."

"Football? It had nothing to do with playing football. I got this after the game."

"How's that?"

"Let's just say I was celebrating a bit too vigorously."

"A fight? You got into a fight?"

Joe nodded. "But those days are long past. I've had enough violence both on and off the field to last me for a while."

"I didn't know you'd even been a fighter. All I remember was the big, handsome hunk in a red-and-white jacket who used to take my sister out. You seemed so—so..." She paused, searching for the word. "Special."

"Every girl's hero, right?"

Willie nodded. "I guess so."

"And heroes don't leave your big sister waiting at the altar, right?"

The waitress arrived with their drinks, and Willie wondered whether she should tell him about her phone call to her sister, Irene. She hated to admit that she'd gotten that wrong, too.

"I called Irene this afternoon," she finally admitted.

He looked at her. "How is she?"

"Fine." She paused and took a sip of wine. "She laughed when I asked her about you, about your engagement. She couldn't even remember what she'd told me. When I reminded her, she said she'd just made the whole thing up. She never wanted to marry you." Willie looked down into her wineglass. "I guess I was the only one who wanted you two to get together."

"Irene said she didn't want to marry me?" His tone was serious, and then she looked at him. He laughed. "Forget about the past, Willie. That Joe Kelly is only a memory, just like that skinny little thirteen-year-old I used to call Silly Willie."

"I didn't know you called me that."

"There's a lot you don't know about me, Willie."

His eyes focused on hers, and he reached across the table for her hand. He touched her lightly, tracing a gentle line from wrist to tip. She didn't want him to stop. As if reading her mind, he went on to the next finger, retracing his path. She took a deep breath.

"You're an incredible woman, Willie."

She could see he knew she was going to balk at such an obvious line, but before she could protest, he went on.

"That's not just a line, so let me finish." He continued to touch her hand. The pressure was so light, yet she could feel it reach through to the rest of her body.

"I came here," he continued, "expecting to find a woman, whom I used to know, trying to do a man's job. I couldn't imagine you as a sheriff." He smiled and held up his free hand. "But before you chew me out, let me say that whatever doubts I've had are swiftly disappearing. I think you're handling the job as well as or better than most men could. And despite our recent differences, I think we can work together."

"I guess you've just forced me to declare a truce, haven't you?"

"That was the idea. I hate to have you as the opposition." His eyes lit up, their cool blue depths suddenly turning warm. "Besides, this morning you nearly scared the pants off me."

"Was that before or after you kissed me?" She smiled. "That was a great tactic. Do you use it often?"

"Only when I meet sexy female sheriffs."

He'd reached the tip of her little finger, and they both looked down, unwilling to break contact. He wrapped his hand around hers and stood. "Would you like to dance? I'm dying to use a socially acceptable way to find out if your outfit feels as good as it looks."

# Chapter 5

Joe led her to the dance floor. The band had just begun a slow number, and Willie felt surprisingly comfortable in his arms. The slight pressure of his hand on her back as he led her around the floor made her aware once again that this was a man who'd made a fortune perfecting his physical skills.

He held her so that he could look at her face, his attention obvious.

"This hasn't turned out to be so bad, has it?" He gazed around. "I think you've caused more of a stir with that sensational outfit than you have coming here with me."

"It probably seems silly to you, but I've spent the past four years trying to persuade this town to see me as their sheriff. It feels strange to let them see me as a woman."

"It's sort of like trying to make people see you as a small-town newspaperman, instead of an ex-football player." He drew his hand up to her hair and traced the ridge of her ear, never letting go of her hand.

"I've been a little hard on you. I admit it." She looked up and noticed the surprise in his face. "I can't believe I actually said that."

He smiled. "If you'd just stop and think about it, you'd see it really isn't so strange that I ended up here running the paper. It's in my blood." He drew her closer. "I remember how much I wanted to be like my old man, even when I couldn't wait to get out of this town. Did you know I majored in journalism?"

Willie shook her head. "I guess I never thought of you doing anything in college except playing football."

He smiled. "I have done a few other things in my life."

He brushed the tip of Willie's chin with his fingers and pressed her closer to him. She felt his hand across her back, and its heat flowed through her body and nestled deep inside her stomach.

"I even have a fairly good mind, believe it or not." He looked into her eyes and brushed her hair back. His touch sent sparks through her hair, and she laughed.

"So you're not just another pretty face?"

"Right." He whirled her around as the band's tempo picked up. "Maybe I knew that in the back of my head I'd always end up here. Too bad it took an unfortunate set of circumstances to bring me."

Willie gave in to the desire to rest her head against his chest. For the rest of the dance she felt his chin near her temple. She could smell the fresh, crisp scent of him, and closed her eyes. He started humming, and to her delight, he was quite off-key. She closed her eyes, and he led her across the dance floor. One slow number finished, and she prayed the band would start up another. They did.

Halfway through the third dance, he started nibbling at her ear. "Stop that," she said, laughing.

"Give me a good reason," he whispered. But he stopped and held her as they moved around the floor.

Finally he spoke again. "See? We can get along," he whispered into her hair.

"That's only because you're such a good dancer."

"So why don't you let this good dancer work with you on the case? We could solve the Great Turkey Caper together."

Willie slowed, losing track of the beat. For a moment she let her heart sink. "Is this what you've been leading up to? You got me up here so you could talk your way into this investigation?" She tried to control the anger by keeping her voice down.

Joe stopped. "And what's wrong with that?"

Willie started to walk off the dance floor, but he stopped her. He took her in his arms and started to dance again.

"Let me go," she whispered, her voice tight.

"You're going to hear me out. I'll be damned if I'm going to let you walk away from me the way you did this morning. You're driving me crazy."

"I'm driving you crazy!" Willie said loudly. Several couples turned and stared.

Joe smiled and led her away. "You heard what I said." He took her back to their table and they sat down.

"How can you say I'm driving you crazy? I'm just trying to do my job. You're the one who's writing all those crazy stories about UFOs and aliens."

"I didn't mention aliens. Bishop's the one who mentioned aliens."

"Whatever. You may not realize it, but people in this town believe what they read in your newspaper. Your father made them believe. Paul made them believe. They don't realize that the *San Juan Independent* is in the hands of an irresponsible, egotistical football player."

Joe shook his head. "There you go again. I've accepted you as the sheriff. Why can't you accept me as a newspaperman?"

"I will as soon as you start acting like one."

He took a sip of his wine. When he spoke again his voice was quiet. "You're just afraid of me, Willie Callen. Afraid that I might be better at your job than you are." Then he edged his hand across the table and covered hers. "Or are you afraid I'll keep reminding you that you're a woman?"

"I'm not afraid," she answered quietly. "And don't flatter yourself, Joe."

Willie looked around. She knew she was in a corner. Joe wasn't going to drop this UFO thing until he had seen it through. If she'd learned anything about Joe in the past few days, it was that he was persistent. She raised her wineglass and drained it. Then she took a deep breath. She'd show him she wasn't afraid.

"I know I'm going to regret this, but I'll let you work with me." She watched his face. A smile softened the hard line of his mouth. "But I don't want you to get in my way." She looked at him, certain that not a hint of a smile showed on her face. "And I don't want you to forget who's in charge."

His grin broadened. "There's no chance of that."

"I hope you realize that the only reason I'm doing this is I know you'll investigate it anyway. I might as well see that you get it right."

Joe smiled. "Anything you say, Sheriff." He motioned to the waitress and ordered another round of drinks.

"Why did you do that?" Willie asked.

"What do you mean?"

"Now that you've got your business out of the way, why don't you just take me home?"

"Willie, Willie." Joe shook his head. "When are you going to learn to relax?" He stood up. "I don't know about you, but I came here to enjoy myself." He reached for her. "Let's have another dance."

Before Willie knew it, she was back on her feet and in his arms. Almost against her will, she felt her stiff body relax as he held her. Without a word, they moved around the floor. Willie was trying to give him the silent treatment, but Joe didn't seem to notice. He was enjoying himself too much. As the number ended, they backed up a bit and bumped straight into another group of dancers.

"Well, well," one of the men said as he turned around. "Look at what we got us here." The voice belonged to Bud Beede. He was standing with her opponent in the sheriff's race, Virgil Jones. Bud was a friend of Virgil's and, as far as Willie was concerned, an absolute jerk.

Bud looked at Willie and then back at Virgil, who was standing behind him. "Looks like if you want to be sheriff in this town, Virgil, you're gonna have to get you some sexier duds." He eyed Willie.

Virgil smiled at Willie. "You look great tonight, Willie."

"Yeah," Bud added. "She does look mighty nice. We got us about the best-looking sheriff in the whole country." He paused for a moment and looked around. "Too bad we need more than looks. Somebody's out there killing off our turkey crop, and the sheriff here is putting on a fashion show."

Willie stepped forward and looked Bud straight in the eye. "What makes you think the turkeys are deliberately being killed, Bud?" Willie asked, keeping her voice even.

"It doesn't take somebody with a fancy college education to figure that one out." He looked around him, satisfied that his cross-examination was drawing a crowd. "The turkeys didn't kill themselves." He paused and stepped closer to Willie. "Of course, Willie here probably thinks it was those aliens that did it." He laughed loudly. A few of the bystanders joined in. "It may be a while before the perpetrators are brought to justice." Again he looked around the room for emphasis. "We all know how hard it is to catch aliens." He laughed at his own joke.

Willie smiled. "If somebody is killing turkeys, you can bet he won't come from outer space."

"That's not what your boyfriend here thinks—is it, Joe?" This time it was Bud's younger brother, Doug, who spoke.

Willie could feel her face heating up and hoped the dim lights covered any sign of a blush.

"I just report the news. I don't make it," Joe answered. "All I'm saying is that some citizens have been seeing some unexplained phenomena." He wasn't smiling.

Bud looked at Willie, then at Joe. "Well, all I can say is it's mighty convenient for the sheriff to have the owner of the county's only newspaper in her pocket." He leered at Willie.

"Or between the sheets," Doug Beede added.

Joe stepped forward. Willie noticed that the scar on his face had turned a deep crimson, and when she touched his upper arm, it felt like a band of coiled steel.

"Hold it, Joe," she said quietly. "This is a free country. People are allowed to say whatever they want, no matter how stupid." She turned around, her arm linked through Joe's. "Let's go back to our table."

"Tell me, Joe," Bud called after they had taken several steps back to their table. His voice carried across the room. "How does our Sheriff Willie compare with all those city women you've had?"

Joe whipped around, tearing his arm away from Willie's. "If you want to step outside, Bud, I'll be glad to tell you all about it." His voice was hard. Joe stepped up to Bud; he towered over him and outweighed him by at least thirty pounds. Willie knew Joe was just looking for an excuse to tear into him.

Willie and Virgil stepped between them.

"Bud didn't mean anything, Willie," Virgil said, carefully keeping his voice cheerful. "He was just having a little fun." He appealed to Joe. "That's what we're all here for, isn't it, a little fun? Maybe the guy's had a bit too much to drink." He turned back to Willie. "Why don't you call off your friend here and we'll just forget this little conversation ever happened?"

Willie looked around. By now, half the people at the dance were watching. I'll just *bet* they'll forget, Willie thought.

"Come on, Joe." She touched him. "Let's go back to our table and sit down."

Joe hesitated, then stepped up to Bud. "Anytime you want to continue this discussion, I'll be glad to cooperate."

His voice was soft and controlled. Then he smiled and took Willie's arm. They walked through the crowd and back to their booth.

For a moment Willie just stared at her drink. Then she took a long swallow and stared at Joe. "What would you have done if I hadn't stopped you?"

He looked at her, his eyes wide with surprise at the question. "I would have smashed that little idiot's head in."

"That's just what I thought," she said and felt herself stiffen. "And I suppose that would have solved everything?"

"Well, what did you expect me to say?" Joe's voice was indignant. "The man was being an idiot. He said our sleeping together was influencing what I was putting in the paper."

"We aren't sleeping together, Joe Kelly." It was all Willie could do to keep her voice down.

"That's only a technicality."

Willie put both hands on the table and leaned forward. "It may be a technicality to you, but it's reality to me."

"What are you getting mad at me for?" Joe looked at her, then smiled. "If you're mad because we aren't sleeping together, that can easily be remedied."

She stood up. "You're as bad as those Beede brothers. No matter what a woman does or says, all you can think about is what she's like in bed." Willie walked away from the booth.

"Oh, no," Joe said under his breath as he followed her. "Will you calm down, Willie? Just because a couple of good ole boys gave you a bad time doesn't mean you have to take it out on me."

She whirled around. "What am I supposed to do? Stay and let another good ole boy like you make it up to me?"

Willie walked toward the exit. A few of the couples were already leaving. She spotted Carl and his bride, Holly, at the door.

"Excuse me, you two," Willie said as she stood behind the couple. Carl turned around.

"Hi, Willie." Carl grinned, then looked at Holly. "We were just calling it a night."

"I was thinking of doing the same thing myself, Carl," Willie answered. "Would you mind dropping me off on your way home?"

"No, Sheriff, it won't be any trouble." Carl stared at Joe, who was standing behind Willie. "I hope you two didn't let Bud spoil your evening."

Holly nodded. "Nobody pays any attention to those Beede boys. I told the people at our table that what Bud said just wasn't true. You and Joe just started going out, I told them. How could you possibly be...?" Her husband glared at her as she let her voice trail off.

"We just told them it wasn't any of our business what you two did. You're both over twenty-one." He looked at Joe again. "Are you sure you don't want to stay, Willie?"

"I'm sure. But I think Joe wants to stay. I don't want to cramp his style." She walked out the door. Carl and Holly followed.

She thought she heard Joe call after her as she walked out to the parking lot, but she didn't turn around to see if it was him. She'd had enough for one night. Maybe all Joe had wanted was to persuade her to let him work with her on the investigation. If that's all he wanted, then he should be satisfied that the night was a success.

Joe leaned his elbows against the bar and nursed his second Scotch. He stirred his drink with a swizzle stick as he stared blankly at the TV jutting out of the wall above the bar. The sound was turned off. As far as he could tell, the images belonged to some late-night talk show. He smiled as he remembered he'd once been a guest on those shows. He raised his glass to the silent host, then drained it. If they could only see him now. Joe Kelly, closing down the bar in Cisco, Colorado.

He thought about ordering another drink, and then he remembered he still had to drive home. And he had to get up and go to work in the morning. The thought that the amber liquid might smother the image of Willie made it tempting, but he resisted.

Willie. Just when he thought he was getting somewhere with her, she turned on him like a rattlesnake. So what if those two clowns the Beede boys had thought they were sleeping together? As Carl had said, they were both over twenty-one. He didn't know what made him angrier—Bud Beede introducing Joe's private life as a topic of public conversation, or the way Willie had reacted to that topic.

The bartender looked at him from the other end of the bar, then walked over. "Look, Joe, whatever it is, why don't you pack it up and take it home?" He pointed to his watch. "It's nearly two, and I've got to close up." He took Joe's empty glass off the counter. "You're not buying anyway."

Joe nodded and put some bills on the counter. Somewhere between the exit to the parking lot and his car, he thought he might do it. By the time he put the key into the ignition and pulled onto the highway, he knew he was going to do it. He turned his car around and headed toward Willie's house.

It didn't take much knocking to get her out of bed. I guess a sheriff gets used to all kinds of late-night visitors, he thought as he stood nervously on her front porch.

When she opened the door, she was wrapped in a blue cotton robe. Her hair fell down around her shoulders like a cloud. He wanted to bury his face in it. Instead, he managed to keep his expression sober until she'd gotten a good look at him.

For a long time she didn't speak, but just stood there, holding the door open. She made no move to invite him in.

Joe finally broke the silence. "I suppose you're wondering why I'm here."

"I suppose I am." Her face betrayed nothing. He couldn't tell whether she was angry, amused or merely annoyed.

"I want to talk to you." He was aware that he looked a bit scruffy. He'd undone his tie hours before, and it hung around his neck like a scarf. And he didn't have to look in a mirror to tell that already a slight stubble was making a shadow across his face.

"It's almost two-thirty in the morning. Can't it wait?"

He shook his head. "No, it can't wait." He stood there, the porch light glaring down on him like a spotlight. "Why don't you ask me in?"

Willie stepped aside and held open the screen door. It was as much of an invitation as he was going to get, so he took it.

He stood in the middle of the room, wondering whether he should sit or stand. Suddenly he was aware of how warm the night was, and pulled his shirt open.

"Can I take your jacket?" Willie asked from behind him. He turned around. He could tell she was studying him. Her practiced eye was probably gauging just how much he'd had to drink.

"Sure," he answered, and as he moved to take it off, he felt his bad knee buckle. Before he knew it he was on the floor.

Willie bent to help him up. "Maybe we'd better postpone this discussion until we're both a bit more . . . uh, sober?" She got him over to the sofa.

"I'm fine." Joe tried to smooth his hair back with his fingers. "We have to talk now. Besides, I haven't had that much to drink."

Willie stared at him for a moment and then folded her arms across her chest as if she'd come to a decision.

"Experience tells me that once you've made up your mind, you're impossible," she began.

"Thank you."

"It wasn't a compliment," she replied, tossing his jacket over the nearest chair. "But since you're set on staying and having a discussion, I suggest you take a shower first while I make a pot of coffee."

Joe grinned. "You mean you're not going to throw me out?"

"Would it do any good if I tried?"

"No." Joe shook his head as Willie pulled him to his feet. His knee was still wobbly, and he had to flex it a couple of times before he could stand.

"Are you okay?" she asked.

"Sure, just point me to the shower."

Willie led him down the hall. He walked past the open door to her bedroom. The huge brass bed was a mass of tumbled sheets. Probably still warm, he thought wistfully as she pushed him into the next room.

It was a pale-pink and beige bathroom, and he could tell just by its scent that it belonged to a woman. It was a delicious, warm smell, like wild roses on a hot summer night. He hadn't been in a bathroom like this in a long time. Willie disappeared for a moment and returned with an armful of towels and a robe. She held it up to him. It was white terry cloth and came to midthigh.

"This will have to do," she announced, her voice businesslike. "Just throw your clothes out in the hall and I'll hang them up."

"You mean I'm not going to put my clothes back on?" He smiled at the thought. Maybe she was going to let him stay the night.

"I can't let you drive home like this. You can barely stand up. All you need is a DWI. That would really get the gossip mills going." She shut the door, then quickly opened it again. "You can sleep in the spare bedroom." She slammed the door and he was alone.

So much for the big brass bed and the still-warm sheets, he thought as he undressed. His knee throbbed, and he sat on the edge of the tub to pull off his pants. For once, his football injury had come in handy, he thought as he looked at the cross-stitching of scars that covered his left knee. It had made Willie think he was almost falling-down drunk, when in fact he was almost cold sober.

The water created a little cloud of heavenly warmth, and he lay down full-length in the tub and let the pellets of liquid beat against his body. There was something utterly comforting in knowing that another human being hovered close by, fixing coffee, worrying about him. Hell, he thought, Willie was probably cursing him, but even that didn't matter.

He closed his eyes and her image rose up in the mist, her soft curves wrapped in blue cotton as she puttered around the kitchen. Every so often a strand of hair fell across her face and his hand was there to brush it out of the way. He could see her face then, her eyes soft as amber, her lips wide and waiting and . . .

Someone was knocking on the door. He felt a rush of cold air as the door opened.

"Are you okay in there?" Willie asked.

Joe smiled. Her voice was music to his ears. He could even smell the freshly made coffee. He shut his eyes again.

"Joe?" she asked. Then the shower curtain was pulled aside. It was Willie, and though her eyes weren't quite as soft as he'd imagined them, they were concerned.

He could tell she was making a valiant effort to keep her gaze from straying below his chest. But he made no effort to cover himself, and instead watched her face as she lost the battle.

"I thought you might have..." Her voice trailed off as her eyes traveled the length of his body. He acknowledged the effects of her attention as he felt himself coil up in a tight knot of desire. Her eyes focused on the evidence of his arousal, and she quickly pulled the shower curtain between them.

"I can see that you're fine."

He chuckled to himself. "I'll be out in a minute," he called after her as she closed the door loudly.

When he appeared in the kitchen fifteen minutes later, she was busy at the sink, washing up some dishes. Her robe barely covered the top of his thighs and stretched tightly across his shoulders, but he walked unselfconsciously into the room and stood next to her.

"I suppose you think that was funny," she said as she rinsed a cup, not bothering to look up at him. "And I thought you'd passed out in my tub and were drowning."

She turned to him and she could read the frustration in his eyes. "I wasn't laughing at you," he said quietly. "And I'm not drunk." He reached up a hand to brush the hair back from her face.

"You could've fooled me. You can barely stand up," she answered, and her hand went up to pull his away. But instead, when their fingers made contact, she let hers rest against his.

"It's a bad knee, an old injury." He stepped back and flexed his knee. "This is one of the reasons I'm sitting behind a desk, trying to put out a newspaper, instead of out there, throwing a football." He laughed when she gasped. "This and the fact that I'm thirty-eight years old."

"It looks terrible," Willie said as she turned away from the sink and led him to a chair. "It looks like it fell off and Dr. Frankenstein tried to sew it back on."

"Oh, it's not all that bad," he said, enjoying her sympathy. She was at the stove now, pouring him a cup of coffee. "I've gotten used to it. Nobody plays football forever. Besides, if it hadn't been for this knee, I probably wouldn't be sitting here now."

Willie looked up from the coffee and brought it to the table. Then her face flushed and she glared at him.

"Joe Kelly, you weren't drunk at all!" She was indignant.

"That's what I've been trying to tell you. I just came over here because I wanted to talk."

"But you let me think you were drunk just so I wouldn't kick you out of here and make you drive home." Joe could tell she was really getting fired up. "Of all the mean, low-down tricks!"

He reached up and wrapped his arms around her. She was so close that he could pull her onto his lap. She struggled for a moment, but Joe had a practiced hand when it came to a tackle, and quickly eased her down until she lost her balance and tumbled into his arms.

"Why did you do that?" she asked, her eyes wide with surprise. They were inches away from his, and he could see her pulse beat rapidly against her throat.

"I think you've given me enough hell for one night." He sighed as he bent over and kissed the spot where he could see her pulse. "There's only so much one man can take."

He moved his mouth until it met her lips. He brushed them lightly and when he felt no resistance, deepened the kiss. Her lips trembled slightly against his, not yet totally giving.

He raised his head and looked into her golden eyes. They were as soft as he'd imagined in his dreams.

"I thought you wanted to talk," she whispered.

"I've changed my mind," Joe answered as he pulled her closer and kissed her again. This time her mouth opened against his, and he knew she'd changed her mind, too.

# Chapter 6

Joe buried his head underneath the curtain of her hair, and Willie felt the soft warmth of his mouth against the base of her throat. Unconsciously she threw her head back as waves of pleasure washed over her body each time his lips touched her skin. Without realizing it, she had wrapped her arms around his shoulders. For a moment she tried to tell herself it was so that she wouldn't fall off his lap, but that only compelled her to admit she wanted to stay in his lap.

She heard him make a low, throaty sound as he nuzzled his way around her neck. She felt her robe slide off her shoulder, but before she could pull it back up, she felt his fingers close around her wrist. He faced her once again and slowly brought her hand up to his mouth. The blaze in his pale-blue eyes could light up the room, she thought. Reflected in the mirror of his dark pupils she saw her own image. It was the image of a tousle-haired woman, soft and open. It was a picture she hadn't seen in a long time.

He lightly bit the fleshy part of her palm just below her thumb, his eyes never leaving hers. The feeling and sight of his mouth on her sensitive skin made her want to close her eyes and give in to the delight. But something compelled her to keep them open.

"What are we doing, Joe?" she finally asked. They were the first words she'd spoken in minutes, and he seemed surprised by the sound of her voice.

He looked up and lowered her hand, not yet willing to release it. "You don't know?" His voice was as soft as his kisses had been.

She shook her head. "What do you want from me?"

"Nothing. Everything." He dropped her hand and wrapped his arms around her waist. "I want tonight."

"I..." she started to say, then realized that she didn't know what she was going to say.

"Look, Willie," he said, his voice quiet and even. "This isn't something I'm going to try to talk you into. It's simple. Either you want me or you don't."

He waited for only a moment, and when she didn't answer, he reached up and gently pulled her robe back onto her shoulder. Obviously he'd heard the catch in her voice, the slight hesitation that said no. She felt a wave of frustration. Willie wasn't so sure that was what she was saying. She was just trying to tell him she didn't know.

He eased her off his lap and tugged at his robe.

"I'm too tired to get dressed and drive home. I'll take you up on that offer of the spare bedroom, if it's still all right with you."

Willie nodded. Joe got up and walked toward the hallway, disappearing as the door swung shut behind him.

She stared at the space he'd occupied. As she closed her eyes, the sensation of his mouth against her skin came back to her. It had been a long time since she'd felt anything like that. Then she smiled. Who are you kidding? she told herself. You've never felt anything like that. No man had ever stirred her the way Joe just had. She felt as if her body had suddenly come alive under his touch, though it was a mystery to her why it had to be this particular man at this time.

She remembered the reflection of herself she'd seen in his eyes. It was the image of a woman, something she'd almost forgotten how to be. Desire swept over her, rising from some hidden depth within her. She wanted Joe. He'd been right; it was simple. She wanted to feel him lying next to her, his arms wrapped around her body.

It was easy for her to walk to the kitchen door and push it open. She almost swore she could hear the beat of her own heart as she walked down the hall. Something told her she was just about to do a very foolish thing, but then it had been a long time since she'd let herself be foolish—too long.

She opened the door to her spare room. He was already lying in bed. The room was all shadows, lit only by the moon and stars outside the open window. His head turned to her as she walked toward him, and he raised himself on one elbow. Even in the darkness she could see the surprise on his face. He didn't say anything; he only watched her, his eyes tracking every movement of her body.

She stood by his bed and let the robe slip off her shoulders. It fell to the floor and lay next to the one he'd been wearing. He threw off the cover and moved over, making room for her. As she slid into bed, she felt the warmth his body had left on the sheet beneath her. She could hear him hold his breath as he reached for her, letting it out when she was finally next to him. She felt his hand reach up and touch her hair, her face.

"I haven't just fallen asleep and started dreaming this, have I?" His voice was a whisper playing against her ear.

"No, you're not dreaming, Joe." She could feel the texture and heat of his skin as it met hers.

"Willie." He sighed as he gathered her close. "Willie. Who would have thought we'd make a pair."

He rolled over so that his body was above hers. She felt the welcome weight of his thighs on hers. She could feel the dark, coarse hair on his chest lightly brushing her breasts. He slid his hand under the back of her head and cupped it, then raised her head toward him and kissed her mouth, her eyes, until she felt that she would vanish into him, lost in the delight of his mouth against her body.

Then he laid her back down against the sheet. She felt dizzy with sensation. His mouth moved down her throat, past her collarbone, until it traced the soft, gentle rise of her breast. She felt her body arch toward him and threw her arms around his back.

Willie couldn't have him close enough, and the sweet, prickly feel of his cheek as it rubbed against her sensitive skin made her want to both laugh and cry. She felt alive, and she wanted Joe.

He sensed her need, and he lifted his head and brushed the hair out of her face, away from her eyes. Each stroke of his hand was a wave of heat she felt flow across her entire body. He held her with his eyes, caressed her. She couldn't see herself anymore, only him. Only Joe existed for her at this moment, and she felt his passion and need echo her own.

"Willie." There was nothing else for him to say. Everything was written on her face.

She gasped as she felt him inside her. She was lost in him, and he in her. They had let their need rule them, body and soul. With each movement she danced with him again, and he with her.

She wrapped herself around him, her long legs covering his, her arms spread across his broad back. The old Willie was about to shatter into pieces, her whole body alive with a pleasure she hadn't thought possible, for at that moment, Willie as she'd known herself had ceased to exist. A new Willie had been created to take her place. She was moving toward that moment where everything is pushed aside by the intensity of present feeling, of immediate emotion. She felt her body against his, saw his eyes lit with a fire she'd never seen. Together they vanished for a time into something new as they reached a peak and hovered there, suspended.

Afterward, Willie lay cradled in Joe's arms. It was a long while before he spoke. She thought he'd fallen asleep, so even was the rhythm of his breathing.

Finally his hand moved to stroke her hair. With the other he stroked the soft inner skin of her thigh.

"Where do we go from here, Willie?" His voice was low, caressing, yet somewhere in it was a touch of uncertainty. That surprised her.

"What do you mean?" But she already knew what he was asking. She turned and looked into his face. "I suppose we just give it time. We wait and see what happens."

He laughed.

"What's so funny?" she asked.

"We could really make quite a team, Willie Callen. If we don't kill each other first."

He laughed again as he pulled her closer. She let her eyes close. "I think you're safe," she whispered. "At least for tonight."

He kissed her and she relaxed in the pillow of his arms and fell asleep.

The sun shone on the quilt between them, making it look like a twisted stained-glass window. Willie moved and felt Joe stir beside her—or was it underneath her? She couldn't tell.

He opened one blue eye and looked at her.

"Good morning." He moved toward her, opened the other eye and looked around him, then back at Willie.

For a moment she felt her heart sink. Why did he look disappointed? she thought. Then he smiled and kissed her on the lips.

"For a moment I wondered if last night wasn't too good to be true."

He rolled over until his body was above her. He reached up and caressed her hair, letting his hand trail gently down her face. Willie could feel desire for him building again. She could feel his body tighten against hers, and she knew he was feeling the same need she had.

"But obviously I wasn't dreaming." He smiled.

"Obviously." She laughed and ran her hands through his hair. It was heavy and black, and for a moment she was caught by the contrast of it against her fingers. Then she let her hand trail down as she traced one of his eyebrows. Their darkness made his pale eyes seem so startling. And so beautiful. Automatically her hand followed the curve of his eye and fell beneath it. Lightly she ran a finger over his scar. He smiled and caught her hand. It was a reminder that he was human, flawed. She liked that.

"So," she whispered as she reached her free hand out to the bedside table, grabbing the alarm clock. It was nearly eleven, and it was Sunday. "What would you like for breakfast?"

"Just what I've got in my arms." He bent down and gently nipped her neck.

"If we keep this up," she said, laughing, as she pushed him away, "we'll never get out of bed."

"What's wrong with that?" He rolled on his back and pulled her on top of him.

"We'll starve to death. That's what's wrong with that."

She eased herself off him and onto her feet. For a moment she felt self-conscious, aware of her nakedness. Last night, the room had been dark, and she'd been ruled by her heart. In the sunlight now, she was aware of how much of herself she had exposed to him. She bent to retrieve her robe.

She could feel his hand brush against her back.

"Don't," he whispered.

She turned around, holding the robe in front of her body. "Don't what?" she asked.

"Feel any regrets." He sat up and reached for her, pulling the robe away. "You're beautiful, Willie. If you hide this from me—" he moved his hand across her body "—you'll only find it easier to hide what's inside. I couldn't handle that. Not with you."

She held his head against her for a long time. When she finally broke away and left the room, the robe still lay on the floor.

By the time they'd showered and dressed, it was afternoon. Willie stood at the stove, humming tunelessly as she fixed breakfast while Joe sat at the table, watching her.

"You act as if you've never seen a woman cook breakfast before." She turned around and smiled. "And I'm willing to bet a year's salary that isn't true."

"If that was a hint you want to know about my past, I'm an open book." He took a sip of coffee. "But I have to warn you that the real Joe Kelly isn't nearly as colorful as he's been portrayed."

"You didn't learn last night's moves on a football field." Willie dished the eggs out of the frying pan onto their plates. She brought them over to the table and sat beside him.

"Listen, Willie," he said, his eyes still focused on her as he reached his hand out to cover hers. "What we experienced was a first for me, too. The last thing I was expecting to find in Cisco was someone like you."

"'Someone like me'?" Her voice was softer, and Willie knew that she wanted to hear more.

"I'm trying to say that in spite of everything, you're incredible." He scooped some egg on his toast and took a bite.

"What do you mean, 'in spite of everything'?" Her voice wasn't quite so soft.

"I mean you're the sheriff, for starters." He looked at her, evidently amazed that she didn't find it as astounding as he did. "I'm not the kind of man who falls for the county sheriff. Even when the sheriff looks like you."

"But I'm a woman. It's just a job."

"I can't believe I just heard Willie Callen say that being a sheriff was just a job." He put his fork down. "It's your life, Willie."

"What if I were a schoolteacher? Would that make it any less 'incredible'?"

"Of course it would. All kinds of women are schoolteachers." He looked at her, and she could tell he had read the confusion on her face.

"But you're not all kinds of women; you're you. All I'm saying is that it's going to take some getting used to."

She shook her head. "I don't understand. What is it about me that is going to take getting used to?"

"The idea that I'm dating the sheriff. The idea of making love to the sheriff."

Willie felt the color rise to her face. "Am I so...so peculiar that I take getting used to?" She stood up and began to move around the kitchen. "Just because I'm not a model or an heiress, or whatever all your other women were, doesn't mean that I take some 'getting used to.'"

Joe got up and walked over to her. He wrapped his arms around her and held her, stroking her hair, soothing her agitation. "There haven't been all that many 'other women.' I was married once, but so were you. Let's forget about that. Let's begin now."

"I want to," Willie said, an edge of hesitation in her voice. "Oh, Joe, this is all so new for me, too. I didn't expect last night to happen." She could hear the quiver of emotion in her voice.

"Willie, Willie," he whispered in her ear. The caress of his breath was so light that she could barely feel it, but it was there, just as he was. "What's this all about?" He turned her around to face him. "All I'm trying to say is that I'm crazy about you. I want to see you. What we had last night, I want again." He kissed her. "And again."

Willie was surprised to feel her eyes sting with moisture. This was all so unbelievable, she thought. She looked at him. "You know the last thing I wanted to do was to start a relationship with you," she said. "It was hard enough for me to deal with you when you were just the publisher of the newspaper." She grabbed a paper towel and wiped her nose. "Now I have no idea what I'm going to do."

Joe smiled. "We'll do just fine, Willie. One day at a time." He lifted a finger and ran it down the tip of her nose, then he kissed each eye. "Neither of us can see what's going to become of this. It's too early to tell. And we're both too cautious to throw ourselves overboard without testing the waters."

"I rarely get this emotional, you know," she said, suddenly embarrassed.

"I like it when you're emotional."

He led her back to the table and they finished breakfast.

Joe wanted to spend the day together, but Willie convinced him that they needed a little time, some breathing space. She used the excuse that Sunday was the only day she could catch up on her laundry, her yard work, all the things she put off doing during the week. The truth was, she could have easily put them off another day.

What she really wanted was to try on the idea of Joe Kelly. She needed time to seriously consider the two of them. Together. It had taken her completely by surprise.

She wandered out in her backyard and found some afternoon shade under a big cottonwood. It was her favorite place. She'd bought this house when she'd come back to Cisco after she'd gotten out of the army. It had been good for her to get away, and it had been good for her to be back home again. A lot of people thought a woman didn't belong in the army, but it was there that Willie had grown up. She'd been married and divorced, but she'd still been a girl when she'd left Cisco.

When she'd come back, it was underneath this cottonwood tree, about a month after she'd been elected sheriff, that she realized just how grown-up she'd become. It was then that she'd finally come to some understanding of what kind of job she'd taken on. It was a job where Willie—who she was and what she wanted—had to come last. Her needs had to take second place to the needs of the people who had elected her. They expected someone who was strong and fair. Someone who was certainly reliable. Someone whom they could depend upon no matter how she felt. Willie knew she had become that person.

Now, almost four years later, under the same cottonwood tree, she was forced to admit that in becoming that person, she had almost erased the woman underneath. It had taken Joe Kelly to uncover the woman.

Joe Kelly. She'd loved his brother, Paul, like the brother she'd never had. And when Joe had first come back to town and announced that he was going to run the paper instead of selling it, she expected to hate him. She wanted to hate him for both the past and the present. But the joke was on her.

When Willie had phoned her sister yesterday afternoon, before she'd gone out with Joe, she'd found out that Irene had said Joe had ended their high school romance exactly as Joe had said. Irene had admitted to telling Willie a little tale about a ring and an engagement, but even then she'd thought Willie was old enough to understand it was just a little fantasy to smooth over Irene's slightly wounded vanity.

After she'd hung up, Willie'd been forced to admit that she'd remembered the past all these years the way she'd wanted to remember it. When she was thirteen her hero had been Joe Kelly. And when that hero had left Cisco and her, she'd made him into a villain. It was as simple as that.

It was forgivable at thirteen, but ridiculous at thirty-four. She said goodbye to one more childhood illusion and looked at her watch. It was almost seven o'clock, and Willie had a lot to do before ten. Before Joe had left, he'd made her promise to come over to his place for a late-night dinner. He hadn't bothered to hide his desire that she spend the night, and surprisingly, she found his honesty much easier to deal with than if he'd gotten her over there and taken it for granted that she would stay. At least this way she could take along a pressed uniform for the next day.

She sighed as she got up and walked toward the house. If her "relationship" with Joe went on for long, it would only be a matter of days before some of the more observant citizens of Cisco would be commenting on whose car was parked in front of whose house. Willie shrugged in resignation. She'd just come to grips with the fact that she was a woman; maybe it was time Cisco did as well.

Joe opened the oven for the third time, nervously checking the progress of his baked chilies rellenos. It had been years since he'd cooked for a woman. He couldn't remember the last time. He wanted everything to be perfect. He knew Willie well enough to realize that the little scene of domesticity that he'd witnessed that morning probably wouldn't be repeated often. There were some disadvantages to dating the sheriff. One never knew when she was going to have to leave during breakfast or the middle of the night.

Satisfied that everything in the oven was going as it should, he sat down at the table and poured himself a glass of wine. It was a little after nine. He looked around the immaculate kitchen. It was the first time in four months that the room had looked so good. Joe wasn't a slob, but he knew he'd never win any Good Housekeeping awards, either.

As he sat in his kitchen, staring at the spotless counters and smelling the casserole cooking, he had to admit that something was up. He hadn't even spent this much energy trying to impress Melissa. And he'd ended up marrying her.

Then the reality suddenly came crashing down on him. He was serious. Serious about Willie, and seriously in trouble. He got up and started to pace the floor. What would life be like if he fell for the sheriff of San Juan County? Willie was good at what she did, but what she did drove him crazy. She could be so bullheaded sometimes, it was frightening. He was used to women who tried to flatter or pout their way around him. Willie did neither. She just came right out and told him how she saw things. She let him worry about his own side of it. Did he really want to let himself in for this kind of punishment?

He looked at his watch again. It was nine-twenty. He'd changed the sheets, put fresh towels in the bathroom. It was obvious that he wanted Willie to come and that he wanted her to stay. He took another sip of wine and told himself that he would work out the details tomorrow.

He took the casserole out of the oven and put the bottle back into the bucket to chill. All he needed was Willie. He was about to step outside for a breath of fresh air when the phone rang.

Even before he picked it up, he had a feeling it was Willie. The feeling was right.

"Willie, where are you?"

"I'm still at my house, Joe." He heard the slight hesitation in her voice. "Look, Joe, something's come up."

"What? I just took dinner out of the oven. The wine's chilled. All I need is you."

"Something's happened over at the Bishop place. I just got a call from LeRoy."

"What's happened, Willie?" Suddenly he was back to being the curious newspaperman. The past twenty-four hours had almost made him forget about UFOs and the turkey deaths. Again he heard the hesitation in her voice. "What is it, Willie?"

"I don't know yet," she answered.

"Willie, didn't we agree that you'd let me work with you on this case? I thought we settled it last night." She was silent. "Look, Willie, you know I'm going to get in the car and come out there." He only had to wait a split second before she replied.

"It was Ed that called. Bishop's son. He said he found his father out between the barn and the stock pens. He's called an ambulance. Maybe it means something; maybe it doesn't."

"You know it means something, Willie. Why else would have Ed Bishop called you?" He paused for a minute, but Willie didn't say anything. "I'm leaving now, I'll meet you out there."

He was out the door and had his car started before he realized that he'd left without his camera. He dashed into the house and got it.

When he pulled up to the Bishop place, Willie was already there with LeRoy. Matt Bishop had just been carried into the ambulance.

Joe didn't know what he expected from Willie. Certainly not a hug and a kiss. What he did get was a curt nod and professional distance. He shrugged his shoulders and stood behind Willie as Ed Bishop watched the ambulance drive off with his father.

"How's Bishop?" he asked Willie.

"He's alive. But that's about all they could tell us. Ed found him over there." She pointed to an area midway between Bishop's turkey pens and barn and the house.

Joe looked at Ed Bishop. The young man was pale and obviously shaken up. Willie had her notebook out, pencil in hand. Tension was visible on her face.

"We might as well get this over with, Ed." She turned to Joe. "This is strictly off the record, Joe. If you print a word of it, I'll deny this conversation ever took place. And I can guarantee that Ed will do the same."

Ed looked at Joe and he nodded, confirming what Willie said.

"Sure, Willie." Joe would argue the point with her later, in private.

She turned and walked with Ed back to the pathway between the barn and the house. LeRoy and Joe followed. Willie pointed to an X on the concrete path that LeRoy had marked in white chalk.

"This is where you found your father?" Willie's voice was quiet and even. "Just go over it one more time, then we can call it a night."

Young Bishop stared at the ground, then up at Willie. He cleared his throat and walked around the X.

"I came home a little before nine. I was over at Mary-Lou's. I would have stayed later. But well..." He stuck his hands in his pockets and looked at Willie. "I came home early."

"Why's that?" Willie asked. "Why did you decide to come home early?"

"Me and MaryLou had a little disagreement. Heck, we had a fight. I thought it was best to let things cool off." He stared at the X again. "It's a good thing I did come home. If I hadn't, there's no telling how long my father would have laid here."

"So you drove up in the yard and saw your father." Willie wrote something down. "Were the lights on? Did your father call out to you?"

"I didn't see my father right away. Both of the outside floodlights were on. The light was on in the barn, too. But that's not what made me think something was wrong. My father worked this time of night a lot."

"When did you think something was wrong?"

"Well, I was going to go into the house to change my clothes, then go out and see if I could help my dad." He looked at Willie and then started to walk back toward the house. He went about one hundred feet, almost to the house, then stopped. There, on the concrete path, was another X marked in chalk.

"I parked my car and walked toward the house. Like I said, I didn't see my father right away."

They all turned back and looked at the path. The X they'd just left was in a dark spot between the floodlights of the house and the barn.

"But I got up to here, and that's when I saw my dad's shotgun."

"You saw a shotgun lying here on the ground?" Willie pointed to the second mark and Ed nodded. "Could you tell if it had been fired?"

"There was a box of shells next to it, and the barrels were open. I don't think my dad ever got a chance to load it."

"What did you do then?" Willie asked.

"I picked up the shotgun and called out for my dad. He didn't answer. Then I loaded the shells."

"Why did you do that?" Willie said jotting something else down. "Did you hear or see anything?"

"No, I didn't hear anything. But I knew my dad wouldn't have tried to load the shotgun for no reason. And I had a feeling."

"A feeling?" Willie repeated.

"Yeah. It was weird, kind of. I felt like I was being watched."

"But you didn't see anything?" Willie asked again. "No, Sheriff. I didn't see anything." He looked toward the barn and into the darkness beyond. "I just loaded the shotgun and walked to the barn. It was quiet. Too quiet. I didn't hear the turkeys we brought in, the ones that weren't killed with the others last week. Usually this time of night I'd hear 'em rustling around up there. But everything was quiet."

He led the group back up toward the first X and stopped halfway between the two marks.

"Then I heard my dad call my name. His voice was just a growl, a whisper. But I heard it right off." He continued walking until he reached the first X. "This is where I found him. Lying on the ground. He was clutching his chest, and I thought he'd probably had a heart attack. But then I saw the gash on his forehead. There was blood on his face."

"Did he say anything?" Willie asked.

"I knelt down. I meant to tell him I was going to run into the house to call the ambulance, but when I got up to go, he got hold of my shirt. He wouldn't let me go until he'd told me."

"Told you what?"

Ed looked around the yard and then at Willie and Joe. He cleared his throat again. "Dad said, 'It was them again. They came back to finish us off.' "

"What did you say?"

"I asked him who 'them' was."

"You didn't know who he was talking about?"

"I had a pretty good idea, Sheriff. I just didn't want to believe it. He said it was the aliens. He said he heard them out in the pens, and when he came out to get them, he got jumped."

"They attacked him?" Joe sounded incredulous. "He actually got that close to these people?"

Ed nodded. "People? Who said they were people? You heard my dad describe what he saw the night our birds were killed. It didn't sound like any people I know." Ed turned back to Willie. "He said they were the same ones he'd seen a couple of nights ago. He said they tried to kill him."

# Chapter 7

Willie looked at Joe. She wished that none of this had happened. She wished Ed Bishop had never called and she was at Joe's house, enjoying his company and the food he'd cooked.

But it had happened. She'd just seen Matt Bishop carried off on a stretcher, unconscious and barely alive. If what his son said was true, then Matt had gotten close enough to make no mistake about who, or what, had attacked him. She just prayed that Matt survived to tell her what he'd seen.

"Did your father tell you anything else?" Willie's voice was low, but she could hear the tension in it.

"No." Ed looked at the ground. "He passed out right after that." Then he looked up. "If you're through, Sheriff, I want to drive into town and see how he's doing."

Willie nodded. "That's all for tonight. I'll probably come back in the morning and see if we can find anything."

She watched Ed as he walked away and got into his car. Neither Joe nor LeRoy said anything until he had driven out of sight. Finally LeRoy broke the silence.

"What do you make of that, Sheriff?" He looked at the X on the ground, then gestured toward the mark closer to the house. "If what young Bishop said was true, we got ourselves an eyewitness account of an alien attack."

Willie eyed her deputy.

"The key word, LeRoy, is *if.* I have no doubt that Ed was telling the truth when he told us what his father said. And I don't question that Matt told him what he thought he saw. But I'm not so sure that what Bishop thought he saw and what actually happened are the same thing."

"But you saw Bishop, Sheriff," LeRoy answered. "You saw what he looked like."

"He had a gash on his head. And he was unconscious. That's what I saw. Only the doctors, and Matt, can tell us what happened."

LeRoy stared again at the X on the ground. "I never expected to have to deal with anything like this." He gave a low whistle and shook his head. "An alien attack."

"This isn't an alien attack, LeRoy. We don't know what it is. And until we do, what you heard tonight goes no further than this. Don't discuss this case with anyone." Her gaze was stern.

"Sure, Sheriff," LeRoy answered. "I understand. But shouldn't you alert the governor's office or something?"

"As far as I'm concerned, this is still a local investigation." Willie's voice invited no comment.

LeRoy looked at Joe.

"The sheriff's right, LeRoy. We can't go around talking about alien invasions. You can imagine the sort of reaction that would cause. Cisco would be turned into a three-ring circus, and we might never find out what happened. We just have to wait and—"

Willie cut Joe off. "You'd better get back to town, LeRoy. I want to look around a bit longer. I'll be in the office in the morning before you go off duty."

LeRoy looked at them both, then turned around, got into his car and drove off. Without saying a word to Joe, Willie walked over to her car and picked up the flashlight. She was aware that Joe was behind her. Was this what the whole investigation would be like—Joe, never less than one step behind? she thought.

"What are you going to do?" he asked as he walked beside her up the path.

"I'm going to do what I told LeRoy I'd do. I'm going to look around here for a while and then I'm going back to town." She went all the way up to the steps of Bishop's house and then turned around. Her back was to the screen door, and the light was on in the kitchen. "I'm going to check on Bishop's condition, see what the doctors think. It would be a help if I could talk to him, but I don't think that's going to happen. Not tonight."

She knew her voice had a hard edge to it. The look on Joe's face told her he'd heard it, too. She focused the light beam on the concrete path beyond the steps and waited for Joe to get out of her way.

Instead of moving, he put his hand up on her left side and rested it against the door. When she made a move to go around him, he put his other hand up, penning her in.

"What's up, Willie?" he asked. "Why the cold shoulder? I thought we agreed that you'd let me in on the investigation."

"You're here, aren't you?" She looked at him, at the dark hair falling across his forehead. He looked as determined as ever. "I suggest you move your arm. I have a job to do."

"What do you mean, move my arm?" In the glare of the porch light she could see his scar darken. Beyond him, the valley was black except for a scattering of lights. She sensed the tightening of his body. "Who do you think you're talking to?"

"I know exactly who I'm talking to." Still he didn't move. "Look, Joe, I'm too tired to argue with you."

"I don't want to argue, Willie. I just want to know what's going on. You're acting as if this is the first time we've seen each other. You're acting as if I'm still some newspaperman who's nothing more than a nuisance."

"Do you expect me to throw my arms around you every time I see you? Or should I cry on your shoulder and ask you what to do?"

She could feel the tension build inside her. Everything she had restrained in front of Ed Bishop and her deputy was coming out now, in front of Joe. And that only made her frustration worse. She didn't want to let him see her like this.

"Should I let you take over the investigation?" she asked. "Is that what you want, Joe?"

He removed his hand from the side of the door and ran it through his hair, sweeping it off his forehead. He took a deep breath.

She glared at him. "Because if that's what you want, you're going to be disappointed."

She started to move off the porch, but he grabbed her arm and put her back against the screen door. It wasn't the force of his grip but the intensity on his face that kept her there.

"What do you want, Joe?"

"I want you to stop acting as if I'm your enemy. I want you to stop thinking that I want your job, because I don't. Just let me do mine."

He let go of her arm. Willie stood there, staring at him. His anger was clearly visible, and his voice suddenly lowered. "And I want you to stop pretending that nothing has changed between us. Because it has, Willie. Everything has changed."

"Just because we slept together doesn't give you the right to assume anything, Joe Kelly."

"Slept together? As I recall, we didn't do much sleeping. You came to me, Willie. Remember that. I think that at least gives me the right to assume we're friends."

She looked into his eyes. They were like blue ice.

He walked off the porch. "You know, Willie, I watched the way you handled Ed, the way you questioned him. And

I'm watching the way you're handling the whole investigation. And do you want to know something?''

She stared at him, not willing to answer. He started walking toward his car, then he turned around. ''You're one hell of a good sheriff,'' he shouted. ''But you're also one crazy, mixed-up woman.''

She wanted to call after him, but instead she watched him get in his car, slam the door and drive off.

Willie stood on the porch. Tension engulfed her, and she felt like screaming. Instead, she kicked the post on the Bishops' porch. It helped to expel her pent-up energy, but it also hurt. She sat down on the steps and held her foot.

It wasn't supposed to happen like this, she told herself. What about the quiet resolution she'd made this afternoon? What about the new Willie, confident that she could handle being both a sheriff and a woman at the same time? She gazed out into the night. It seemed that the ''new'' Willie had disappeared down the road along with Joe Kelly.

She got up and walked toward the barn. Ed had been right about the place; it was quiet. Maybe too quiet. She opened the gate to the large turkey pen at the side of the barn. There was no evidence that only days before it had been covered with several hundred dead birds. She walked across the empty yard and looked at the washed troughs. Willie remembered Ed saying something about some other turkeys, a flock that they'd had on the other side of the barn when she'd been there several days earlier, collecting evidence. She flicked the flashlight on as she moved behind the barn, out of range of the powerful floodlights in the main yard.

She felt it as soon as she turned the corner and went to the dark side of the barn. It must have been what Ed was talking about when he said he felt something weird. Willie slowly turned around and aimed the beam of light into the barn's shadowed interior.

She could make out the shapes of machinery and bags of feed. There were several bins filled with grain. The night was still silent. She couldn't hear a sound from the barn's interior, but she could feel a rush of goose bumps pucker her arms. Willie put the flashlight into her left hand. Her right hand moved slowly down to the gun at her hip and unsnapped the leather strip across the handle. She heard the pop of the snap. A metallic click followed as she took the pistol off safety.

She heard the sound of tires crunching gravel and the hum of an engine somewhere out on the road. Then the sound was gone. Another farmer passing by? She was about to go to the front of the barn and look, when she thought she saw something move inside the building. A small sliver of sound, like something falling on dirt, came from within. She wrapped her hand around the grip of her gun, still in its holster, and shone the light inside.

"Is anyone here?" she asked. Silence answered her. But what did she expect, aliens with laser guns? She walked inside the barn, a surge of adrenaline quickening her heartbeat.

It was a big building, used mainly for storage. There were four doors, two large ones at each end, and smaller ones on either side. She'd come through the large back door. The noise she'd heard had come from her left, near the side door. She moved toward the rectangle of dim light marking the opening. Thankful that Bishop was a fastidious farmer, she found a clear path through the center of his barn.

As she neared the side door, she sensed a stirring just outside. She could see the dark outline of an opened metal gate across the door. Again the soft sound of something moving against the hard-packed dirt just outside the door broke the stillness. Willie drew her gun from her holster and stood by the side of the door. She turned off the beam of the light, knowing it would make her an easy target. Then she hid her body at the side of the door and moved her head around the corner to get a look outside.

The light from the moon hit the other side of the barn, so she couldn't see much. She could tell that the area outside the door was a pen, smaller than the one she'd walked through to get inside the barn. A flutter of movement near the ground caught her attention. Something was moving. In fact, several things were moving. The pen was littered with small dark-gray heaps. She switched on her flashlight. The pen was filled with turkeys. Dead and dying turkeys. Willie expelled a deep breath and put her gun back into her holster.

With his father injured, it was obvious why Ed hadn't thought to go check on the remaining turkeys. She walked out into the pen and bent down to examine one of the birds. It looked like the ones she had seen at the Wheeler place last week, and here. Not a mark on it, but definitely dead. She stood up and looked around, trying to reconstruct the order of events.

Bishop had probably heard someone out around his pens. Not willing to give up the rest of his flock without a fight, he had come out with his shotgun. Someone had stopped him before he'd ever gotten to the pen in the back of his barn. He hadn't even had a chance to load the rifle. But he had tried. Had he seen someone coming? The "alien"? The thought of running into the silver-suited creatures of Matt's description gave her some more goose bumps.

She turned around and walked back to the barn door, switching off the flashlight. What she'd heard had been the dying turkeys. Now that she'd seen what it was, she could find her way back outside without the light.

Willie was two steps into the barn when she heard footsteps coming up the path outside. She crouched for cover behind some feed sacks. She had her hand back on her .38 when she saw the form of a large man outlined in the barn door. He was coming from the bigger pens out front, and his body was silhouetted against the floodlights. She drew her pistol and waited.

The man was holding something in his right hand, and she caught a reflection of light shining off metal. He stood still. He must have sensed her presence. Willie felt her finger edge toward the trigger as she raised the gun. The man started to move his right hand. Again she saw light glint off metal. It was now or never, she thought as she took a deep breath and then expelled it.

"Police. Hold it right there," she called out. "Drop the gun."

"Willie?" The voice was instantly recognizable.

She stood up, her pistol still pointed toward the figure. He dropped what he held in his hand.

"Joe," she exclaimed. "What are you doing with a gun?"

He bent down to retrieve the object he'd dropped.

"It's only a flashlight, Willie." He held it out and looked at her. "Will you put that thing away!" He pointed to the gun.

She put her gun in her holster and walked toward him, adrenaline still pumping through her body. "Do you know you almost got yourself shot!" Her voice quavered with emotion. "Of all the stupid things. What were you doing sneaking up on me like that?"

"I wasn't sneaking up on you."

She moved closer. Tiny beads of sweat made his forehead glisten. "That's what I call it. You nearly scared me to death."

"I scared you! You're the one who had the gun."

"A man was just attacked out here!" she yelled. "I have a gun because I'm the sheriff."

"I know you're the damn sheriff!" he shouted back. "It's impossible to forget when you keep reminding me."

"Why did you come back? Were you hoping to get some juicy evidence you could put in the paper?"

He shook his head and stood there, staring at her, as if he couldn't believe what he was hearing.

"No, damn it," he said, his voice still fired with anger. "I came back because I wanted to talk to you."

She looked at him. Here they were, screaming at each other like a couple of fools. It was crazy. She leaned against the frame of the door.

"Listen to us, Joe. I could have killed you, and all we can do is get into a shouting match."

He stood on the opposite side of the opening. He put the flashlight into his back pocket and wiped his forehead with his sleeve.

"What were you doing here?" she asked again.

"As I said, I came back to try to work things out. I got about two miles down the road and realized I didn't want to leave it the way we did." He managed a half-hearted chuckle. "If I'd had any idea that you'd try to blow my head off, I would've reconsidered and gone home."

"I wasn't trying to shoot you, Joe. How was I supposed to know you'd come back and apologize?" Her voice had collapsed into a whisper.

He moved toward her. "I didn't say I came back to apologize." He reached up and put his hand above her head, resting it on the barn door. He was leaning toward her, only inches away but not touching her. "I said I wanted to work things out."

She felt her anger rise again. But this time she realized that it was directed not at Joe but at herself. She'd already admitted to herself she'd been unreasonable. That was why he'd driven off in the first place.

"You're right, Joe," she said quietly. "You don't have anything to apologize about."

"What was that?"

"I said you don't have anything—"

"No, the first part."

"I said 'You're right, Joe.'"

"That's it." His face brightened. "I may never hear it again, but it's a beautiful sentence." He lifted his hand to her face and wiped away the slight moisture above her lips. "Tell me why I'm right, Willie." His voice was low. "I need to hear it from you. I need to know I'm not crazy to come chasing after a woman in the middle of the night. A woman who just pulled a gun on me."

She looked into his eyes. "You really want to hear it. Now?"

He nodded. "I'm not going to let you off the hook."

She reached up and wrapped her hand around his. "You had every right to be angry. I behaved badly. I know you're not trying to do my job, and I know you're my friend."

He moved closer. "Anything else?"

"You were right about another thing, too."

His lips were almost touching hers. "What's that?"

"I am one confused woman."

He smiled. "Maybe I can help you get unconfused."

He kissed her, his lips light and gentle, demanding nothing, asking everything.

He slipped his hand between her back and the door frame, pulling her against his chest. She felt the rhythm of her heartbeat against his. "Is this confusing you, Willie?"

She shook her head.

"Good," he answered. "Why don't we both go home and call it a night." His arm was around her as they walked toward their cars. "We can sort the rest of this out tomorrow."

The sun slanted through her window, and Willie squinted in the light. Recollections of last night flooded her sleep-starved brain as she swung her legs over the side of the bed and took a deep breath before she stood up. Just let me get through the day, she thought.

It was 6:00 a.m. and Willie had slept exactly three-and-a-half hours. After she'd said good-night to Joe, she dropped by the hospital to find out about Matt Bishop. The doctor on duty couldn't tell her much, except that Matt's condition appeared to be stable. He also told her that the head wound was superficial and the real problem was most likely a heart attack.

Willie took a cold shower, put on a fresh uniform and told herself she felt better. When she stepped into her office,

LeRoy was sitting at his desk, staring at the blank report form in front of him.

"Morning, Sheriff," he said, barely looking up. He looked as tired as she felt. "I'm just wondering what I should put on this form."

"Put the truth." She hung her hat on the hook.

"But I thought you told me you wanted this thing kept quiet."

"I meant don't talk about it. That report should state exactly what you saw and heard last night." She sat down at her desk. "Just because a witness says he saw something doesn't mean it happened that way. We all have a habit of seeing exactly what we expect to see."

LeRoy shrugged his shoulders and started writing. It took him the rest of his shift to finish. Willie called the hospital and was elated to hear that Matt Bishop had regained consciousness. The doctor told her she'd be able to see him later that morning.

Wes and Carl had come in, and she was just about to go out for a quick breakfast when the phone rang. It was Joe. He was already at work, and he told her he'd meet her in five minutes at the Desmond Diner across the street. As she hung up she took a deep breath and smiled. The morning wasn't turning out so badly.

Joe already had a corner booth by the window when she walked in. His face lit up when he saw her. A cup of hot coffee was waiting as she slipped into the booth opposite him.

"You're looking pretty good for someone who's had about as much sleep as I have," he said.

"And you're a liar, Joe." She smiled. "It's good to see you. I was hoping you'd call, but I didn't think you'd be at work so early."

"After a night like the last one, I normally wouldn't be. But I wanted to see you." He reached across the tabletop to touch her hand. "And at six-fifteen I was awakened by an interesting phone call."

The waitress came to take their order. When she left, Willie said, "A phone call? Should I be curious?"

"Probably. But I'm surprised you haven't heard about it by now." He took another sip of his coffee.

"What do you mean?"

"It was from Lucy Wiemer."

Willie put her cup down. "Don't tell me she already heard about what happened over at the Bishop place last night. The people in this town must have some sort of secret communications system! And it's probably organized by Hannah and Lucy Wiemer."

He shook his head. "She hadn't heard about Bishop when I talked to her. But she did say something about him. She said she'd gotten some kind of warning."

"Warning? What did she tell you?"

Joe took a deep breath and was about to begin when he looked out the window. "Oh, no," he said in a low voice. "I think you're about to find out firsthand."

She looked outside and saw the short, wiry figure of Mrs. Lucy Wiemer disappear into the diner. Willie turned around and saw her as she came in and headed their way.

Willie turned back to Joe and closed her eyes. "Whatever it is, I don't think I want to hear about it this morning," Willie whispered.

Joe rose to his feet as Mrs. Wiemer came and stood in front of them.

"Hannah told me that I'd find you over here, Sheriff."

"Good morning, Mrs. Wiemer," Willie responded. "Would you like to join us?"

She ignored the question and turned to Joe. "Have you already told her?" she asked, her voice lowered to a stage whisper.

"I was just about to," Joe answered.

Willie looked at the woman who'd been one of Cisco's resident eccentrics for as long as she could remember. She was in her mid-sixties, Willie guessed. Small and thin, she exuded the energy of a woman half her age. Over the past four years, Mrs. Wiemer had spent a good deal of that energy calling Willie.

She'd been one of Willie's strongest critics, her main objection being that a woman didn't belong in the sheriff's office. Over the past couple of years she'd dropped that complaint and both she and Willie had settled into a civil tolerance of each other.

Now she hovered over their table, dressed in a flowered housedress. Her wispy white hair was barely combed, Willie noted, which was unusual for the normally well-groomed Mrs. Wiemer.

"I had a dream last night," she told Willie.

It was just about the last thing Willie expected to hear. This was the news that couldn't wait?

Mrs. Wiemer looked from one to the other. Joe kept his face respectfully attentive, and Willie tried to do the same.

"Yes?" Willie said. "You had a dream?"

"It was about that spaceship. I saw it coming for us. And I saw what they did to Matt."

"You saw what happened at the Bishop place?" Willie tried to keep her voice calm. The waitress had brought their food and was tidying the next booth. Willie was aware that the woman hadn't moved since Mrs. Wiemer had joined them.

"I saw it all," Mrs. Wiemer said, not following Willie's lead and lowering her voice.

Willie stared at her barely eaten food, and then at Joe. "Look, Mrs. Wiemer. What happened to Matt Bishop is still under investigation. Why don't you go over to my office and wait for me? I'll finish breakfast as fast as I can, and then I'll come right over."

"But I think this is something everyone should know." The older woman looked at Joe. "That's what I called Joe about this morning. I was instructed to tell everyone." In a determined voice, "This is something everybody should know," she said again.

Willie looked at Joe.

"Willie's right, Mrs. Wiemer." Joe stood up and took the woman's arm. "I think something this important deserves a nice, quiet place. I know Willie wants to listen undisturbed." He turned to Willie. "Why don't you have the waitress make our breakfast to go? I'll take her over to your office."

Before she could say anything, he was walking out of the diner with Mrs. Wiemer on his arm. For once, she was glad that Joe had interfered. She had no idea what Lucy Wiemer had in mind, but she didn't want the Bishop case and his story about his "alien" attacker discussed in Cisco's busiest diner.

Willie followed a few minutes later, balancing their takeout breakfast as she crossed the street. The fatigue of the past couple of days was rapidly catching up with her. The last thing she needed was to hear Mrs. Wiemer retell her dreams. It was even more difficult to believe that she was actually going to listen.

Joe had settled Lucy in a chair in front of her desk, and he was sitting by her side. Carl was sitting at his desk, pretending to go through some paperwork. But Willie wasn't fooled. He wasn't going to miss any of this. She handed Joe his breakfast and sat down.

"Now, Mrs. Wiemer, why don't you tell me what you told Joe this morning?" She tried to erase any skepticism from her voice.

Mrs. Wiemer smoothed her housedress over her lap and gently puffed her hair with her hand, aware that she had the complete attention of both Joe and Willie.

"Excuse the way I look this morning, but I thought I should get over here and warn you. In fact, the whole town should be warned. That's why I called Joe first thing this morning."

She smiled smugly and folded her arms across her meager bosom. Willie looked at Joe and could tell he was trying to exercise the same polite self-control she was.

"Well, Mrs. Wiemer, I'm sure that as soon as you tell us, both Joe and I will do all we can to help the citizens of Cisco."

The older woman nodded, clearing her throat. Willie waited, aware that she was playing this for all it was worth.

"I dreamed about the UFO last night." She looked at Willie, then turned to Joe, obviously expecting some kind of reaction.

"And?" Willie asked, then saw by Mrs. Wiemer's frown that she'd expected more. "What UFO was that?"

"Why, the one Joe's been telling us about in his paper! The one that's killed Grady Wheeler's and Matt Bishop's turkeys."

"Mrs. Wiemer," Joe interrupted her. "I was just reporting what Matt Bishop thought he saw. There was nothing in my article that stated there was any conclusive evidence of a UFO sighting."

"Well, now you have it, don't you?" Mrs. Wiemer leaned forward, making her point.

"How's that, Mrs. Wiemer?" Willie asked.

"Last night in my dream, they spoke to me. They told me that if we didn't listen, they were going to come down and get us, one by one. And it's already started to happen."

Willie and Joe looked at each other. Willie knew he was thinking the same thing she was. Lucy Wiemer had finally gone off the deep end.

"First they got the turkeys," she continued. "Now they tried to get Matt."

"What do you mean they tried to get Matt?" Willie wondered how Mrs. Wiemer had found out about what Matt had told his son.

"Why, they attacked him. I saw it all."

"You saw it all?" Here was a new twist in the case. "What did you see?"

"Last night those silver-suited spacemen came to finish off Matt's turkeys. He tried to shoot 'em, but he never even got the chance. He went after 'em with a shotgun but never got the thing loaded. They got him. Stopped him in his tracks and killed his turkeys as well.''

Willie took a deep breath. No one knew that the turkeys were dead except Joe and her. It wasn't even in the report yet, because LeRoy had left before she'd discovered the dead turkeys. ''How did you see all this? Were you there? Did someone tell you this was what happened?''

''You aren't listening to me, Sheriff.'' Mrs. Wiemer turned to Joe and gave him a look of mock annoyance. ''I already told you how I know. It was all in my dream.''

## Chapter 8

Carl cleared his throat in an attempt to swallow his laughter. Willie briefly glanced at her deputy, and he began a flurry of paper shuffling. She looked back at Joe and Mrs. Wiemer and had no trouble keeping a smile off her face. What Lucy Wiemer had just told them was no laughing matter. She looked at the woman directly, commanding her attention.

"Mrs. Wiemer, I consider the attack last night on Matt Bishop a very serious matter. If you have any information concerning this investigation, I want you to tell me now." Willie's voice was stern, sharpened by fatigue.

"I just told you," Mrs. Wiemer said demurely. "I saw the whole thing in a dream."

"And in your dream, did you happen to identify the person who attacked Matt?" Willie noticed that Joe was studying Mrs. Wiemer as she spoke to Willie. She couldn't wait to hear what he thought about her alleged "source" of information.

"It wasn't a person; it was a thing. A thing in a silver space suit. It had a big cover, like a helmet, over its head. It looked like what the astronauts wear." She moved her hands over her head to demonstrate.

"And you say Matt went after this 'thing' with his shotgun?"

"I said he tried to. He came running out of the house with both barrels open, trying to load the shells. That's when the thing attacked."

"Did you happen to 'see' the attack? Did you see it in your dream?"

"I saw it hit Matt with a long, heavy object. It looked like a fire extinguisher or something. It was the same shape and size. It only hit him once, and Matt fell to the ground. Then the thing ran off."

"Mrs. Wiemer," Willie said slowly as she got up and moved around to the other side of the desk. She stopped and leaned against it, directly in front of the older woman. "I've known you all my life, haven't I?"

Mrs. Wiemer nodded, pleased at Willie's recognition of her familiarity and social prominence in the small town of Cisco.

"And I've lived in this town for most of my life. There hasn't been a time when I haven't had some connection with Cisco and its people over the last thirty years."

Willie glanced at Joe and then Carl.

"And it's been the same with Joe and Carl, hasn't it?" Puzzled, they both nodded in agreement. "Among the three of us—Cisco being what it is—we know of just about anything that's happened here in the last forty years." She stopped and put her arms by her sides, then stood up, towering over the other woman. "And I'm willing to bet that not once during those last forty years has one of us heard about Mrs. Lucy Wiemer having any clairvoyant powers."

Mrs. Wiemer straightened to her full height. Willie still dwarfed her by well over half a foot.

"Do you doubt that I'm telling you the truth?" The little woman quivered slightly, her face turning crimson. "Are you calling me a liar?"

"I'm not calling you anything, Mrs. Wiemer. We have a felony investigation going on here, and I want to know where you got your information."

The old woman looked to Joe for assistance. Willie noted gratefully that he remained quiet and kept his face neutral. Then Mrs. Wiemer turned back to Willie.

"I told you. It was all in a dream. I had a dream, and I came here to warn you." Her mouth was set like a tight little slash in her face. Willie could tell she wasn't going to give up.

"To warn us? What did you want to warn us about? Matt Bishop was attacked last night. The crime has already been committed." Willie wanted her to know that she didn't give up easily either.

"There will be others. That's what the aliens told me. They told me to tell the people of Cisco that if they didn't give up their worldly possessions and follow them at the appointed hour, we'd all be destroyed."

"What do you mean that if we don't follow them at the 'appointed hour,' we'll all be destroyed?"

Mrs. Wiemer shrugged. "They haven't told me the particulars yet. I just understood that Matt Bishop was an example of their power."

"It doesn't take an impressive amount of power to kill a bunch of turkeys and injure a sixty-nine-year-old man," Joe said. "I agree with Willie. You've got to tell her where you got your information."

"You two just don't understand, do you?" Mrs. Wiemer grabbed her purse and turned toward the door. "I expected it from her," she said, pointing to Willie. "But I thought you'd have more sense, Joe Kelly. I thought you'd know exactly what I was talking about because of your article about the UFO sighting. I wanted you to put an article about my dream in the paper. But I guess I'll just have to warn everyone myself."

Mrs. Wiemer stalked out of the office. Willie sighed and sank into her chair. "So much for keeping this investigation quiet," she said.

"You're not going to let her go, are you?" Joe asked.

"What do you expect me to do, arrest her?"

Joe walked around to Willie's side of the desk. "Obviously she knows something," he said. "She described exactly what happened, right down to the shotgun and dead turkeys. There's no way she could have gotten that information unless she talked to someone who was there."

"Or was there herself."

"You don't believe that, or you would have arrested her."

"No, I don't believe she was there any more than I believe that she saw it all in a dream."

"So everything she said was true?" Carl finally asked. "It happened exactly like she said?"

Willie looked at him. "Exactly."

"Oh, boy." Carl shook his head. "I think we've got some problems, Sheriff."

"I think you're right," Willie answered.

Willie went to the hospital to see Matt. He was conscious, and his condition was weak but stabilized. He confirmed everything his son and Mrs. Wiemer had already told her. Willie realized that the old man probably wouldn't be in the hospital, recovering from a heart attack, if it hadn't been for his visitors, but it also meant that whoever had been with him last night hadn't meant to kill the old man. They'd just wanted to kill turkeys. Killing Matt Bishop would have been an easy matter. Yet here he was, alive to tell the tale of his "alien" assault. Willie couldn't help thinking that it was a significant observation.

She also called Denver and asked the lab what was taking so long. They casually told her that dead turkeys had a rather low priority. After listening to a couple of tasteless dead-turkey jokes, she informed them that they were holding up evidence in a possible attempted-murder investigation. Then a clerk in the forensic lab admitted that he'd sent the carcasses over to the state Department of Agriculture lab. Willie exacted a promise that they would retrieve the birds and have the analysis completed by the following day.

The rest of the afternoon was spent fielding an increasing number of phone calls about Matt Bishop and the attempt on his life by those "alien creatures." It was obvious Mrs. Wiemer was making good on her promise to inform the citizens of Cisco of the danger they were in. Willie left her office at four forty-five, instructing LeRoy to tell curious citizens only that the case was under investigation. She also told him that she was not to be disturbed except in a case of emergency. Willie felt as if she would drop unless she got a good night's sleep.

All she remembered of the evening was a hot shower, a warm bowl of soup and sleep, blissful sleep. Just before she drifted off, she thought of Joe. She remembered that she'd promised to call him, to let him know how things were going. She sighed. That could wait until morning. Joe would understand. She smiled. Joe was turning out to understand quite a bit about her. And she liked being understood. She liked it a lot.

Joe stared at the twisted blue sheets that covered his bed. Then he turned and stared at the rumpled, exhausted man staring back at him from the mirror.

"Damn it," he muttered. "Why didn't she call like she'd said she would?"

He glanced at the clock. It was almost midnight. And he should be asleep. If she'd have called, he'd be asleep, not pacing the floor, wondering how she was going to react to his front-page story in the next day's paper. If she'd have called, he'd have given her the courtesy of talking it over with her. Of course, then he would have done exactly what he'd intended to do all along, but at least she'd have known beforehand. Now, she'd find out when she read it in the paper.

He sat on the edge of the bed. It wasn't what he'd done that bothered him. It was what Willie's reaction would be that was keeping him up. He'd printed Lucy Wiemer's story on the front page, something he'd promised Willie he wouldn't do.

He got up and stood in front of the mirror. Was that the face of a man who'd broken his promise? Yes, he supposed it was. But it was something that had to be done, he argued with himself. That afternoon, he swore, nearly half the citizens of Cisco had called him, demanding to know what Lucy Wiemer was talking about. And he knew that tomorrow the number would probably be doubled. He'd even gotten a call from someone at a Denver TV station who wanted to know if it was worth his while to come down and interview the old lady who'd dreamed about UFOs and the end of the world. Joe told the man it wasn't, subtlely intimating that Lucy Wiemer was something less than mentally stable.

Willie had to realize that all this wasn't going to blow over just because she wanted it to. It was news, and he had to print it. Joe was confident that when people read the story, they would see how ridiculous Lucy Wiemer's claims were and realize that the whole thing was being handled competently by their sheriff. Joe wasn't so sure how Willie would see it, though.

He went downstairs and stared at the contents of his refrigerator. Milk seemed to be the best it could offer, and he poured himself a glass. He took it outside and sat on the front porch.

A soft late-night August breeze brushed his bare chest as he sipped the milk. Few things were quieter than nighttime in a small town. He'd been back for months and he still hadn't gotten used to it. He could actually see the Milky Way spread out across the sky like a giant cluster of diamonds. Stars that had been made invisible by the lights of the city seemed to pop out of nowhere and light up the Colorado night. There were no sirens, no sounds of traffic or people. Only the occasional howl of a dog or the hoot of an owl against a background of singing crickets broke through the silence of the night.

He stared up at the sky and the vast tunnel of darkness before him. Here, in Cisco, there had been no long-lost buddies calling him up in the middle of the night wanting to know what was happening. No one approached him with a deal he couldn't refuse. And he could finally listen to the sound of himself, the sound of a solitary man trying to make sense of his life.

He stared into the night and thought of Willie—not Willie the sheriff but Willie the woman. A woman who wasn't afraid to admit she was wrong. He liked that. He drained his glass and smiled. She was the first woman to pull a gun on him and the first woman to tell him that he'd been right, all in the same night.

When Willie called him the next morning, Joe didn't have the heart to tell her about the article; she'd find out soon enough herself. He told himself that she'd seemed so cheerful, so optimistic. He didn't want to spoil it for her.

An hour and a half later, when she called his office for the second time, he knew by the way she said his name that she'd gotten hold of the paper. She'd made the word *Joe* sound like the lowest form of life on the planet.

"Wait a minute, Willie," he told her. "It's only fair that you hear my side of it."

"As far as I'm concerned, your paper says it all."

"Willie, I got a dozen or more calls yesterday. One was even from Denver. It certainly wasn't any worse than second- and third-hand gossip about what Mrs. Wiemer had said. At least this way people aren't going to make it sound any stranger than it already is."

"What you did, Joe Kelly, was legitimize an old woman's delusions—or her lies. Something you told me you wouldn't do."

"And you told me you'd call yesterday, to let me know how Bishop was doing and whether you'd heard the results on the lab tests from Denver."

"I suppose you're going to tell me that if I'd called, you would've discussed it with me. And then I suppose you'll try to tell me that what I said would've made a difference."

Joe was quiet on the other end of the line.

"Just go ahead and tell me, Joe," she said. "Because I'd love to call you a liar." She hung up.

Joe stared at the phone. The woman was unbelievable, he told himself. She was crazy. She was . . .

Before he could think of another adjective, Tom Hubbard, the mayor, walked into his office. He nodded gravely, then sat down.

"What can I do for you, Tom?" Joe asked, knowing perfectly well why he'd come. "Is it about that article on Lucy Wiemer I ran?"

"It's about Lucy and it's about the crisis we've got on our hands."

"Crisis?" Joe couldn't help but sound startled. Was there something he didn't know?

"Crisis. This UFO thing has gotten completely out of hand. Between what Lucy Wiemer's been spreading around town and what you've printed, we have a problem. Add that to the eyewitness account of Matt Bishop and we have a crisis. I've had half a dozen calls from upstate and a few from some national newspapers. It seems everybody wants to know about this. I've called an emergency town council meeting for tonight at seven. I'd appreciate it if you were there."

"Then you've already talked to Willie about this?"

He nodded. "She was the first one I talked to this morning."

Joe frowned. No wonder she was as mad as a hornet when she called him.

"She still insists she's got things under control. She told me she didn't like the idea of a town council meeting, that going public might jeopardize the whole investigation." The mayor looked down at his hands, which were wrapped around each other in his lap. "You know I think Willie's done a fine job. I'm supporting her in this election. But..." Joe could tell that the mayor was uncertain of just how much to say.

"But what?" Joe prompted him.

"But I think this just might be more than she can handle." The mayor looked at Joe and then back at his hands. "What if Lucy's right? What if all this does have something to do with aliens and UFOs?"

What had he done? Joe asked himself, growing uneasy. If this was the mayor's reaction to the story, what must the rest of the town be thinking?

For the rest of the day, Joe thought at least half a dozen times about going over and talking to Willie. He tried to convince himself each time that if only she would listen to his side of it, she'd understand. But he failed. She was mad, and mad she was going to stay. At least until things blew over. By late afternoon, it looked to him as if things wouldn't blow over for quite some time.

Mike, his absent reporter, called in from Phoenix. He told Joe he'd heard about Cisco and its UFO problem on the local news. Mike's mother was still in the hospital, and he himself sounded pretty sick about missing out on all the action.

Around three, a man arrived in a rental car he'd driven all the way from Grand Junction. He identified himself as a reporter from the *National Exposé* and seemed genuinely surprised that Joe was less than happy to see him. He was followed by several others an hour later. Someone from an L.A.-based magazine called *Personality* phoned to say she was sending out a reporter. The magazine called itself a news and feature journal. Joe called it an extended gossip column. And he should know, since there'd been a time when he'd been a regular subject of that gossip.

He was about to go home and get something to eat before the town meeting, when the reporter from *Personality* walked into his office.

No one could have been more surprised than he to see Diana Lawrence in Cisco. And that surprise was obvious to Diana.

"Joe, sweetheart," she said as she crossed the room. "How long has it been?"

She didn't wait for an answer but gave him a passionate kiss on the lips. Debbie watched from behind the front desk as Joe tried to ease out of her arms.

"Let me see now," he said as he stood back, pretending to look fondly at the dark-haired woman in front of him. "Just how long has it been?" She was dressed in an electric-blue jumpsuit, which had shoulder pads like he hadn't seen since his days on the football field. "Was it three years ago in Miami? That long?"

"Two years ago in Dallas," she said loudly enough for Debbie to hear. "And here we are, together again."

"Yes." Joe looked at her, then at Debbie, who was still staring. "Why don't we go into my office while Debbie finishes up?" He opened the door to the back room and Diana walked in.

Diana glanced around the room, then turned to Joe.

"How quaint. You've actually got a rolltop desk." She smiled and sat down. He followed her lead, and she looked at him with eyes the same color and intensity as her jumpsuit.

"What on earth are you doing here, Diana?" Joe managed a smile.

"When they told me that you were somehow involved in this silly UFO business, I knew I just had to have this assignment. Since my editor knows what good friends you and I are, she agreed, of course."

"Of course."

"So," she said, sighing, "I'll have to count on you to fill me in." She looked around again. "And I suppose I'll have to actually attend that town meeting tonight." She pulled a cigarette from her purse and lit it, then inhaled deeply. "Oh, well. There's a first time for everything."

Joe watched as she stood up and started walking around the room.

"I heard that you've actually got a female sheriff in Cisco. Is that true?" She took another drag on the cigarette as she glanced at some pasteups on the table in the center of the room.

"As you just said, there's a first time for everything."

She looked down at him. "Rumor has it that she isn't all that bad-looking, either, that she could be pretty photogenic. Maybe there's another story here. 'The Sexy Sheriff of Cisco.'" Diana held up her hand as if to outline the imaginary headline. "Do you think she'll go for it?"

"Why don't you ask her?" Joe did his best to keep a straight face as he visualized Willie's response. Diana would be lucky to leave Cisco alive.

She started to walk around the room once more. "This is quite a change from pro football and the celebrity circuit you used to travel." She leaned against another desk, smoke billowing around her head. "Tell me, are you really taking all this seriously? I just can't imagine the Joe Kelly I knew putting out his little paper twice a week in Nowhere, Colorado."

Joe stood up and walked over to the door. "You can tell your readers that as hard as it is to believe, Joe Kelly is taking all this seriously."

He held the door open and Diana walked out. Debbie had left, and Joe started closing up.

"Can I drop you off at your motel?" he asked as they walked to the front of the office.

Diana stopped and fingered the collar of his shirt, stroking his cheek with one lacquered red nail. "I was hoping you'd offer to show me the sights—if there are any. If not, at least you could offer to take an old friend to dinner."

Joe stared into her bright-blue eyes. With all that he had on his mind, the last thing he wanted was to spend the next hour and a half with a woman he'd known only briefly in a life he'd left behind. But Joe wasn't in the habit of being rude to women he'd had a relationship with, so he smiled and ushered her out of his office and into the late-afternoon heat.

They were fifteen minutes late for the town meeting. Joe had to park nearly three blocks from the courthouse, and when he and Diana walked into the crowded council chambers, it was still buzzing with pre-meeting conversation.

Tom Hubbard was up in front, trying at the last minute to help set up a microphone. Willie was seated to his right, dressed in her uniform and talking to Wes, her deputy. Tom caught sight of Joe and waved, motioning for him to come to the front of the room. When Joe started to move forward, Diana tugged at his sleeve.

"I have to go up front," he told her. "It seems the mayor wants me for something."

"Is that her?" she asked, pointing to Willie. Joe nodded.

"She looks a bit stern to me, but then she would photograph well. She has great cheekbones." Diana turned to Joe. "Do you know her?"

Joe just stared at Diana. His relationship with Willie—or, more correctly, the relationship he was trying to have with Willie—was something he didn't want plastered all over the pages of some national rag.

"Of course you know her," Diana said with a laugh. "Everyone here knows everyone else. Isn't that how it works in these little towns?"

"Right." Joe turned and walked to the front of the room, toward the mayor and Willie.

"I thought you weren't going to make it," the mayor said as he pumped Joe's hand. "This is turning into something else, isn't it?" He glanced around the room.

"It's something else, all right," Joe agreed.

He was standing less than a foot away from Willie, and she looked up.

"I think the term is 'circus,'" Willie said.

"What?" Joe bent forward.

"You heard me, Joe Kelly. You've turned this town and my investigation into a three-ring circus. Are you satisfied? I see you've even brought along your own audience." Willie looked out at the crowd and Diana.

"Now wait a minute, Willie—" Joe began, but didn't get a chance to finish. They both heard the amplified taps of the mayor's finger against the microphone as he signaled that the meeting was about to begin.

"We won't waste any more time," the mayor announced. "We'll get this show on the road."

"Show" is right, thought Willie as she stared straight ahead. Joe was so close that she could almost feel him breathe as he stood against the back of her chair. She'd never seen so many people at a town meeting in Cisco. The fact that some of them were reporters from out of town didn't help to ease her jumpiness.

She knew they were here for one reason, to get a story. And they weren't going to leave Cisco without it, even if they had to make one up. She could almost feel her blood pressure rise as she realized once again that one man was to blame, and he was standing behind her. She tried to concentrate on what the mayor was saying—something about the situation being well under control, that her office and his office were doing everything possible. But all she could feel was the presence of Joe Kelly as the front of his thighs touched her back. Did he have to stand so close? she wondered. Then she heard the mayor say her name and she turned toward him.

"So," he said, staring at her. "As I said, I'll turn the rest of the meeting over to our able sheriff, Wilhelmina Callen, and you can ask her any questions."

She stared out at the cameras and strange faces and felt her body refuse to obey her brain's command to stand. The thumping of her own heart was thundering against her ears when she finally felt a familiar arm help her to her feet. It was Joe, right behind her. She took several deep breaths and began.

"First of all, I want to say that I was just informed that Matt Bishop is out of danger and on his way to recovery. His head injuries from the assault are minor. The seriousness of his condition is the result of a heart attack, not the assault directly. Mr. Bishop has a history of heart disease."

Willie paused. That wasn't so hard, she told herself. "We are investigating other circumstances surrounding this case. Just before this meeting, I got word from our lab in Denver that the carcasses of both Matt Bishop's and Grady Wheeler's turkeys contained toxic levels of an insecticide. The poison attacked the birds' respiratory systems and they suffocated. We are still investigating local use of this particular insecticide. We find it significant, however, that Matt Bishop's description of the object he was struck with fits that of a canister commonly used to spray this type of insecticide."

She looked around her audience, trying to avoid the glare of camera lights.

"So you see, what we have here is obviously a very earthbound crime. I find it hard to believe that visitors from another planet would come to here just to kill turkeys with an insecticide manufactured in Ohio." She smiled confidently. "I expect my office to have the case wrapped up soon. I think it is safe to rule out UFOs and alien attacks."

Willie was about to sit down, believing that she had finished, when several voices from the crowd started to shout questions. She couldn't hear any of them completely, and she felt the confusion returning.

"What about the UFO sightings, Sheriff? Do you have an explanation for them?" A man in a white summer suit and silk tie asked the question. He was next to a man holding a camera with the familiar logo of a Denver station. "Can you tell the people of Colorado that these sightings have no factual basis?"

"I wouldn't say they have no factual basis," she began. "Several reliable witnesses have reported the same type of visual phenomena. But I'm sure that when other elements of the case come together, we'll be able to determine their origin."

"Then you're saying that these UFOs are of an unknown origin?" a man from the back shouted.

"No, I'm not," Willie started to answer, but another voice drowned her out.

"What about the articles in the local paper, the ones that Joe Kelly published? Don't they support the theory of visitors from another planet?" She was surprised to recognize Bud Beede's voice. "What would you do in case we had these visitors? Do you think you could handle it?" Bud looked around the room. "Would you know an alien if he came up and bit you?"

Before she could even think about replying, another voice piped up. "And what about the dreams of one of our most prominent citizens, Mrs. Lucy Wiemer?" Willie glared through the light of the cameras and realized that the speaker was Homer Beede, Bud's father and Lucy's younger brother. "Don't those dreams support the possibility of an alien visit? Joe's article quotes her as saying she has a message from outer space. Shouldn't we at least listen to that message?"

Willie wondered what he really thought of his sister's dream. It was clear to Willie, although she wasn't sure how clear it was to anyone else, that Homer's sudden interest had nothing to do with his sister's dreams. Homer was a vocal supporter of her opponent, Virgil Jones. He must see this as an excellent opportunity to make Willie look incompetent. She could feel her anger building. The Beedes were using this meeting to cloud the issues in front of a bunch of strangers.

Willie didn't know where to begin, so she just stared at the crowd as they fired questions in her direction. The mayor nudged her arm. She looked at him and shrugged. How could he expect her to address such confusion? She was about to try, when she felt Joe's hand touch her shoulder. Joe leaned forward.

"Why don't you let me give it a shot," he whispered. Willie was so stunned that she found herself just nodding and stepping to the side of the podium.

"It's all yours," she whispered.

"Let's do this the easiest way," he said in a voice that boomed above the crowd. "One question at a time."

For the better part of the next hour, Willie watched as he fielded the reporters' questions with ease and skill. She moved from guarded acceptance of his takeover to outright admiration. He was asked about Lucy Wiemer and Willie noted, to her surprise, that she hadn't shown up at tonight's meeting. Willie thought Mrs. Wiemer would have welcomed the opportunity to reach a wider audience.

By the end of the meeting, Joe had them laughing. When the crowd had exhausted the UFO question, they started asking him what kind of a chance he thought Miami had of getting to the Super Bowl in January. Joe finally gave the floor back to Tom Hubbard, who thanked everyone for their interest and closed the meeting.

Willie realized that she was grateful to Joe for saving her hide up there in front of all the voters and reporters. Suddenly it didn't seem to matter much how it all had started. Maybe this would be the end of it, a human-interest story buried somewhere after the hard news and just before the weather.

She was waiting for the crowd to clear and for her courage to build when the dark-haired woman she'd seen Joe come in with approached him and put her arm possessively against his broad shoulder. He looked slightly startled and then he smiled. Willie felt an unfamiliar feeling, like the pull

OPEN YOUR DOOR
TO SILHOUETTE...
Send us this bouquet
AND WE'LL SEND YOU
4 SILHOUETTE
INTIMATE MOMENTS®
NOVELS
FREE
PLUS 2 FREE GIFTS

of a knotted rope, inside her stomach. Suddenly, it was easy to remember why she was angry with Joe Kelly.

When he looked up at her, she couldn't hide her contempt. Willie was surprised to see the woman pull Joe toward Willie. Joe grabbed the woman's arm. When she insisted on moving forward, he put an arm around her shoulder and whispered something in her ear. Whatever it was, it stopped her. She looked up at him and smiled. Joe put his arm around the woman's waist. Without looking in Willie's direction, he turned her around, and together they disappeared out the door.

# Chapter 9

Willie tried to keep her emotions under control until she reached her car. It wouldn't be hard, she told herself. She just had to walk out of the council chambers and down the steps of the courthouse. But she stood there a few minutes longer, wanting to be sure that Joe and the woman were gone.

A few people came up to her, offering their support and congratulations on how she and Joe Kelly had handled the meeting. She accepted the comments with a few of her own. Luckily the reporters seemed to have been satisfied and had already left.

She'd made it halfway to her car when Bud Beede planted himself in front of her. He was flanked by his father, Homer, and his younger brother, Doug.

"Good evening, Sheriff," Bud said, tipping his hat. "It was quite a meeting, wasn't it?"

"Yes, it was, Bud. Quite a meeting." She looked him in the eye and started to move forward, but he held his ground.

"Looked like you were going to drift downstream without a paddle, when Joe Kelly took over."

Willie didn't reply, and Bud looked around. "By the way, where is old Joe? I thought he'd be with you."

Still Willie was silent.

"I think I saw him leave with one of those reporters," Homer offered. "I think it was that tall dark-haired lady, the one in the blue suit."

"Did you get a look at her?" Doug asked no one in particular. "I wish she would've tried to interview me," he added wistfully.

"As long as we're wondering where people are," Willie said, addressing Homer, "I noticed your sister, Lucy, was absent from tonight's meeting. I hope all the excitement hasn't been too much for her."

"Well," Homer answered slowly, "funny you should mention that. Lucy was feeling a bit played-out this evening, what with all the interviews and everything. We convinced her she should stay home."

"My aunt isn't a young woman," Bud added. "She needs her rest."

"Give her my best wishes," Willie said as she moved around Bud, heading for her car. He reached out and grabbed her arm. It took all the self-control Willie could muster to stop herself turning around and jerking his hand away.

"Do you want something, Bud?" she asked, returning his scrutiny.

"I hope you're still not sore at me for last Saturday night," he said, assuming his best errant-boy grin. "It was just that I had a bit too much to drink, and, well, you know how that goes."

She reached over and took his arm off hers. "Yes, I know how that goes."

"Anyway, it looks like there isn't much to what I said." He must have read the slightly puzzled look on Willie's face as she tried to remember exactly what he had said. "You know, what I said about you and Joe. The way he was looking at that big-city reporter, it looks like Joe Kelly is still playing the field." He grinned at her. "I apologize for shooting off my big mouth."

"Apology accepted." There was a lot more Willie could have said, but she didn't. "Good night, Bud." She nodded to the two other men. "Homer, Doug."

She got in her car and drove off without a backward glance. Willie had closed her front door behind her before she felt the tears trickle down her cheeks. She didn't even bother to turn on the lights but sat down in the nearest chair and wept.

Afterward, she knew the tears weren't just for Joe. They were for all the tension and nerve-racking anger she had tried to hold back in the past twelve hours.

She walked into the bathroom and washed her face with cold water. When she faced the mirror and saw the red-eyed woman looking back at her, she started to laugh out loud.

"Face it, Willie," she told her reflection. "Maybe it was all in your head. There was no relationship to begin with. Maybe you were just another one of a long line of women in Joe Kelly's life." Then she laughed again, knowing that wasn't true, either.

She turned out the light and walked into her bedroom. The sight of her bed, still unmade from the morning, made her feel like crying all over again. This time she held it back as she changed out of her uniform and into her nightgown.

Willie washed her face again, trying to wipe away the last trace of her tears. Then she wandered into the kitchen, fixed herself a cup of tea, then sat down with it in front of the TV.

A knock on her front door opened her eyes. She was staring at the last guest on a late-night talk show when she heard it again. She grabbed her robe before she answered the door.

It was a few seconds before Willie remembered who the woman was, but then the bright-blue suit triggered her sleepy memory. Willie's surprise must have been obvious, because the woman nervously cleared her throat.

"You don't know me, but I was at the meeting tonight," she began.

"Yes, I saw you," Willie mumbled. Why was this woman on her porch? Why wasn't she with Joe?

"My name is Diana Lawrence, and I'm a reporter for *Personality* magazine." She handed Willie a business card, then paused to let it all sink in. "I'm sorry to bother you so late, but I drove by and saw your light on. I just thought if you could spare a few minutes, we could talk."

She was still staring at the woman when it occurred to Willie that she should ask her in.

"Sure." She stepped to one side, then looked at her watch. It was past eleven. "Can you be brief? I have to get up early."

"Of course," she said. "This won't take long. May I sit down?" Without waiting for an answer, she sat down in the armchair next to the sofa.

Willie turned off the TV. "Can I get you something? A cup of tea, perhaps."

The woman shook her head. "No, thank you, I've just been out for drinks and I'm on my way back to my motel."

Willie sat down on the sofa. "What can I do for you, Miss Lawrence? I've said everything I'm going to say about this case."

"Oh, it isn't the case that I want to talk about." She paused, looking at Willie. "It's you I came to talk about."

"Me?"

"Yes. I think you'd make a great personality profile for our magazine."

The look on her face showed she was serious, but still Willie couldn't help but let a laugh slip out.

"What on earth gave you that idea?" Willie asked. "I'm just a sheriff in a small Colorado town. I'm about as interesting as Cisco on a Tuesday night."

Miss Lawrence managed a slight smile. "Come now, Sheriff, you're being far too modest. I think you're extremely interesting." She read the skepticism on Willie's face. "You're a very attractive young woman, and I think millions of Americans would love to hear the story of how you became sheriff of San Juan County."

"I was elected," Willie said.

"Of course you were, but I think the story behind the sheriff is what our readers would want." She waited for a moment, and Willie knew that she was trying to decide what tack to take. "You're a single woman, aren't you, Sheriff?"

"Look, Miss Lawrence, I think—"

"Call me Diana, please."

"Okay, Diana. I think my marital status has very little to do with my being sheriff."

"Of course it does."

"It does?"

"Yes. I mean what's your love life like? How do the men in your life view your job as sheriff? Do you think it makes them feel, well, less like men?"

Willie stared at the woman.

"Face it." Diana shrugged. "Being sheriff is not a very 'feminine' occupation for a woman to have. The kind of thing our readers want to know about is how it affects your personal life." She waited, then continued when Willie didn't answer. "We don't have to do the interview tonight, of course. I'd want some pictures—you know, of you in your uniform, then maybe some shots of you in something more causal, relaxed. I think you'd photograph well." She smiled. "What do you say? I think we could do a terrific piece."

Willie silently counted to five before she answered. "You mean, you want to do an article about my personal life?" Willie thought she'd done an admirable job of keeping her voice calm. Diana was still beaming.

"Yes. That's the sort of thing we're big on."

"Whatever gave you the idea that I'd agree to this?" Willie's voice wasn't so even now and the smile came off Diana's face.

"I talked over this idea with Joe Kelly—he's an old friend of mine—and I—"

"Joe Kelly put you up to this?"

"Well, he didn't exactly put me up to it. It was my idea. I just threw it around with him."

"What did he say when you were 'throwing it around' together?"

"He suggested that I ask you. And that's what I'm doing. Asking you." Diana smiled again.

"That was all he said?"

"Sure. I tried to get him to talk about it, but he kept telling me to ask you." She glanced at her watch and gathered up her purse. "Listen. Don't give me an answer tonight. Think about it. I'm staying at the Canyon Rim Lodge, and I'll give you a call in the morning."

"That won't be necessary, Miss Lawrence," Willie said as she stood up. "Don't call me back."

"What?"

"I said don't call me back." Willie walked to the door and opened it. "I've decided I'm not interested."

"But it would make a great piece. Think of it. I know you're up for reelection and—"

"Diana," Willie said, lowering her voice confidentially as she let her hand rest on Diana's arm, "I don't think the men in my life would understand. Besides, it's a small town, and if I talked about one of them, I'd have to talk about them all. I might leave one of them out." Willie smiled. "The men in my life would never forgive me."

"But—" Diana started to say.

"Good night, Diana. It was so nice to have this chance to talk." Willie closed the door. It was a few seconds before she heard the sound of footsteps as Diana Lawrence walked off her porch.

Willie leaned against the door and started to giggle as she heard a car engine start, then fade away down the road. To think that she'd imagined that Joe was spending the night with Diana. The woman she'd just spoken to wasn't Joe's type. She was attractive, yes. But Willie couldn't believe that Joe would ever be interested in a woman like that.

Willie walked over to the sofa and sat down. She laughed again when she realized how funny it was that Joe had sent Diana Lawrence over in the first place. He must have known what Willie's reaction would be to the proposed article. In fact, Miss Lawrence had gotten off easily. If a man had suggested that Willie do a piece about her "personal" life, she'd have thrown him out a lot more quickly and used considerably less tact in the process.

Suddenly she had a strong desire to share the joke with Joe. He was probably laughing right now. Besides, she still hadn't thanked him for this evening. Bud Beede had been right about one thing; he had bailed her out. She looked at her watch. It wasn't yet twelve. Not too late, considering the late-night call he'd paid on her a few days earlier.

She'd thrown on some jeans and a cotton shirt and was in her car in less than ten minutes. Her courage weakened, however, when she approached his house. There wasn't a light on. He must be asleep, she thought. But she told herself she'd come this far, so she parked.

The moon was a silver crescent in the middle of a star-spattered night. Cautiously, she moved along his front path in the darkness. She was almost at his front steps when she thought she heard something move.

"Hello, Willie."

She looked up. Joe Kelly was sitting bare-chested on the front porch.

"Hello, Joe," she answered. "I hope it isn't too late for a visit."

In the darkness she saw the motion of his arm as he indicated the spot next him on the steps. "Have a seat."

She sat down.

"It's a beautiful night, isn't it," he said. "I'd forgotten how beautiful the sky is in the summer. But then maybe I never noticed it before."

Willie was silent. She could hear him breathe, and in the darkness she could see the rise and fall of his chest. She could tell he'd just showered. His hair was wet, and he had on white pajama bottoms. They sat there, gazing up at the stars, until Willie realized that Joe wasn't going to start a conversation. He was waiting for her.

"Aren't you going to ask me why I'm here?" she finally said. She saw him shake his head, and he turned to face her. Shadows played across his bare chest, and she had to clench her fist to keep herself from reaching out and touching him.

"A friend doesn't need a reason to stop by," he replied.

"Not even when it's midnight and the last time you saw that friend she was ready to kill you?"

He smiled. "I knew you'd get over it—wanting to kill me, that is. But isn't this a little soon, even for you?"

"I came over to thank you."

"You're welcome." He paused and smiled. "What did I do?"

"You know perfectly well what you did. You saved my tail this evening. Those reporters were ready to eat me alive. I didn't know what hit me."

"Don't forget the Beedes. They don't exactly seem ready to start a Willie Callen fan club."

"I'd like to forget the Beedes." She turned to him. "I mean it. Thanks. You could have just let me flounder up there."

"As I recall, you did hold me partially responsible for those reporters being in Cisco in the first place. I guess I am. If I hadn't printed that story, nobody would have taken Lucy Wiemer's 'dream' seriously." He reached out and put an arm around her shoulder, drawing her closer. "Are we still friends, then?"

"Yes," Willie whispered. "It looks as if I'd better hold on to all the friends I've got. They seem to be getting scarce."

With one hand he lifted her chin, bringing it closer to his mouth. He kissed her lightly, almost teasingly. "Aren't you going to ask me about someone?"

"Who?" Willie said in her most innocent voice.

"You know who. I saw that look you gave me tonight as I left with that female reporter. If looks could kill, I would have gone up in smoke."

"How did you know how I looked? You didn't even bother to glance in my direction."

"Of course I did."

"No, you didn't. You were too busy eyeing Diana and her blue jumpsuit."

He kissed her again. "I thought you were going to be nice."

"I am." Willie opened her mouth and kissed him back. It was a long, deep kiss, without the hint of a tease. Somewhere in the middle of it Joe's lips became still. He withdrew and looked at Willie. "You called her Diana."

"Of course I did. That's her name." She started to take up the kiss where he'd left off, but again he stopped.

"I know that's her name. How do you know?"

"She told me."

"Diana came over to your house? Tonight?"

"She paid me a late-night visit. I understand it was after the two of you left the meeting and went out for drinks."

Joe looked at her cautiously. "Why did she come to see you?"

"You know what she wanted, Joe," Willie answered. "In fact, she told me it was all your idea."

"And you believe her?"

"Of course." Willie smiled. "I told her I'd be glad to do it. In fact, that's another thing I have to thank you for: the chance to tell America all about the personal life of Willie Callen."

Joe looked at her and shook his head. "You're not serious, are you?"

Willie just grinned wickedly. "You don't think my personal life would make great reading? Your friend Diana thought it would make a fascinating story. She was especially interested in how the men in my life felt about my occupation." Willie shrugged. "I just told her she'd have to ask the 'men' in my life." Joe groaned. "So I gave her your name."

"No." He shook his head. "You're teasing me."

"Of course I am." She laughed and he joined her, his relief obvious. "Why didn't you introduce us after the meeting?" Willie asked. "I could have saved her the trip out to my house. Instead you had to let me think the two of you—" she paused, searching for the right words "—that the two of you were old and rather intimate friends."

"You don't know Diana. I didn't want her to get within ten feet of the two of us together."

"Why not?"

"Because that woman has incredible sexual radar. She would have known within ten seconds that something was going on between us." He brought her closer, moving his hand up to her neck, caressing her, easing the tension he felt there. "Our relationship is the last thing I want to see discussed in *Personality* magazine. I'm surprised she didn't try to pump you for information about us."

"She didn't get the chance."

Joe eased her forward with the slightest pressure on her neck. Slowly his lips met hers, tasting them as if for the first time. In midkiss Willie stopped and pulled away. "You seem to know Diana Lawrence pretty well." Joe shrugged and drew her back. Willie resisted. "What does that mean? Do you or don't you know her?"

"Past tense. I did know her. Long ago and for a very short time."

"How short?"

"Believe me, it was short." He could tell she wasn't going to let him off the hook. "Okay. It was a couple of years ago, right after Melissa and I had split up. I was lonely. Diana had done a few stories on me before. She's the kind of journalist who believes in getting to know her subjects well, if you know what I mean." Joe attempted a smile. "So, she got to know me. It was one of those times when I didn't even have to wait until the morning after to realize that I'd just made a mistake."

"She isn't your type?"

He shook his head. "Definitely not."

Willie wrapped her arms around him. "Good. Because if she was, I knew one of us was in big trouble."

"You should realize by now that I like women who carry thirty-eights and wear Stetsons." He laughed. "That isn't entirely true. I like you. I don't think another woman with a thirty-eight or a Stetson would even turn my head."

Once again he covered her mouth with his. This time she felt his arms wrap around her, and he lifted her onto his lap. Willie started to laugh as she watched her long legs dangle off his and onto the porch steps. It had been a long time since she'd sat on anyone's lap. She let her head rest against the warmth of his bare chest, her cheek brushed by the coarse, curly hair that swirled in a V there. She let his arms enclose her. It was the first time in her adult life that she'd actually felt petite in a man's arms.

She tried to suppress a giggle.

"What's so funny?" he whispered. "I'm trying to seduce you. The least you can do is take me seriously."

"Oh." Willie was quiet for a moment and then started to laugh again. "It's just that I had this wildly romantic vision of you carrying me upstairs."

"What's so funny about that?" Joe stopped nuzzling her neck and looked at her. Even in the dark, Willie could imagine the softness in his eyes as they studied her face. "Did you laugh when Rhett carried Scarlett?"

"Of course not," she sighed. "But I'm a slightly bigger package than Vivien Leigh. And big girls never get carried up stairs."

Joe looked at her for a moment, then laughed.

"There's always a first time," he said. Without warning he slipped one arm under her knees and kept the other behind her back. In one movement he was on his feet and Willie was in his arms.

She gasped. "You can't do this!"

He carried her across the porch and stopped in front of the door. "Of course I can. But you'll have to open the screen door." She opened it and he carried her in.

"Joe, if you try to carry me up those stairs, you're going to break your back."

"Hush," he told her as he started up the stairs. "As I remember, even Scarlett had the good sense to keep her mouth shut."

"She swooned," Willie said, laughing.

"Please don't swoon," Joe said as they reached the top of the stairs. "You'll miss out on all the fun." He walked down the hallway and into his bedroom. "And so will I."

He reached his bed and held her in his arms above the freshly turned down sheets. Slowly he bent his head toward hers, stopping just before their lips met. He let his lips linger over hers, teasing, until she stopped them with a kiss of her own. It was an open kiss, an invitation. She let him know that even though she had been carried to his bed, she would have eagerly walked there beside him.

Finally she felt him lower her onto the bed, her head cradled by his arm and the pillow. He slipped in beside her, gently rubbing the back of his finger against her cheek. There was a light on at the bedside table. His face was in shadow, but she could read the desire in his eyes. His dark hair reflected the light behind him, forming a halo of brightness around his head.

"Do you mind if we leave the light on? Last time I didn't get a chance to look at you." He kissed her again and his hand trailed down to the small of her back, pushing her body to his. With his other hand he traced the curve of her outer thigh. She could feel its heat through her jeans. "I want to look at you, Willie."

She smiled and ran her hand through his hair. It was surprisingly soft. She tugged at it lightly bringing his mouth to hers. She kissed him again, delighting in the feel of him. She could sense the quickening of his heartbeat, and her own pulse followed suit, pounding throughout her body with increased urgency.

Twisting underneath him, she felt suddenly confined by her clothes. With infinite care, Joe undid each button on her blouse and let it fall open, revealing her pale breasts beneath. It seemed as if minutes had passed, time he spent caressing her body with his eyes. Then he bent forward and kissed her, letting his tongue define the soft, rounded flesh of each breast as he eased her blouse over her shoulders and down her arms. Then he pulled her to him, and she shuddered as she felt the sudden warmth of his bare body next to hers. She wrapped her arms around his shoulders, pulling him closer to her, craving the texture and heat of him next to her. His coarse chest hair made her skin tingle as it rubbed against her.

His hands moved lower, tracing the curve of her waist. She heard the zipper on her jeans and felt a sudden release as he slid it open. He was at once both gentle and rough as he pulled the denim fabric down past her thighs, then off her legs, carelessly tossing her pants over the bed. Having freed Willie of her clothes, Joe tugged at the drawstring around his own waist, all the while embracing her with his eyes, holding her with his gaze, until his pajamas fell easily past his hips and onto the floor.

He stood there a moment, naked. In the muted light Willie could see the outline of tight muscles defined under the skin of his powerful thighs. Then he came to her, covering her body with his own. Willie brought her legs up over his and stroked the length of his muscled legs with the soft skin of her inner thighs. Joe pressed himself closer and she could feel the desire as he kissed her face, her neck, her breasts. Slowly he let his mouth move lower, until he was tracing the outline of her belly with his tongue.

Willie's legs were now wrapped loosely around his back and she let his mouth wander lower still. She groaned and locked her legs more tightly around his body, the excitement carried through her on the liquid heat of her blood.

Spirals of pleasure and anticipation shot from her center and traveled the length of her body. He moved his mouth slowly, until she felt his lips gently urging her to hold nothing back. All her senses merged into one, and nothing existed for her but Joe and what their bodies were doing.

Joe had given her this powerful sensation of intense passion. It was rolling in like a wave, ready to wash over her. And when the release finally came its strength startled her. Her body tightened and clung to Joe and then she felt herself relax. She was floating with the wave, letting it carry her away.

When she finally opened her eyes, she was cradled in Joe's arms. He began kissing her all over again, his hands roaming the length of her body. She felt he couldn't get enough of her. He wanted to experience every tremor, every taste, she had to offer. Willie returned his kisses, and as she did, she felt her desire for him begin to build again.

"Willie," he whispered as he bent over her, his body moving, floating above hers, an echo of her own movement. "What's happening to us, Willie?"

She didn't know what to say. All she knew was the exquisite fire glowing within her. He pressed closer, finally filling her desire with his own. As she felt him inside her, she wanted to cry out. It was overwhelming; she felt as if she were drowning in him. It was impossible to tell where Willie's body was separate from Joe's, because each of their rhythms belonged to the other.

Willie felt Joe pull her along. She felt her own body travel to its boundaries, stretched to the limits of response. Joe helped her ride the crest of pleasure. She knew it matched his, and the look of exquisite ecstasy on his face told her he had reached the point of release.

They lay together, locked in each other's arms, their bodies still intimately joined. Willie could feel his heartbeat against hers; when finally he rolled over beside her, it was slow and even.

"It's hard to believe that anything could be better than this," he said quietly. "We need to forget about all the tangled pride and inflated ego we find in each other and just remember this." He traced the curve of her cheek with his finger, then kissed the path he'd drawn. "You could become a habit, Willie." His kissed her again, and Willie felt his lips, heard his voice, through the haze of beginning sleep. "Yes, you could become an incredible, beautiful addiction."

# Chapter 10

Willie was running from the light, running as fast as she could. Still it came closer. She cursed under her breath; it was stupid to have come out here alone. But it was too late for regrets. She had to find a place to hide. She turned her head from side to side, searching. The back fields of the farm were barren, no trees or hillocks in sight. No gullies broke the flat landscape until a small rock appeared out of nowhere.

She glanced back. Fear raced through her as she saw the aliens. Tall creatures dressed in white space suits with shiny dark helmets over their heads were only steps behind her. She tried to bury herself behind the rock. She couldn't make herself stop shaking as she listened to the footsteps coming closer and closer. Suddenly she felt the heavy, mechanical hand grip her shoulder. She sat up and screamed.

"Willie," Joe said soothingly, trying to hold her in his arms. "Hey, Willie."

"No! Let go of me!" she screamed. "Let go of me or I'll shoot." She struggled to find her gun and was horrified to realize she wasn't even wearing her holster. "No..." she said again.

"Willie, baby," Joe whispered into her ear, "it's all right. It was just a dream. I'm here. Everything's okay." He held her and rocked her gently. "It was just a dream, sweetheart."

Willie opened her eyes and looked around. She held on to Joe and laughed weakly. "I guess all this stuff is really getting to me. Some sheriff I am, falling apart at the first sign of real trouble." She shook her head. "You should have been there." She looked at him. "Maybe this whole thing's getting to be too much for just me."

"Are you kidding? You're doing a great job. Anyone's entitled to a bad dream now and then. Besides, you're not going to call in the second string just because the game gets rough. Who do think is better equipped to handle this job? You or some of the good ole boys upstate?" He smiled. "If you think they are, then you might as well hand your badge over to Virgil Jones." He laughed. "He'd probably deputize the Beede brothers."

"Over my dead body!"

"That's the spirit," Joe said, still holding her.

Willie smiled. "You know, nothing's been the same since you came back to town." She pulled away for a moment and looked at him squinty-eyed. "Are you sure you're not an alien? Maybe I should look for some empty pods around here." She laughed and started to lean over the edge of the bed.

"Have I changed that much?" Joe asked, suddenly serious.

"No. Yes. A little." She reached out and smoothed a length of dark hair off his forehead. "The situations we've been through have made us both change. I guess we just grew up." She let her finger trace the top of his ear. "But I wondered whether you were an alien because," she said as she brought her finger down the side of his neck, "last night was out of this world. No wonder I ended up dreaming about extraterrestrials."

Joe laughed softly. "That reminds me of a story I read in one of my competitors' papers. You know, the one you're always accusing me of wanting to write for. A woman reported that she'd been kidnapped by aliens and subjected to a—shall we say—physical examination that succeeded in satisfying her far more than any of her earthly encounters."

Willie laughed. "Do you actually read that stuff? 'Preacher Explodes into Flames before Startled Parishioners'; 'Cannibals Shrink the Heads of Aliens.' It's incredible that anybody believes it."

"I didn't say I believed it. I don't think many people do. It's just that we humans are a notoriously curious breed."

Joe pulled gently on the sheet she held against her naked breasts. When he'd finally gotten it down, he circled one pale pink nipple with his finger. She leaned back on the pillows, sighed deeply and brought Joe down with her as she covered his shoulders with her arms.

He rolled over her and moved his hand from her breast, trailing along the middle of her stomach to the downy softness of her belly, his tongue opening her lips to his. Willie sighed and moved languidly beneath him, relishing the sweet arousal that spread through her body.

Joe's touch could restart the fire inside her, both filling her with tension and relieving it at the same time. When he touched her, when he made her feel this good, she didn't want to think about anything else. Not about the aliens, not about the election, not about Joe's paper.

Right now only she and Joe existed, fulfilling each other's deepest needs. Then an uncomfortable thought crept in.

He was fulfilling her deepest needs, but he hadn't said much about what role she was playing for him. It didn't seem possible that a man who made love like Joe was just doing it to get something from her. But the doubt had taken root in Willie's mind, and she found it hard to shake.

"Willie?" she heard Joe saying softly as he rolled over and sat up on his side of the bed.

"Wh-what? Why did you stop?" she asked.

"Making love is a lot more fun with two people." He smiled. "Still bothered by your dream?"

Willie sat up, pulling the sheet around her, finding it hard to ignore Joe's broad, flat, hairy chest just a few inches away. It was the same chest she had spent the night pressed against, a position she'd found most comforting.

"Yes. I guess it'll keep bothering me, waking and sleeping, until I get to the bottom of this whole thing. And I've got to do it as soon as possible if I want to remain sheriff. When there's a new problem, people forget what you've done in the past. And for this county, it's more than just a problem; it's a crisis. If any more turkeys die, the area's turkey-producing reputation could be destroyed. We both know what that could mean."

"Yeah. No turkeys, no Cisco," Joe said glumly. Then his face brightened. "That also means we'll have to solve this baffling riddle before the election and save the reputations of both the turkeys and the local sheriff!" With that Joe leaped out of bed and headed for the shower.

Before Willie could open her mouth to ask "What do you mean *we'll* have to solve this riddle?" Joe had the water running and was singing "Purple People Eater" at the top of his lungs.

Willie just smiled, waiting for her turn in the shower. What have I gotten myself into? she wondered. Why did I have to fall for a guy like Joe, someone who never seems to take things seriously and— She caught herself. *Fall for.* Had she fallen for him? She wanted to think that the attraction was purely physical, that he'd merely met a long-ignored need of her body.

But in her heart she knew it was something more: the way he could make her laugh and lighten her mood, his dedication to their town and the paper, and the incredible way he could physically touch the deepest part of her. Yes, she admitted reluctantly, it was something more than that schoolgirl crush she'd had long ago.

But how did Joe feel? She felt overwhelmed again. First the election, then a turkey crisis caused by aliens, of all things, and now Joe Kelly. Would she be strong enough to make the right decisions? The last thing she needed now was a love affair gone wrong. But the thought of giving up Joe and staying away from him made her feel even weaker. He stimulated her mind as well as her body.

Thinking of stimulation, she smiled and hopped out of bed. She opened the bathroom door and steam poured out. She could see the outline of Joe's body through the frosted glass of the shower stall. She slid it over and stepped in.

Willie dabbed at her damp hair with a rumpled towel as she glanced at the front page of the *San Juan Independent*, going over Joe's story again. The aroma of fresh-brewed coffee filled the little kitchen. It was much tidier than Willie had thought it would be. She wondered if Joe had a housekeeper.

Once in a while she looked up from the paper when she thought Joe was too busy to notice. She watched as he moved around the kitchen. It amazed her that a man like him could be so at home in this setting. Again she realized that one by one her stereotypical thoughts of him were falling by the wayside.

She'd had him pegged so neatly when he'd first returned to town. Now all those ideas were proving to be false. Willie was bothered by this. She took a great deal of pride in her ability to read people, to be able to tell what they were thinking, what they might do next. It had proven useful to her more than once in her job. Now here was this man who was a genuine enigma. Willie had been prepared to dislike him from the start—in fact, she had. But something about him had forced her to look beyond the picture she'd created. She was glad she had.

She had to laugh to herself. She'd spent the night in his bed and in his arms. If that wasn't doing an about-face, she didn't know what was. She wondered now whether that had been wise. Cisco was, after all, a small town and, as in all small towns, news traveled fast. It wouldn't do her re-election bid any good if the population knew she'd been sleeping with the only newspaper editor in town.

"Damn them!" she said softly. "It's about time I thought of myself for a change."

"Damn who?" Joe asked, turning from the stove, where he was forking the last omelet out of the pan and onto a plate. "I'm hurrying as fast as I can. I know you're my guest and—"

Willie laughed. "Okay, I can take a hint. Where are the plates and silverware?" Joe showed her, and she began to set the table. "Don't worry. I'd rather eat here than anywhere else. You're way ahead of the competition."

"Thanks a lot," Joe said huffily, "considering my only competition in Cisco is Hermione Desmond, the seventy-five-year-old doyenne of Desmond's Diner. Hermione is the only reason, I might add, that it's always full of people. You know, I think she may be single-handedly responsible for the fact that tourists pass through Cisco only once. If they taste her coffee, they'll take a hundred-mile detour to avoid it on their return trip!"

Willie laughed. "Now, don't speak ill of an institution. That's the reason I always pack my own jug of coffee. Desmond's Diner might be the best place in town to pick up news, but it's the worst place to eat." Joe sat down across the table from her, placing the steaming plates of eggs and toast in front of them. Then he poured her a cup of aromatic coffee.

"Let's see if you're any better a cook than Hermione. Who knows? Maybe your house will become the new meeting place in town. You won't even have to leave home to get all the news that's fit to print."

"If I'd known you were such an expert, I'd have had you writing a dining out column for the paper." He smiled at her, and Willie could tell he was eagerly awaiting her reaction to his cooking.

She took a mouthful of the omelet. She closed her eyes to savor every taste. Eggs, cheese, ham, peppers, onions, and a few seasonings unknown to her. She continued to chew slowly, emitting an "Umm" and a "Hmm" every so often. She opened her eyes a pinch and saw the expression of exasperation on Joe's face. After what seemed to her like minutes, she swallowed and put down her fork. She picked up her napkin and dabbed at the corners of her mouth.

"Willie, if you are trying to drive me crazy, you're succeeding admirably," Joe said with a hint of impatience. "Well? I'm waiting for your verdict."

"It's been a while since I had one of Hermione's omelets. A couple of days ago, I think . . ."

"Quit stalling, Sheriff. How is it?"

"It's wonderful." Willie laughed at Joe's broad smile of pride. "It's the best omelet I've ever had, and I've had a lot in my day. Where did you ever learn to cook? Oh, never mind. You're hired."

"Hired?" Joe asked, confused.

"Yes, hired. When can you start? It's obvious that you were never meant to be a newspaperman at all. You were meant to be a housekeeper and cook for some poor lost soul like me."

"You hardly strike me as a lost soul, but I wouldn't mind playing house with you at all," Joe responded with a comical leer.

"I said *keeping* house, not playing," Willie reminded him, and then stopped as the true meaning of her words struck home. Maybe that was the difference between them. An unbridgeable distance? Joe was playing around, and Willie wanted something permanent. Maybe she'd sensed the difference all along and that was the reason for their unspoken tension.

Suddenly the light mood had vanished, and Joe and Willie stared quietly at their food, moving it around slowly with their forks.

Joe was the first to break the silence. "Well?" he said, pushing his plate aside. "What's the plan?"

Willie looked up, surprised. "What plan?"

"I assumed you had a plan. How are you going to find out who's killing the turkeys of San Juan County?"

"I don't have a plan. I had other things on my mind last night."

"Then I think we should come up with one," he said.

"What's this *we*? I don't remember deputizing you. Why are you so interested in helping me out of this? Virgil Jones might accuse you of taking sides."

"I know a newsman is supposed to be impartial, but it's too late for that. Let's face it. I don't have the same affection for Virgil that I have for you. He's just not my type."

Willie laughed.

"I want to help you. You're my friend. Besides, this could be a big story for me, an exclusive. My byline all over the country, the world..."

Willie eyed him suspiciously.

"Well, all over the state, anyway."

Willie had her doubts. What interested Joe more—the byline or her friendship? But she had to admit he was right. It looked like a local job, and she could use all the help she could get. She liked her deputies, but they had to be used for other duties, and quite frankly, she didn't think they'd be as helpful to her as Joe would.

Was she just rationalizing to find a way to be with Joe as much as she could? She knew Joe was intelligent, and she could count on him to come up with some good ideas. Besides, she was tired of trying to stay one step ahead of him. What better way to keep her eyes on him than to have him working with her?

"Okay. I'll admit I can still use your help. You always seem to end up where I am anyway. You might as well make yourself useful."

Joe faked a low bow. "Your enthusiasm is overwhelming, Sheriff."

Willie smiled, her mood lightening again at the thought of working with Joe. "I think the first thing we need to decide is where the 'aliens' will strike next. Let's look at where they've been and see if we can establish some sort of pattern."

Joe smiled. "That's a great idea. Exactly what I had in mind, too, I might add. I knew there was a reason you were elected sheriff."

Willie chose to ignore this. She pulled some paper and a couple of pencils from Joe's nearby desk. She laid the blank pages between them. Sipping her coffee, she began to draw a small map, showing the location of all the farms in the upper part of Spanish Valley.

They studied the map together, marking off the farms that had been hit. Willie filled Joe in on the history of each farm and farmer and the general relations among them as neighbors.

Willie drew in Wheeler's farm to the north of Bishop's place, next to land owned by Homer Beede and a farmer named Royce Jacobs. Royce had a much smaller turkey-growing operation than either Wheeler or Bishop. Most of his land was planted in pinto beans and hay. Homer Beede had some turkeys, but he raised mainly cattle.

"Several years ago Wheeler, Bishop and Jacobs challenged some water rights that Homer Beede had been using for years," Willie told Joe. "All of the farmers get water from the Dolores River, but that usage is regulated by the state. Only so much water is available in the valley."

"And the other farmers thought Beede was getting more than his share?"

"Exactly." Willie drew a circle around the Jacobs and Beede farms. "The word around town was that there was going to be a big court battle. Everyone was surprised when Beede settled out of court by relinquishing a rather generous share of water rights that had been in his family for several generations."

"What did Beede get out of it," Joe wondered out loud, "besides the goodwill of his neighbors?"

"Not much." Willie shrugged. "But the whole thing was settled so amicably, it's hardly grounds for suspecting Homer and his boys of killing off their neighbors' turkeys. The Beedes are obnoxious, but unfortunately, that isn't a crime."

"But why would Beede give up something like that so easily?"

"Because even though his family had been using those water rights for years, there was definitely a legal basis for his neighbors' claims." Willie looked down at the map. "One thing is for certain. We need something more to go on than an old water rights dispute."

"I think it's a good beginning." Joe looked down at the map. "My bet for the site of the next 'alien' visit is the Jacobs place."

"I had a feeling you were going to say that." Willie smiled. "So where does that leave us, pardner?"

"Looks to me like we'll just have to do a little old-fashioned reconnoitering. Let's pick a likely spot on the Jacobs land and stake it out. Tonight."

"You're serious, aren't you?"

"Yes. Do you have any better ideas, Sheriff?"

"No, I guess I don't. I'm just not sure I know exactly what you mean by, uh, 'reconnoitering.'"

"Not to worry, Willie. I'll be all business tonight. Maybe you should even deputize me, to keep the local tongues from wagging."

"I plan to keep this a totally secret operation, so the local tongues shouldn't have anything to wag about. I agree we should have a stakeout, that it's probably the only way we'll ever be able to find out whoever is doing this, but..."

"But what?"

"I don't know if you'll be any fun to be with if you're going to be all business...." Willie smiled at Joe.

He laughed wickedly and leaned across the table to kiss her. "Well, I'll make sure that even if we don't see any turkey-killing aliens, the entire evening won't be lost. I'll regale you with tales of my football days and show you a few tricks I learned along the way."

Willie rolled her eyes. "Sounds like a terrific evening. I guess I'd better get prepared for this one."

"Just bring your sleeping bag. I'll get the other gear and the food together. We'll take my old pickup, which I seldom use. That way we'll be in an unmarked vehicle."

"You know an awful lot about preparing for a stakeout—unmarked cars and everything. Are you sure you haven't done this sort of thing before?"

"Positive, my love. But you probably have something to do to get ready, too."

Joe's statement shook Willie from her daze. She jumped up from the table, fumbling to braid her hair.

"Darn it, I'm going to be late for work. That'll really start tongues wagging. Hannah's favorite pastime is watching me come in and wondering what I did the night before." She hurried upstairs to the bedroom.

"I've got a lot to do before tonight," she said, raising her voice so he could hear her in the kitchen. She took off his robe and searched the floor for her clothes. "Assuming that our villains are not from some distant planet, they must be using one of those new super-silent helicopters to get around. I suppose they could rig one of those up to look like a UFO."

She pulled on her jeans and buttoned her blouse. "I'll get Carl or Wes to check all the places in the area where a helicopter like that could be rented. There shouldn't be too many places close by. Grand Junction, maybe Denver."

"They might have used an alias when they rented it," Joe shouted from the kitchen. "Any ideas who can pilot one of those things?"

Willie returned to the kitchen and sat down. "Several of the locals were in Vietnam." She was tying her shoes, then she stopped and looked at Joe. "The Jacobs boy, Bud Beede and Virgil Jones were among them. I'll check whether any of them flew a helicopter."

"Wouldn't it be an interesting coincidence if one of them did?"

Willie smiled and nodded. "Very interesting." She finished tying her shoes and walked over to where Joe stood at the table. He put his arm around her and pulled her close.

"I hate to see you leave," he whispered. "We could go back upstairs and forget all about aliens and helicopters and we could. . ." He let his mouth linger over hers, brushing it lightly, urging it open. "We could leave the turkeys to their fate and continue where we left off." He kissed her, and she felt the tip of his tongue taste hers. It was a delicious thought, but she shook her head. "No?" he asked.

"No," she answered. "Duty calls." She pulled away and headed toward the door.

"What time do you want me to pick you up?" he called after her.

She turned around. "Come by thirty minutes after dark."

"See you then, pardner," he said as she disappeared out the door.

Joe's old pickup rattled its way to the top of the tiny hill, the one everyone in Cisco called Desert Point because it had a wide view of not only the farmland below but the desert beyond. The hill was deserted as Willie had hoped. The young kids in town all went to the reservoir to neck.

Joe stepped on the brakes and the old heap ground to a halt. Willie let out a sigh. This old truck had been Paul's; in fact, she thought it must have been in the Kelly family for generations. She wasn't sure they would make it up the minor incline, and she prayed they wouldn't have to depend on the ancient truck to make a quick getaway. She was beginning to think it would have been much better to have taken Joe's Blazer than to risk being stuck.

"Well, here we are. Ready to reconnoiter," Joe said as he parked the truck near the top of Desert Point. He reached for Willie's hand and brought it to his lips for a quick kiss. The action caught her off guard and she remembered, not for the first time that day, the passion of the night before.

"We might as well make ourselves comfortable," he said, opening his door and sliding out. Before she knew it, he was on her side of the truck. He opened her door and held out his hand, helping Willie step down. Their eyes met and held for what seemed like minutes, then Joe slipped his hands up Willie's arms and pulled her into his. Willie felt a knot of excitement twist inside her stomach.

Her hands found the nape of his neck and she drew his head closer. Their lips met. They were tentative at first, then they opened to each other. Joe's thighs pressed Willie against the truck as he ran his hands along her body. They kissed again, and Willie felt her need for him ache inside her.

Suddenly Willie jumped and the embrace was broken. Forcing itself between her legs and Joe's was a young turkey. A soft *gobble* came from its beak. Willie laughed, the tension and romance of the moment broken.

"Damn turkeys are everywhere!" Joe said, backing away. "Let's get our gear into the back of the truck. That's the reason I brought it. We'll have a perfect view of the valley. We can enjoy the refreshments I brought, and best of all, we can get away from these blasted birds!"

Willie looked around. "I knew there must have been some reason you brought this prehistoric machine." She helped Joe lay out the sleeping bags in the bed of the truck. He pulled out a backpack and withdrew a bottle of wine and some sandwiches.

He offered her some wine, but she shook her head. "I don't think we should be drinking on duty." He nodded and put it away, then took out the canteen. "I forgot. I'm on the right side of the law now. Usually newspapermen are required to drink on duty." He smiled and offered her a sandwich. She took a bite.

"Have you considered my job offer any further?" she asked, settling back on the sleeping bags.

"Job offer?"

"To be my housekeeper," she reminded him.

"I'm an honest, upstanding man. Can you imagine what the townspeople would say about me if they knew I was working for a single lady? My reputation would be ruined. I'd never be able to show my face on the street again. It's all right for you, you being the sheriff and—"

Willie laughed. "Shut up and have a sandwich," she said, stuffing one into his mouth.

She sighed and laid her head back against the crook of his shoulder. Joe wrapped his arm around her and moved even closer.

"This is my favorite place in the whole valley," Willie said quietly. "I used to come up here when I was a kid and look at that desert beyond the farms and wonder what lay out there in the world beyond Cisco."

Joe brushed her hair aside and kissed her forehead. "You left, but you came back. Why?"

Willie snuggled deeper into his arm. "I guess I'm just a small-town girl at heart. No other place seemed to fit. After the army, Cisco meant a lot to me." They were quiet for a moment, staring at the starry sky and listening to the wind move over the valley below.

"Why did you come back, Joe? You really had a life away from Cisco. I never did."

"I did, but everything changes. After my divorce, after football was finished, something was missing. It never would've occurred to me to come back. But then Paul died and I was faced with having to come home." He kissed her hair. "I know just what you mean when you said that Cisco seemed to fit. It was the same way for me. It felt right." He was very quiet as he pulled Willie close against him.

Willie pulled his hands to her lips and kissed them gently. Then she turned and rested her body against his as he lay in the bed of the truck on one of the sleeping bags. Joe lifted her face and their eyes met. Neither said a word; neither had to. He drew her closer and they kissed.

The kiss was slow at first, then it deepened. Willie found the buttons on Joe's shirt, and she undid them quickly, running her fingers over the flat, broad chest beneath.

They lay together in the bed of the truck, aware of nothing except each other's bodies. Everything seemed so new, as if they'd never made love before. Willie moaned as Joe ran his finger over her breasts. She opened her eyes to look into his when suddenly her body stiffened and she groaned. Joe sensed it wasn't a groan of ecstasy but one of disgust.

"Willie, what's wrong?" He tried to continue, but she wouldn't let him. "What's the...?"

Willie didn't speak but continued to stare over Joe's shoulder. He couldn't help but notice the look in her eyes and prepared himself for the worst as he turned around slowly.

Joe looked over his shoulder, blinked and looked again. Then he burst out laughing. Willie pushed him off as he continued to laugh.

Surrounding the bed of the truck was an audience of turkeys staring silently at Willie and Joe, apparently intrigued by the sight of two humans making love. Joe continued to laugh, unable to speak, and Willie shoved him away.

"It's not funny, Joe," she said, then she, too, started to laugh. "You birds deserve whatever you get," she shouted at them, waving her arms, trying to shoo them away. They remained unmoved. She turned to Joe. "Who do they remind you of?" she asked. "Some of Cisco's more prominent citizens?"

Joe tried to control himself. "You know, you're right. That one over there does look like Hermione Desmond, and the one over there looks like the mayor's wife." He started laughing again. "That one's Hannah. She's sitting next to Lucy Wiemer."

Willie took her rolled-up jacket and began hitting him. It only served to increase his laughter. "I don't think they were all female," she said, laughing. "I think there're a few old toms in the lot."

Suddenly she stopped as she pointed to the valley below. She was quiet. Joe stopped laughing, too.

"I'm sorry, Willie. They just all looked so funny sitting there, like they were enjoying a matinee or—"

Willie put one hand over his mouth and pointed with the other. In the farmland below them was a circular object surrounded by flickering lights, hovering over the land. As the object descended to the ground, Willie and Joe sat stunned. They saw, just barely, the silhouettes of two beings dressed entirely in white, with enormous heads, as they emerged from the craft.

Joe jumped up first. "Come on, let's get going." They leaped over the sides of the truck, scattering turkeys. Joe hopped into the cab and turned the key, but the only response was a sickly rattle. "Damn it, don't fail me now," he pleaded, and tried once more. This time the old engine flared into life, and Joe threw the truck in gear and took off down the hill.

"Turn off your lights," Willie commanded him. Joe looked at her as if she were crazy.

"How am I supposed to see where I'm going if my lights are off?" he asked.

"Use the lights of their craft as your guide. We don't want them to see us coming."

"In case you didn't notice, Willie, this old jalopy isn't exactly silent. They'll be able to hear us long before they'd be able to see our headlights."

"I don't care. They might not be able to tell what or where the noise is coming from if it's dark. We'll have a better chance of catching them."

"Whatever you say, Sheriff. Just don't blame me if we end up in a ditch instead of next to the UFO."

"Hurry up. You know darn well it's not a UFO. It's got to be one of those silent choppers rigged to look like one. It would be easy enough to do. A string of lights, a— *Ouch!*" She glared at Joe in the dark. "What are you trying to do, kill us?" Willie rubbed the spot on her head that had just connected with the roof of the bouncing truck.

"I told you I can't see where I'm going without the headlights. It's not my fault if I hit a few potholes and dips. This isn't exactly a major highway. Maybe we should have brought horses instead." Joe gripped the steering wheel tightly as he tried to make out the road in the dark.

"If it wouldn't take up too much time, I'd have you stop and I'd take over," Willie retorted, scanning the area ahead for the men and the glowing machine.

"Any more smart comments and I'll let you. If I'd known you were going to be such a nag, I'd never have volunteered for this hazardous duty. I'd—"

"You enjoyed the earlier part of it!" Willie said.

"What do you mean by that?" Joe let his eyes leave the road to glance at Willie, and the truck veered dangerously toward the edge of an irrigation ditch.

Willie screamed as Joe fought to get the truck back under control. "Nothing, Joe. Really, I didn't mean anything. I'm just anxious about getting these guys. You're doing a really great job. I know I couldn't do better myself. But hurry up, or we'll lose them!"

# Chapter 11

Damn it, Willie, this old truck's going as fast as it can. If you think you can get us there any faster, I'll be glad to stop and let you drive," Joe told her as he concentrated on the road. "I don't know how you expect me to drive in the dark on this goat trail the county calls a road. We won't find out anything if we have an accident and kill ourselves."

"All right, all right. You've made your point. I'm sorry." She searched the road, straining to keep her eyes on the bright light ahead of them. "Maybe I should've brought Wes along."

"What's that supposed to mean?" Joe turned to look at her and the truck swerved to the right. Willie reached out and put her hand on the steering wheel.

"Take it easy, Joe. Watch where you're going." He slowed down. "All I meant was, Wes is trained to do this. It's part of his job. What if something happens?"

"I think I can handle anything we're going to run into tonight, Sheriff." He turned toward her. "Besides, waiting with Wes wouldn't have been quite so much fun, would it?"

Willie was glad it was dark. Joe couldn't see the flush she felt spreading across her cheeks. He probably could handle anything. She hoped so, anyway. She knew she'd never forgive herself if anything happened to Joe.

Then Willie realized that the reason she was so jumpy had more basis in good old-fashioned passion than in aliens. Was that passion for Joe so intense that she was letting it interfere with her common sense? Willie had never been one to do everything by the book, but careering along a back road on her way to a stakeout, a civilian in tow, wasn't exactly accepted procedure. That the 'civilian' was also her lover didn't make matters any better.

Willie's internal debate was stopped when she braced herself against the dash as Joe drove his truck into a shallow ditch.

"What did you do that for? How could you miss the road?"

"I didn't miss the road, Willie," he explained with forced civility. "I'm parking the truck. Or did you want me to pull up and park it under their noses?"

"Okay. Stop being such a wise guy." She leaned over and kissed his cheek. "You did a great job for a rookie." Quietly she opened the door. "I'll approach them on foot."

She got out of the car and strapped her holster and .38 to her hip. Then she started up the incline, toward the "UFO." She heard Joe's door open and felt him fall in behind her.

"What do you mean 'I'll approach them'?" He touched her shoulder. "We're doing this together."

"Okay. But just stay out of the way. Especially if things start getting rough."

Without looking back, Willie crept along the edge of the dirt embankment, keeping low, praying that Joe was doing the same. They moved along for about a hundred yards. Willie guessed that the little gully where Joe had parked his truck was the eastern boundary line between the Jacobs and Beede farms. They were now on Beede property.

Joe held apart a barbed wire fence as Willie crawled through. She stopped and did the same for Joe. The lights on the UFO were shining just above a little hillock to the east, and wordlessly they dropped on their stomachs as they reached the top.

The subject of their investigation was at the northern end of the slight depression that lay below them. It was too far away to see anything clearly except the pulsating lights. They heard an odd soft whirring sound. But closer, no more than sixty yards away, were two "aliens" dressed in silver-white suits. Their heads were entirely hidden under large helmets with reflective front covers. Each of the beings held a large metal cylinder.

"Look," Joe said as he pointed to the scene below. "That must be the stuff that's killing the turkeys."

Willie nodded. She could see a few of the birds lying on the ground already. The rest of the flock was starting to weave around.

"Stupid birds," Willie muttered. "They don't even have enough sense to try to run." She shook her head and caught a whiff of the same faintly metallic odor she'd smelled at the Wheeler and Bishop farms.

"Give me your camera," she whispered. "I want to get a picture of this." Without looking at him, she held out her hand.

"Camera?" Joe said the words softly against the hillside. "No camera," he sighed. Willie turned to him. "I'm sorry. I forgot the camera."

"Any other time you have it wrapped around your neck as if it grew there," she said in a low, angry voice. She crawled forward, using the scrub oak on the hillside for cover. "You stay put," she whispered. "Maybe you can draw a picture."

She unstrapped her gun and took it off safety, then eased her way down the slope. She was outside the circle of light the UFO threw off, but she knew she wouldn't be too hard to spot if someone happened to look her way. But the aliens seemed too intent on killing turkeys to look around them. She'd gone about fifty feet when she felt something behind her. Reflexively she drew her gun and whirled around.

Joe was staring into the barrel of her .38.

"Joseph Kelly," she said through clenched teeth. "If you don't want to be the next headline in your own paper, stay out of my way!"

"Okay. Just put that thing back where it belongs." Willie put the gun in her holster and moved forward, with Joe right behind her. "You didn't think I was going to let you have all the fun, did you?"

Willie ignored the remark and kept crawling down the hill. The creatures in white were definitely two men. Both appeared taller than average, well over six feet. But then the boots they were wearing looked large and very thick-soled, as if they were meant to make the wearer stay well off the ground. The loose fitting suits eerily reflected the pulsating colored lights of their vehicle, which sat several hundred yards behind the men. Willie couldn't see inside the craft, but she'd bet her next paycheck that a man sat at the controls, waiting.

The vehicle was incredible. If Willie had believed in such things, she'd have called it a UFO herself. It was certainly unidentifiable. It appeared to be round, about fifteen feet in diameter. The outer edges were defined by constantly flickering lights. It made a soft, almost purring noise, and she could see no source of propulsion, no wings, no propellers or rotors. Nothing.

She turned to Joe. "Well, what do you think? Have we been invaded by turkey-hating Martians?"

Joe squatted next to her, his back to the dirt hill. "I think it's the Venusians who hate turkeys," he whispered back. "Well, Sheriff, what's the plan?"

"I was just about to ask you for suggestions."

"I guess their killing turkeys doesn't warrant you rushing in with your gun," Joe said jokingly.

"Why don't we try to block off their escape?" she said, moving her head toward the pulsating UFO.

"Good idea. I'd like to get a closer look at the thing, anyway," Joe said. "If I can't take a picture, I'm at least entitled to a thousand words."

"Okay. So you move around toward their vehicle, and I'll try to close in on our two turkey killers." Without waiting for a reply, Willie and Joe went off in opposite directions.

At the bottom of the hill, Willie jumped over the small irrigation ditch and moved toward the two men in white. Their backs were toward her and they hadn't seen her yet.

When she was about twenty-five feet from her quarry, the lights on the UFO began to pulsate more quickly and with a definite rhythm. The soft sound coming from the machine shifted to a slightly louder, higher pitch. Willie knew at once that the pilot of the craft had spotted her and was warning the others.

The two men turned around. At the sight of Willie, her .38 reflecting the lights of their craft, they paused. But only for a moment. They glanced at each other, then started toward her, the nozzles of their cylinders on full force as they started spraying the toxic liquid in her direction.

Willie stepped back. The sight of the two tall beings, devoid of facial features and covered entirely in white suits, momentarily froze her. She saw her own reflection in their shiny face masks. Every bad science fiction movie she'd seen flashed before her and she saw the headline in Joe's paper: "Aliens Attack Sheriff with Deadly Spray" or "Sheriff Kidnapped by Aliens, Last Seen Being Taken Aboard UFO." Then her training took over and she held her ground.

"Police. Stop right there, or I'll shoot," she said, raising her gun and placing her feet solidly apart.

The men stopped and looked at each other, then turned around and glanced at their getaway vehicle. Slowly they turned back to Willie. Without warning, the one on the right hurled his cylinder at her.

Willie jumped to one side. She felt the hard metal cylinder graze her left leg. She glanced down, not seeing the other man as he thew his cylinder. It hit her squarely on her right shoulder, knocking her to the ground. Her gun, still in her hand, discharged with a bang.

The two men ran toward the flashing lights, one of them stopping to pick up the cylinder he'd thrown at Willie. Suddenly the whine emitted from the craft shifted frequency. Willie knew this signaled takeoff. She took a deep breath and steadied herself, raising the gun. She pointed it at the man on the left, aiming for his left thigh.

A microsecond before she squeezed the trigger, she saw something emerge from the darkness, a blur of motion. She lowered her gun. A second later, Joe tackled Willie's target.

The man in the silver suit was on the ground with Joe on top of him before his companion knew he'd gone down. Willie scrambled to her feet, the pain searing her shoulder, and ran toward the men.

Joe was trying to figure out what to do to the well-protected man he'd just tackled. He didn't see the other man raise his metal cylinder over his head, nor did he hear Willie's shouted warning. He only saw a flash of lights and the night sky before he fell over, stunned by the blow.

The two men ran the short distance to their craft. It was already hovering as they climbed aboard. Willie raised her gun and fired, hoping to hit something that might abort a takeoff.

She heard something shatter. A semicircle of bright lights in front went dark, and as the craft ascended, she could clearly make out a metal frame strung with utility lights. It was supported on the familiar landing gear of a helicopter.

Willie turned around and ran to where Joe lay. He shook his head, rubbing the back of his neck.

"Are you all right?" She knelt beside him and felt the knot already forming where the metal cylinder had hit him.

"I'm all right." He looked up at her. "How are you? It looks as though we both connected with the same thing."

"My shoulder's a little stiff, that's all." She helped him to his feet. "Some stakeout this turned out to be. We let them slip right through our hands."

"Don't be so hard on yourself, Willie. They put up a good fight." He turned his head from side to side. "Who would have guessed that a couple of aliens could be so tough!" He looked at Willie and grinned.

"It'll make a great story, though: 'Sheriff and Local Editor Wrestle Aliens—Aliens Win.'" Willie sighed. "Virgil Jones will love it." She stood in the middle of the field and looked around. Turkeys were scattered over the ground, some dead, some just moving in circles.

"It's one story Virgil and the rest of Cisco are going to have to wait for." Joe looked at Willie. "I don't think it would be in the best interests of this investigation if I were to print what happened here tonight." He rubbed the back of his neck. "It would also make me look like a fool."

"How's that?" Willie asked, pleased and a bit surprised that he was giving up a good story in favor of her investigation.

"I'm a big football hero, remember?" He grinned. "And big football heroes are supposed to have the strength of ten. My image will be tarnished if it gets out that I was defeated by a couple of guys in white suits."

Willie laughed. "We wouldn't want to do that, would we?" She walked away from Joe and began to look around.

"What are you looking for?" Joe asked, still rubbing his sore neck.

She bent down, then got up. "At least the evening won't be a complete loss," she said. She held up the metal cylinder that had hit her. "We can find out exactly what this is and who might use it locally."

"While you're at it, why don't you find out what it'll do to us? I think we both got a heavy dose tonight." He looked down. "It's a good thing we're not a couple of turkeys." He laughed and put his arm around Willie's shoulders and they walked back to his truck.

Willie had Joe drop her off at her house. There she picked up her Cherokee and drove into town. When she walked through the main floor of the courthouse, Joe was already there, flirting with Hannah, acting as if he were fishing for the latest information.

Hannah usually worked a split shift, taking several hours off in the middle of the day so she could stay late and cover some of the night hours. The middle-aged woman was laughing coyly, her fading strawberry-blond hair piled high on her head, bobbing as she giggled. Many times in the last four years, Willie would have loved to fire Hannah. She was one of the most notorious gossips in town, occasionally abusing her privileged position in the sheriff's office when her other sources ran low. But she was also the mayor's sister and had been the county dispatcher for the last twenty-five years. She'd probably be sitting just where she was tonight for the next twenty.

"Oh, come on, Joe. You know the sheriff would have my head if I gave away any information." Joe said something to Hannah that Willie couldn't hear and Hannah smiled. "Okay, I guess I can tell you…." Hannah suddenly stopped as she caught sight of Willie standing just inside the door.

"Evening, Sheriff," she said quickly, a flush covering her already rosy skin. "Joe here was just trying to weasel some extra news out of me. Course, I told him we don't play favorites around here. He'd just have to wait until you showed up and—"

"Thank you, Hannah," Willie interrupted her. "I appreciate your dedication." Willie smiled and looked at Joe as if they hadn't just spent the previous two hours together. "Good evening, Joe," she said as she glanced at her watch. "Don't you ever sleep?"

Joe shook his head. "No. That's the amazing thing about newspaper people. Just the scent of a big story can keep us going for days." He smiled, and Willie turned back to Hannah.

"Any calls?" Willie asked.

"The switchboard's been lit up all night. Folks all over the valley claim they've seen a UFO." Hannah gathered the slips of paper on her desk. "But then what do you expect with those reporters in town and Lucy Wiemer going off the deep end? If you ask me, this whole town's going UFO crazy."

"Any important calls?" Willie sounded a little impatient now. Hannah handed her a stack of messages. "Bud Beede called twice. He wanted me find you. I tried your home but couldn't raise you. LeRoy's still down at the Wagon Wheel, checking out a drunk-and-disorderly. I told Bud we'd send someone out soon as we could."

Willie glanced up at Joe. "Did Bud say what he wanted?"

Hannah shook her head. "Said he wanted to talk to you or a deputy as soon as possible. He said he wanted someone to come out to his place right away. He seemed pretty annoyed when I told him I couldn't get hold of you and that all the deputies were busy."

Hannah paused for a much-needed breath. "Then he made some smart-aleck remark that if Virgil were sheriff, he'd be around when people needed—"

"Thanks, Hannah," Willie said, interrupting her. "Is there anything we can do for you tonight, Joe?"

Joe looked at Hannah and winked. "Yeah," he said. "I want to see if I have any better luck getting information from you. Your dispatcher here is a tough nut to crack." Hannah smiled as Joe followed Willie into her office.

He shut the door behind them.

"What are you doing here?" she asked, moving behind her desk. "I thought you'd had enough excitement for one night. How's you're head?"

"My head's fine." He wrapped his arms around her shoulders and lowered his lips to hers, stopping less than an inch away.

"I wanted to see if I could get you to play favorites," he whispered as he let his lips brush hers. "Or is it true what Hannah says? Do you treat all reporters the same?"

He kissed her, and Willie felt her mouth open to his. After a long moment, she gently pushed him away.

"I don't think we should do that here, Joe. Hannah could walk in any minute, and she probably will. Next thing we know, it'll be all over town that she found us naked on top of my desk."

Joe laughed and moved away. "You're right," he said as he picked up several reports from her desk and glanced at them. Willie took them away and put them back on her desk.

"Can I help you, Mr. Kelly?"

"Yes, you can." He sat down on the chair in front of her desk and crossed his long legs. His jeans were faded and stained at the knees from the scuffle he'd had in Beede's field. His blue cotton shirt was open at the neck. He let his pale-blue eyes linger over her as she talked. "As a concerned citizen, I wanted to discuss this case with you. You see, I have some theories and I'd like to—"

"Excuse me," Willie said as she noticed the light on her phone and picked it up. "Put him through," she said to Hannah, then she covered the mouthpiece with her hand. "It's Bud Beede," she whispered to Joe.

"What can I do for you, Bud?" she said into the phone. Joe leaned forward. Willie listened for a moment, then nodded. "I appreciate your call, Bud. I was just on my way out to your place now. But if you say it can wait..." She paused again. "I'll send Wes out in the morning to get your statement." She hung up, then looked at Joe.

"Let me guess," he told her. "Bud Beede wanted to report something strange was going on at his place tonight. Something that has to do with bright lights and unidentified flying objects."

"Exactly." She stood up and walked over to the window that looked out on a darkened Main Street. "But curiously, he said the whole thing could wait till morning. In fact, he specifically requested that we don't come out tonight, said nothing could be done now."

Joe raised his eyebrows. "Interesting."

Willie walked back to her desk and looked through the messages Hannah had given her. She pulled one out.

"This is the first message. It was called in at nine thirty-five. We saw the lights over Beede's place about the same time." She looked down at the message. "The first one was called in by Lucy Wiemer. She lives with her brother Homer."

Willie sat down. "It could just mean that they saw what we saw. There wouldn't be anything unusual with that."

Joe nodded. "It just seems odd that Bud would have changed his mind about wanting someone to come out tonight."

"Isn't it," Willie agreed.

She looked through the rest of the messages. "What were you trying to weasel out of Hannah when I walked in on you two?" Willie inquired without looking up.

"I was asking her she knew of anyone in town who could fly a helicopter. I told her I was thinking of taking some aerial photos of our little town for the paper."

Willie looked up. Why hadn't she thought of asking Hannah? She would've had Carl call all over trying to get the same information. She rarely asked Hannah about anything, because she didn't like to encourage what she considered the woman's one bad habit—gossip.

"What did she say?"

"She launched into a story about her boy Roger being a medic in Vietnam and how he was now a doctor in Denver. She said it was the one good thing that came out of the war, as far as she was concerned."

"What else?" Willie asked, knowing Joe was withholding something. "If I remember right, Roger went in with Virgil Jones, Bud Beede and Sam Jacobs."

"Right. They all served in the same unit because they volunteered together."

"Sam didn't come back," Willie remembered.

Joe nodded. "But Virgil and Bud were both chopper pilots."

"Both of them?" Willie paused for a moment. "Did she say whether either of them still flew?"

"Hannah says they get together once a year with her boy. They rent a helicopter and take a trip. Last year they went up to Montana and rented a helicopter. She wasn't sure whether it was Bud or Virgil who did the flying." Joe paused. "It shouldn't be hard to find out whether both of them have a current pilot's license."

Willie nodded. "I'll have Carl on it first thing."

She stood and stretched, then stopped, her arms up in the air. She looked at Joe. "You don't think this whole thing is just a ploy to make me look incompetent and sway the election toward Virgil, do you?" She folded her arms across her chest.

Joe shook his head. "I can't believe anyone would want to be sheriff that badly—Virgil included." He walked over and stood behind her. "And I can't believe anyone would want to see you out of office that badly, either."

He started massaging her shoulders and neck. She sat down at her desk and let him continue. The strength and gentleness of his fingers surprised her as she felt the tension being eased away.

"I went to school with Virgil. He can be a pain in the butt and a know-it-all sometimes, but I don't think he's capable of doing something like this." He let his hands slide over her upper arms. "The guys we tangled with tonight are playing hardball."

"What do you think about Bud Beede?"

Willie felt a slight tightening of his grip at the mention of Beede's name.

"Bud and I never got along." He moved back up her shoulders and started working on her neck. "He's a year older than I am, and I played football with him. He used practice as an excuse to try to beat me up. I think he never got over the fact that he couldn't do it." Willie moaned with pleasure as he worked his fingers up the side of her neck and and into her hair. "But that was twenty years ago. I can't hold that against him now." Willie felt little goose bumps spring up along her arm. "But I can hold against him what he said about us at the Sportsman's Club last Saturday night."

"Don't forget the town meeting," Willie said. "It seems to me he was pretty eager to draw attention to himself and criticize the way I was handling this whole situation."

"He was, wasn't he?" Joe worked his fingers back down her neck. "But it was his farm that was hit tonight. Why would Bud want to kill his own turkeys?"

Willie shrugged. "That's a good question. Well, because of his cattle crop, he doesn't stand to lose as much as Wheeler or Bishop, so it wouldn't help the..."

Joe stopped the massage. "Wouldn't help what?" he asked as Willie's pause grew longer. He waited.

It struck Joe that Willie's sudden silence was the result of an idea coming to her. "Come on, Sheriff, let me in on your secret," he prompted her.

Willie spoke slowly. "As I was saying, the Beedes raise mostly cattle, so even a total loss of their turkey crop wouldn't be as devastating for them as it would be for, say, Grady Wheeler or Matt Bishop."

After a thoughtful pause, she went on. "In fact, it's likely Wheeler and Bishop would lose their farms if they lost the turkey crop. With all the UFO rumors and the deaths from a toxic substance, they'd hardly get anything for their farms and probably nothing for their remaining crops."

"So?" Joe encouraged her to continue as he began to follow her line of reasoning.

"So? Don't you see how suspicious it would look if only one farm in the county didn't get hit by the 'aliens'?"

Joe nodded, the impact of Willie's words finally hitting him.

Willie went on. "It's also one heck of a coincidence that our local prophetess, one Lucy Wiemer, is Homer Beede's sister. Personally, I think Lucy's biggest problem is senility. It would be easy for the Beedes to convince her of the reality of the UFO and aliens and use her to spread the word through the town."

"While it's all reasonable, Willie, you forgot to point out one important thing," he reminded her.

"Hmm?" Willie asked, breaking out of her thoughts to look at Joe. "What's that?"

"Motive."

"Motive," Willie repeated slowly. "Well, it would be one way for Homer Beede to get even with Wheeler and Bishop and get their land and water rights once and for all. And at a bargain price."

Joe looked amazed at her ability to figure things out.

Willie sighed heavily as she moved in her chair. "Now all we need is to get some hard evidence." Then she was lost in thought again.

"And you have to get some sleep." He leaned down and kissed Willie on the ear, then pulled her out of her chair.

She rose and started to straighten up her desk. She felt Joe's hand cover hers. "Can't it wait until tomorrow?"

She looked up to see his beautiful blue eyes ready to send her off to dreamland where she stood. "You're right. It can wait until tomorrow."

He walked with her to the outer office. Hannah was busy on the phone and barely looked up as they walked by and said good-night.

When he reached her car, he started to open the door, then stopped. "Why don't you let me drive you home, Willie? I can bring you in to work in the morning." He ran a hand through her hair. "You look beat. We'll just sleep together. Much as I'd love to, I promise I won't try to touch that beautiful body of yours tonight."

"You mean you won't try to make wild, passionate love to me?"

Joe raised his hand. "I solemnly swear."

She looked at him. "Then forget it, Joe Kelly. I can drive myself home." Laughing, she climbed into her car and started the engine. Joe ran around and got in the other side.

"Okay," he said as he closed the door. "With the right incentive, I could be persuaded to change my mind."

# Chapter 12

Joe looked down at Willie, her tawny hair dark in the moonlight and spread over his chest like a silken banner. Her breathing was deep and steady, and he could feel its warmth against his skin. Gently he brushed the hair from her face, taking care not to wake her.

Every time he thought of her, his mind sifted through a catalog of emotions. She could evoke in him more feelings of tenderness than he thought he possessed. And she could put him on the defensive quicker than a three-hundred-pound linebacker. One thing was certain: she'd made the quiet little town of Cisco, Colorado, come alive for him again.

He watched as she lay in his arms. Even when she was sleeping, he could feel the emotions churning inside him. He wanted her. If his feelings stopped there, it would be easy enough to understand. Over the last twenty-five years he had wanted a lot of women. He had wanted some of them badly enough to pursue them. But with Willie it was different. It went past wanting, into something else. Some other, unnamed emotion tugged at him, leaving him unsatisfied.

He sighed and looked at the woman with whom he'd just made slow, tender love. He wondered where it would all lead. After this case was solved, after they'd settled into an amicable tolerance of each other's professions, then what? It was a question he couldn't answer.

The last few years of loneliness swept past him. The longer he was with Willie, the more he'd felt that loneliness ease. But who was he kidding? he told himself. She was interesting, fascinating. That was the problem. He'd really never known anyone like her.

Joe looked down once more at the woman he held in his arms and wondered whether he could handle a serious relationship with such a complex human being. He sighed and felt the weight of fatigue. He closed his eyes and knew that eventually he'd have to sort it all out.

The phone rang again and Joe pulled himself out of sleep, reaching for a bedside table that wasn't there. It rang again, and he realized that the table wasn't there because the pale, smooth arms that were tangled with his belonged to Willie. He was in her bed. He started to answer it, then thought he should wake her. Gently he shook her shoulders.

"Willie," he called. "Willie, wake up."

She groaned. "What time is it?" Before he could answer, she realized it was her phone that was ringing, rolled over and reached for it.

"Hello?" she said.

Joe could hear the sleep still in her voice. He leaned back against the pillows, trying not to listen but knowing he couldn't help it.

"She's what?" Willie sat upright and ran her hand through her hair, looking at Joe, then back at the phone. She glanced at the bedside clock. "It's six in the morning, for crying out loud!"

Joe leaned close to Willie, his hand against her naked back. "What is it?" he whispered. She responded with a finger to her lips.

"Call Homer. But don't do anything until I get down there." She waited a few moments, nodding. "Yes, I know she's waking up half the town, but until I get there, just let her be."

She put the phone down. Joe watched her as she leaped out of bed. Her strong body was all angles and curves; she was fully awake now. She was too preoccupied to make even a pretense of being embarrassed about her nakedness. Joe couldn't help but smile as she paced the room.

"What's up, Willie? Did Homer finally find his dead turkeys?"

She shook her head. "This town's going crazy," she said, glancing at him. "I wonder if it's possible to have a whole town committed."

"Probably not," he told her as he got out of bed. He walked over to her closet, then searched through her clothes until he found a clean, pressed uniform. She continued to pace as he took the pants off the hanger and handed them to her.

"She's finally done it," Willie said as she saw the pants. "Thanks," she mumbled as she slipped on a pair of panties, then the slacks.

"Who's gone and done what?" Joe asked, handing her the shirt.

"Lucy Wiemer." Willie slipped on her bra and then her shirt. "She's on the courthouse roof. She's got a loudspeaker, and LeRoy says she's ranting and raving about the UFO that's coming to save Cisco. What's amazing is that she's already got a group of people over there. And LeRoy says that they're actually standing there, listening to her!"

Joe laughed and Willie looked at him. "It's 6:00 a.m. I've got a little old lady on top of the courthouse, ranting about flying saucers, and you think it's funny?" She threaded her belt through the loops and put her gun in its holster. She grabbed her boots from under the bed, sat on the edge and pulled them on. Then she looked up at Joe and smiled.

"I have to admit the situation has certain elements of humor." She brushed her hair. "Let's just hope Lucy sees it that way when we pull her off the roof."

She stood up and her let her eyes linger on Joe's body. "I love you the way you are, Joe. But you'd better get dressed if you want to ride into town with me." She tossed his pants to him. "It's against regulations to let a naked man ride in an official state vehicle."

Willie walked out of the room, and Joe pulled on his pants. He could hear Willie brushing her teeth in the bathroom as he put on his running shoes. He left the laces for later as he searched under the sheets for his shirt. He found it just as he heard the front screen door close.

"Wait for me, Willie," he called, and ran out after her.

Joe got into the car, buttoning his shirt as Willie backed out of the driveway. He looked at her. The clean, sculptured planes of her face were calm. Her features were too strong to be called pretty, but here, in the early-morning light, Joe realized that she was a genuinely beautiful woman. Even without makeup, her face looked vividly alive.

He could detect only a slight tension in her hands as she gripped the steering wheel. He was just beginning to appreciate what she'd been handling for the past four years.

"What do you make of it?" Joe asked, bending to tie his shoes. "Maybe she's gone off the deep end. Maybe she is senile, like you said last night."

Joe watched Willie's face, and suddenly there was a ripple in its composure.

She turned to Joe. "That's got to be it!" she almost shouted. "That's what's been bothering me about Lucy for a long time."

"What? You mean it never occurred to you that a woman almost seventy years old could go a little crazy?"

Willie shook her head. "That's just it. It didn't occur to me before because I've known her for so long. Lucy Wiemer has always been a little crazy. I guess I just never noticed how bad she's gotten."

"But she's on top of the courthouse with a bullhorn, trying to sell people on salvation from a UFO. That's hardly normal behavior."

"No, it's not. But maybe she has a reason we don't know about." She tapped the steering wheel.

"What are you getting at, Willie? I think old Lucy has gone south and she's trying to convince the rest of the town to go with her."

Willie shook her head. "Maybe. Or maybe that's what she wants us to think. Or at least that's what she wants *someone* to think." She stepped on the accelerator and the Cherokee picked up speed. "I've had almost daily contact with Lucy since I became sheriff. And I'll admit that at times she's been the biggest pain you could imagine..."

"I can imagine. She's been hounding my office, too."

"The woman's crazy, but she's also as sharp as anyone in town, as contradictory as that may sound. Nothing gets past her. Sometimes I think a person can't breathe in Cisco without Lucy Wiemer knowing about it."

"I agree, but what's your point?"

"Someone that crazy and that aware doesn't go scared overnight. Not even if there is a UFO rumor running rampant." She glanced at Joe. He was finally starting to understand what she meant. "If a UFO landed on Lucy Wiemer's front lawn, what do you think she'd do?"

Joe smiled. "She'd give 'em hell for ruining her grass. Then she'd call you and give you hell for letting them ruin her grass."

"Exactly." Willie pulled into her usual parking space in front of the courthouse. "Either Lucy Wiemer has totally, truly and thoroughly lost her mind at last or..."

"She's trying to tell us something," Joe finished her sentence for her. He started to open the door and looked out at the crowd of about fifty people who'd already gathered on the front steps of the courthouse. Above them, on the roof of the two-story building, was the tiny figure of Lucy Wiemer, wielding a bullhorn. More people were wandering over from across the street.

"Aren't you afraid of the gossip, Sheriff?" Joe asked before he opened the door.

"Gossip?"

"Don't you think it's a little obvious, our arriving together at six-fifteen in the morning?"

Willie laughed and looked around. "I think Lucy on the roof is upstaging our entrance. Nobody would notice—or care—if we arrived naked on horseback. This is Lucy's show."

They got out of the Cherokee and were halfway up the steps of the courthouse before LeRoy noticed their arrival. Carl was trying to keep the crowd off the steps and on the lawn. LeRoy was busy trying to talk to Homer.

They saw Willie at the same time.

"Sheriff," Homer said. "What are you going to do?" He turned back and glanced up at his sister. "She says she'll jump if we try to get her down. She says she's going to say what she has to say, even if it kills her."

Willie glanced up at the elderly woman, then back at Homer and her deputy.

"Then I guess we'd better let her say it." She turned to Joe, then looked back at the men in front of her. "I just hope she doesn't take too long. That bullhorn's making an awful racket. The noise will make it hard for me to get my work done."

Homer looked at her in amazement, then smiled. "I must say you're taking this pretty well, Sheriff. LeRoy here wanted to haul her off the roof, no matter what." He turned to LeRoy and couldn't resist a little smugness.

"I don't see what harm she's doing, Homer. Citizens her age are entitled to a little eccentricity now and then." She lowered her voice a bit. "Just make sure she doesn't make it a habit. I don't want everybody up on the courthouse roof."

She turned to LeRoy. "You and Carl, keep the crowd back. See that they don't get Lucy too excited. We wouldn't want her to fall off, would we?" Willie turned and walked into the building, a slightly shocked LeRoy gazing after her.

Joe followed her into the courthouse. Hannah was already at the switchboard, but before she could open her mouth, Willie anticipated her and responded.

"Good morning, Hannah." She stopped in front of her desk. "As you've probably noticed, Lucy Wiemer is on the roof with a bullhorn. If anyone calls, tell them we're already aware of this. If people want to know what she's doing or saying, tell them to come down and see for themselves."

"But Sheriff," Hannah said, "aren't you going to do something about it?"

"Yes, Hannah. When she's ready to come down, let me know, and I'll send Carl up to help her."

She walked into her office, Joe still behind her. She went over to the window that looked out over the front of the courthouse and opened it. Lucy's voice came through loud and shrill, if a bit fuzzy. Willie glanced at Joe.

"You are taking this well, Sheriff," Joe said, walking over to the window. He leaned one leg against the sill and looked out.

"Lucy Wiemer is just exercising one of her fundamental rights—free speech." Willie grabbed a notepad off her desk. "The fact that she's also disturbing the peace and possibly endangering herself is another matter. What really interests me is that she's telling us that next Monday night at eleven fifty-five, a UFO is going to land on the southwest corner of Matt Bishop's farm. I think that's a significant bit of information in this case, don't you?"

Joe nodded. Willie never ceased to amaze him.

"I also find it interesting that Homer Beede actually agreed with me. He wanted me to let Lucy stay up on the roof." She turned away from the window and looked at Joe. "Under normal circumstances, I would have expected Homer to be furious with his sister. She's making a spectacle of herself in front of the whole town, acting foolish enough to embarrass even a Beede."

"Apparently that's exactly what he wants."

Willie nodded and smiled. "I wonder why." Then she looked at her notes, scribbling down what Lucy was babbling. She glanced up at Joe. "Shouldn't you go get your camera? This is front-page news."

Joe smiled. "You're right." He walked out of her office, turning around when he reached the door. "And to think that my old friends told me Cisco would be dull."

It was nearly an hour later before Lucy decided to come off the roof. By that time, she'd had every man, woman and child in Cisco gathered on the courthouse lawn. Willie had Carl help her down. He carried her bullhorn down the narrow staircase that went through the attic and onto the roof. Later he assured Willie that the agile old lady could have easily made the trip herself. She'd gotten up there, hadn't she?

Willie spent the rest of the day making and answering phone calls. She sent Wes out to the airport with the cylinder cap she'd recovered from the previous night's escapade with Joe. She called the state lab beforehand, telling them that she'd have their heads if they sent this one over to the Department of Agriculture. They promised to have something in by the following afternoon.

Around noon, Homer Beede called. It came as no surprise to her that he'd just discovered nearly two hundred dead turkeys on the western end of his property. He claimed they were valuable, prizewinning birds. Willie could think of no prize that they'd won, but she didn't argue the point. She sent Wes out to get a full report. Tactfully she asked after Lucy, and Homer told Willie his sister was sleeping peacefully.

Neither she nor Carl had any luck finding out where the "aliens" had rented their helicopter. She was about ready to call it a day when Joe sauntered in.

Carl was filling out a report on the Beede turkeys, and he and Willie looked up. Willie could tell by the smile on his face that he'd turned up something.

"Hello, Joe." Willie smiled. "What can we do for you?"

"The question is what I can do for you." He glanced over at Carl. "Any luck with the helicopter?"

Willie shook her head. "Not yet."

"Maybe I can help you. I just found out which of our citizens can fly one."

Willie and Carl said, "Who?" in unison.

"Both Virgil Jones and Bud Beede are licensed helicopter pilots. And both have flown within the last six months."

"How did you find that out?" Willie asked.

"Elementary, my dear sheriff." He pulled up a chair and sat in front of her desk. "I just called Roger Wilson, Hannah's boy. We had a nice, friendly chat about old times. We even got around to talking about not-so-old times. He told me that this spring, he and Virgil and Bud and Doug Beede all went on a camping trip up to Montana, just as Hannah said. When I asked who had flown the helicopter, Roger told me they both had. Apparently both Bud and Virgil have kept their hours current, and both have valid licenses."

Joe took a slip of paper out of his pocket and handed it to Willie. "This is the outfit in Montana they rented the helicopter from. Roger told me that they'd arranged for it through the company below."

Willie read the address. "This is in Denver."

"Right."

Willie thumbed through the papers on her desk. "I don't think we've called this one, have we?" Carl walked over to the desk and looked at it.

"That's the one that told me to call back."

Willie nodded and let Carl take the paper. "Thanks for the information, Joe."

He looked at Carl, then stood up. "Sure," he said. "I guess I'll see you tonight, then. At seven."

Willie looked up. "Tonight? What's happening tonight?" She couldn't remember having made a date with Joe.

"Don't tell me you forgot," he said.

"I forgot."

"The debate. At the high school." Willie still looked confused, and Joe moved a few steps closer. "You know, the ritual where candidates for public office get up in front of an audience and try to sound intelligent and well-informed."

"I thought that was next week," she said. "That's tonight?" Joe nodded. "What idiot set that up?" she muttered as she shuffled papers on her desk.

"The idiot standing before you," he said. "Come on, why don't I take you out to dinner. I can give you a few pointers on satisfying a bloodthirsty public."

Willie looked at her watch. "It's five forty-five. I'll barely have time to go home and change as it is."

"So don't change. You look fine. The perfect authority figure."

"Don't you think wearing my uniform is taking unfair advantage of Virgil?" Willie asked as they walked out of her office.

He looked at her for a moment, considering the question. "So take unfair advantage," he told her. "This is politics."

Willie sat on a stiff-backed chair just left of center stage in the San Juan High School auditorium. A few feet away, at the bottom of the stage stairs, was Virgil Jones, her opponent for sheriff. Virgil ran the town's only funeral chapel and was a part-time real estate agent. His only qualification for the job of sheriff was that he'd been a volunteer on the county's search-and-rescue team for the past ten years.

Virgil was busy shaking hands with some of the people in the front row of the well-filled auditorium. Willie recognized some of the group as regulars at Desmond's Diner;

they were the local good ole boys. Virgil finished and came up the steps. Willie stood and they shook hands.

"Good evening, Willie," Virgil said. "I heard you had quite a day, what with this UFO business and Lucy Wiemer going crazy on top of the courthouse."

"It's been interesting, Virgil." Willie and Virgil sat down as Mayor Hubbard got up to speak.

Tom was dressed in his dark-blue suit, the one he'd worn to the town meeting a few days before. Willie quickly scanned the audience and noticed a few out-of-towners, probably reporters. This "UFO business," as Virgil had called it, had suddenly made the sheriff's race in a little back-road town news. Willie noticed that Diana Lawrence wasn't in the audience. Apparently the election wasn't big enough for *Personality*.

"Good evening, ladies and gentlemen," Tom began. "It's great to have such a large turn-out for tonight's debate. As you know, our incumbent, Sheriff Wilhelmina Callen, comes to us with a lot of experience." He turned and nodded toward Willie. "She is a college graduate with a degree in business from the University of Colorado at Boulder. She completed two years of law school at the same university. Her law enforcement experience includes three years as a military policeman in the U.S. Army. For the last four years she has been the sheriff of San Juan County." He smiled at Willie and then turned to Virgil.

"Her opponent, Virgil Jones, is also a local high school graduate. He's had courses in criminal law and psychology at Colorado College in Glenwood Springs. He is currently our local undertaker and a businessman. For the past ten years, he has served as a captain on the San Juan County Sheriff's search and rescue posse.

"I'd like to turn the debate over to the man who will conduct this debate, the most distinguished alumnus of San Juan County High and owner and editor of the *San Juan Independent*, Joe Kelly."

Willie nearly choked. Joe hadn't mentioned that he was going to be conducting this debate. But then she thought, Why not? He'd set the thing up the first place.

Joe seated himself opposite Willie and Virgil on the stage and shuffled through some notes. He looked up and smiled.

"Are you ready?"

Willie and Virgil nodded.

"I've been compiling a list of what seem to be the major concerns of our local citizens. These questions were taken from letters to the editor over the past year and from personal conversations." He pulled out a card. "Our first question is about the current policy toward speeding within the city limits. This has often sparked some controversy, because school children must cross Main Street daily. Some citizens feel that the speed limits aren't adequately enforced. What plans, if any, do you have to beef up enforcement of local speed limits?"

Joe looked up. "Sheriff Callen, why don't you go first?"

Willie took a deep breath. During dinner, Joe had hinted that this question might be asked. It was one she could answer with ease.

"Over the last four years, our department has shown a fifty-percent increase in citations for speeding within the city limits. My deputies are regularly posted along Main Street and in other high-traffic areas to catch speeders. I want to take this opportunity to remind parents that almost sixty-five percent of the drivers caught speeding within the city are under eighteen years of age. I feel that this problem could be cleared up if we could work together with the parents of these young people."

She sat down. Virgil took his time walking the three feet to the microphone. "Well, you've heard from our current sheriff, Miss Willie." Willie almost cringed at this old-fashioned term of familiarity. Virgil, the Beede men and their cronies were the only ones who called her that. She figured she could be grateful he hadn't called her "little Miss Willie," but maybe he was saving that for later.

"There's nothing more important than the safety of our young folks, as far as I'm concerned. As you know, I've got three of my own at home. These damn speeders—pardon my language, ladies." Virgil laughed as he looked around, ending his circuit of the auditorium with Willie. "These damn speeders have got to be stopped. If elected, I promise to put all the resources available to me as sheriff on this problem."

Willie sighed, trying not to roll her eyes. She hoped that if this was a sample of what the night would be like, the voters had enough sense to notice that Virgil seemed to be at least eighty percent bull.

Joe stood up and asked the next question. "What do you plan on doing to limit the budget? As we know, it has increased over thirty percent in the past four years. Will this trend continue?"

Willie stood up again. "Our population base has increased almost forty-five percent over the past five years. This has brought an increased tax base. So what looks like an increase in budget is really just an increase proportionate with the growing population of San Juan County.

"Actually, when viewed in that light, our budget has actually decreased. We currently need another dispatcher, at least on a part-time basis. I've worked that need into next year's budg—"

"Sheriff," a voice from the back of the room interrupted her. It was Grady Wheeler. He stood up.

"Mr. Wheeler, you'll have an opportunity for addressing your questions to both Sheriff Callen and Virgil when we've covered our topics," Joe told him.

Another man, Jake Hauser, stood up several rows down from Grady Wheeler.

"Listen, Joe," he said, "I don't see the point of talking about budgets and teenagers out on a joyride, when we've got real problems."

Several murmurs of "Yeah" were heard in the audience.

"That's what I want to know, Sheriff," Grady added. "When are you going to get to what's on everybody's mind? When are you going to talk about our dead turkeys and the aliens that's killing 'em?"

Joe started to say something, but Willie held up her hand. "I think everything that can be said about the investigation was said at the town meeting." She looked directly at Grady. "You know as well as I do that I can't discuss everything about a case while it's under investigation."

"These are special circumstances," Jake interrupted her again. "Lucy Wiemer's telling us that these UFO folks are going to come into town next week. What are you planning to do about it? They got away once with almost killing someone. Just thank God Matt Bishop is going to be all right. Are you going to let them try again?"

Willie looked at Joe and took a deep breath. "If and when alien beings come into town, I assure you that the sheriff's office will do its best to protect the citizens of this county."

She turned to Virgil, who was sitting back, enjoying the scene. "What would you do in case of an alien attack, Virgil?"

Willie sat down and watched as a surprised Virgil stepped up to the microphone. "Well, Miss Willie," he said slowly, trying to think of a coherent response. "Are you saying you think this county is under direct threat from aliens?"

"I'm just asking a question by popular demand," she answered.

"I think questions of aliens and UFOs are out of the scope of this debate," Joe interjected.

Grady stood up again. "I want to know what Sheriff Callen is going to do about this UFO that's been killing our turkeys! I could be wiped out." He looked around. "Last night the Beede place was hit. Homer lost half his birds." He turned back to the stage, his attention on Willie. "What are you going to do, wait until they wipe us all out?"

Several other farmers stood up. "Yeah, Sheriff, what are you going to do?" they chorused.

Willie took a deep breath. Virgil was still in front of the podium.

"The sheriff's doing all she can, folks. This UFO thing just might be too big for her to handle, that's all," Virgil said. "I don't think she really knows that much about it. It isn't as if UFOs have license plates that can be traced." He smiled and looked at Willie sympathetically. He might as well have said, "The little lady's doing all she can, so lay off."

Virgil cleared his throat. "Of course, I'll understand if my opponent doesn't want to go into what she has on the case so far, if she has anything at all." He turned around again, empathy in his eyes. "To be sure, this is a difficult case. Maybe the mayor and city council ought to ask for some outside assistance."

"Is that what you'd do, Virgil?" Willie asked, then walked over to the microphone. She stood beside Virgil. "I would like to discuss this case. I would like to tell everyone what we have. But to do so would seriously compromise the investigation."

Several other people from the audience stood up and started shouting questions. Finally Joe joined them at the microphone, stepping in front of both Willie and Virgil. "Now, folks, I think the sheriff has made it pretty clear what her stand on this issue is," Joe said. "Why can't we leave it and go on to something else?" Willie and Virgil went back to their seats.

"Why are you protecting the sheriff, Joe?" Bud Beede stood up. "You two got something going?"

What a fiasco! Willie thought. All she needed was for the debate to deteriorate into a public discussion of her private life.

"That's not the issue, Bud," Joe countered.

"Well, then, if you're not keeping her busy, why hasn't she done anything about this UFO and the turkey killings?

My aunt Lucy's ready to go crazy. She's trying to warn us, and the sheriff refuses to do anything about it."

"She's been plenty busy with this investigation," Joe said. Willie could see the scar on his cheek deepening to crimson. His blue eyes looked positively lethal. "She hasn't done anything about the UFO because there is no UFO!"

Homer Beede got to his feet. "You can't tell me there isn't any UFO, because I saw it last night."

Everyone's eyes turned to Homer and then to Joe. Willie prayed that Joe wouldn't lose his temper.

"What you think is a UFO is actually a helicopter," Joe told Homer through clenched teeth.

"Are you calling me a liar, Joe Kelly?" Homer asked. Immediately Bud and Doug stood up. Virgil sat up and watched, his composure finally beginning to crack. "Next thing you're going to call my sister a liar!" Homer started walking out of the auditorium, his sons following.

"There're two people in Cisco who can fly the kind of helicopter I'm talking about, Homer," Joe said. The older man turned around and glared at him. "And they're both in this room."

Virgil looked around. He went over to Willie. "This has gone too far, Willie. You've got to stop Joe. Next thing you know, he'll be accusing someone. He has no business doing that."

Willie agreed. Joe had said enough. She walked over and took his arm.

"Joe," she whispered through clenched teeth. "When I said *I* couldn't discuss the case, I didn't mean that I wanted *you* to!"

Groups were gathering all over the room. Joe looked at Tom Hubbard and motioned for him to come up and close the meeting. Joe had compromised her case, Willie thought angrily. When she turned around to take her seat and wait for the disaster to end, she looked around for Virgil. He was nowhere in sight.

# *Chapter 13*

Willie walked up to Joe. "I think you've created enough chaos for one night," she said as she grabbed his arm. "Why don't we get out of here!"

He looked back at the mayor, who was too busy talking to some people in the front row to notice Willie and Joe as they slipped out the side entrance.

They'd walked half a block down Main Street before Willie finally broke the silence.

"Well, have you got any more bright ideas? After that little spectacle, probably neither Virgil nor I have a chance of winning the sheriff's race. I think half the town will write in Lucy Wiemer's name."

"She'd probably win. And this town would be getting what it deserves." Just when Willie was thinking she'd heard an edge of bitterness in his voice, Joe turned to her and burst out laughing.

"What are you laughing at?"

"Didn't you see it, Willie? Didn't you see what happened?"

"I saw a few of our more vocal citizens goad you into revealing some very sensitive information concerning my investigation, that's what I saw."

"Willie, didn't you notice the quick exit the Beedes made as soon as I started even hinting that we weren't dealing with a UFO?"

"I noticed. And I noticed that Virgil Jones suddenly made himself scarce. So you succeeded in making our two major suspects very nervous. We still don't have any hard evidence."

She walked along, letting Joe enjoy himself, when suddenly the whole thing hit her. She wondered whether it was true, whether Joe was really capable of such a devious, underhanded ploy. She looked at him and knew he was. "You did that on purpose. You knew what was going to happen all along, didn't you!"

"Of course I did. Those people are as predictable as—"

"Those people are people. They aren't here to be manipulated by you!" Willie was furious. She wanted to slap him or kick him in the shins. Instead, she just stood her ground in front of the courthouse. "What went on in that meeting will upset people for days, maybe weeks. And it compromised my investigation."

Willie walked over to her Cherokee. Joe grabbed her arm and swung her around. "But don't you see? Now we know who's behind this whole UFO business."

"No, Joe. We don't know anything." She jerked her arm away. "There's just one little thing you're forgetting. It's called evidence. The county attorney demands it before he will even press charges, and a jury demands it before conviction."

"But Virgil Jones and his buddies the Beedes acted guilty as sin."

"Acted, Joe." She shook her head. "Acted doesn't mean anything. What you did tonight was like hanging out a big banner over the courthouse that told Virgil and the Beedes they were our chief suspects." She opened her car door. "I could have forgiven it if it had happened by accident. But you deliberately set out to make it happen. You manipulated half the town and almost publicly accused Homer and his boys of being behind this whole UFO mess. That was just plain stupid."

She got in the car and left Joe standing on the sidewalk, his mouth slightly open.

"But the worst part of it is that I have to accept part of the blame, Joe." She started the engine. "I never should have let you get so involved in this investigation."

"How do you figure that?" Joe's voice was tense.

"We're at cross-purposes, you and I. You want a good story, something that will be interesting enough to make people buy your newspaper." She paused. "My job is to discover the truth. It doesn't have to be a good story. It doesn't even have to be interesting. Just the truth. And you can bet that before I go and accuse a citizen of anything, I'm going to have some hard evidence to back it up. I only hope I can still get some in this case."

Willie put the Cherokee into reverse and backed out of the parking lot.

Joe walked to his truck. It had been parked across the street, behind the newspaper office, since the night before last. He'd left it there when he and Willie had returned from the Beede place and their run-in with the "aliens" and the UFO. It had been years since Joe had lost his temper, but he hauled back and swung his foot at the fender of the dilapidated truck.

How could he have been so stupid? What had he been thinking? Much as he hated to admit it, Willie was right. He'd risked the whole case, and for what? To prove that he could make Homer Beede and his boys act foolishly? They certainly hadn't needed his help to accomplish that.

He got in and sat behind the wheel. The parking lot was deserted. He could hear the September crickets chirping in the darkness. He hit the steering wheel with his fist. Even he hadn't been totally honest with Willie. In his effort to "brag" about what he'd done, he'd let her believe it had all been planned, which wasn't exactly true. He hadn't decided on saying anything about the local helicopter pilots until Bud had made that crack about him and Willie. A stupid thing like that had made him risk Willie's investigation.

Joe started the engine and headed for home. The nagging thought of Willie kept tearing at his mind. He'd been stupid, and he certainly couldn't blame Willie for being angry. As he drove down the highway, he suddenly realized that he wasn't going toward home. He was headed in the opposite direction, toward Willie's place.

When he pulled up in front, her house was dark. He would have thought Willie had already gone to sleep, except that he noticed her Cherokee was gone. It was almost eleven at night. Where would she have gone? Then he got into his car and headed out toward Spanish Valley, following his instincts, to where they'd been the night before.

Joe pulled up to Desert Point almost an hour later. The narrow road opened up into a flat, unpaved lookout. Toward the east end, almost out of sight, he saw Willie's Cherokee. He parked his truck next to it and got out. Willie wasn't inside, and it took a few moments for his eyes to become accustomed to the starlight that illuminated the hilltop.

He thought about calling her name, but he didn't. She probably wouldn't answer anyway. He looked around and tried to put himself in Willie's place. If he'd come up here for some peace and quiet, where would he be?

Joe noticed a gentle slope on the east side of the hill, just beyond where he'd parked his truck. At the bottom was a group of flat-topped boulders overlooking the valley and Cisco beyond. He walked to the edge of the hill and saw Willie's silhouette against the night sky.

He knew she heard him as he picked his way down the rocky hillside. But she didn't turn around; she just sat there, staring out into the night, her arms wrapped around her legs.

He sat down next to her, leaving enough space between them to keep the peace. He waited a few minutes before he spoke, letting her get used to the idea that he was there.

"I came to tell you I'm sorry."

She didn't say anything. No response, no acknowledgment.

"You were right and I was wrong. It was a stupid thing I did tonight."

Still nothing. His instincts told him not to touch her. He had to let her respond in her own way. He picked up a dried-out twig of scrub oak and began to snap it into one-inch lengths. He could wait here all night if he had to.

"I didn't do it entirely on purpose," he said quietly. "I let Bud and Homer goad me into it. I just didn't want to admit that to you."

"Why not?" she said finally, still looking straight ahead. Her voice was quiet, the anger gone. "Does it bother you to admit you're human like the rest of us?"

Joe smiled. "No," he said as he shook his head. "I became aware of that painful reality years ago." He snapped off another piece of twig. "I just didn't want to point that fact out to you."

She turned to him. "I don't need a paper hero, Joe." She sighed. "I wanted you to be that when I was thirteen, but not now."

"What do you want now?' Joe looked at her, her face a complexity of planes and curves, shadow and darkness.

"I want a real hero. Someone who knows he's flawed like the rest of us but who goes on in spite of it."

"Someone who isn't afraid to admit he's wrong?" Joe asked.

"Exactly."

Joe could hear the smile in her voice. He dropped the twig and reached for her hand. When he found it, he could feel her fingers wrap around his.

"I've never known a woman who wanted the flawed version of Joe Kelly. They all seemed to demand the one whose body never broke down, who could do no wrong."

"Maybe that's all you wanted to show them," Willie said. "It's pretty frightening to give somebody a reason to walk away."

Joe took a deep breath. "Is that what I've given you tonight? Have I given you a reason to walk away?"

Again Willie looked at him, and even in the darkness he could see her head move from side to side. "No, Joe. When you came here, you gave me a reason to stay."

They were perched on a flat boulder. He closed the gap between them as he wrapped his arms around her, pulling her to him. He swore he could hear her heart pound against his chest and thunder in his ears.

"Do you think we can still patch this case together after the mess I've made?"

"We?" she answered, and for a moment Joe thought she was going to tell him to forget about the case. But suddenly she laughed. "I'm glad you said 'we,' because after tonight's disaster, you owe me."

He turned her toward him and covered the length of her face with his hand. The skin of her cheek was like velvet in his palm. He brought her face next to his and then kissed her mouth, letting it open naturally, easily, against his own. Her lips were softer than her cheek, their warmth a willing revelation of desire.

"I want you, Willie," he said simply.

The night wind brushed his face, and he felt a strong desire to hold her, to love her. He could feel her body shiver against his. He broke away from her, took off his jacket and draped it around her shoulders.

"Why don't we go back up the hill?" he suggested as he pulled her up. She walked up ahead of him, and he watched her move through the darkness. She got to the top of the hill and stood between his truck and the Cherokee, waiting. When he reached her, she started to slip his jacket off her shoulders. Joe felt a fierce urgency. He hadn't lied when he'd said he wanted her. She looked so vulnerable standing there, his big jacket slouched over her shoulders. The fact that she was the strongest woman he'd ever met made her all the more sensual, all the more desirable.

He reached up and slipped his hand between the jacket and her shoulders. He could feel the warmth of her body underneath her uniform. "I want you, Willie," he said again. "I want you now."

He knew she could feel his heat, because she undid the buttons on his shirt, slid her hands inside and wrapped them around his bare back. That little action drove him so crazy, he wanted to pull her down right there.

Instead, he remembered the sleeping bags still in the back of his truck. He lifted her over the side of his pickup. He was beside her before she could open her mouth. When she did, he was there to cover it with his own. Willie stretched out next to him. She pulled at his shirt, tugging it off his shoulders. He could feel her short-clipped nails as they moved across his chest.

"This is crazy, Joe," she whispered, running her hands over his stomach. "We both have beds we can share and we're rolling around in the back of this truck like a couple of teenagers." She laughed as she let her tongue tease his mouth.

"It is crazy," he agreed. "But it's great, isn't it!" He rolled on top of her and felt the weight of his body on hers. The cool wind slipped over his back. He wanted to feel it ripple over his whole body. He pulled off his shoes and then his pants. He was naked and she was still dressed. He lay down and pulled her on top of him.

"Keep me warm," he whispered as he nipped at her ear. "Cover me with your body." He pulled her shirt over her shoulders, and then he felt something hard prod into his hip. "What the—?" he muttered as he reached down. His hand wrapped around her holster, and he pushed her up, unbuckled her belt, and released it from the loops of her pants.

"This has got to go," he said, letting it slip beside her in the truck.

She sat down next to him and pulled off her boot. He laughed and she looked up.

"If anyone had told me I'd go for a woman who dressed like a man, I would've told them they were crazy." He laughed, pulling the other boot off.

"I don't dress like a man," she told him, taking a swipe at his midsection with her boot. "I dress like a sheriff."

He reached for her. "I won't argue the point. Dressed or undressed, I find you irresistible."

He pushed her slacks and panties over her hips, until all she wore was her open shirt. He could see her badge reflecting the moonlight. When he slipped her shirt off, she was as naked as he was. Again he pulled her on top of him, their bodies cushioned by the down sleeping bags.

He could feel her skin come alive under his touch, her body moving against his, its heat matching his. He closed his eyes and found her lips, moving his body under hers by instinct. He breathed in the scent of her, relished the fresh, salty taste of her body. He touched her warm breast with his tongue, then rolled on top of her, never letting her soft flesh leave his mouth.

He wanted the night to go on forever, wanted them to be locked in the secret world on top of the hill. And yet he needed release from the incredible tension within his body. He wanted to possess the woman underneath him.

He felt himself slip inside her, her moist warmth surrounding him as if she were made just for him. He heard her sigh, heard her whisper his name, and it made his passion for her stronger. He wanted to go on forever. He wanted, he wanted...

Finally he could stand it no longer and the night shattered into a thousand stars. Willie moved under him, and he held her, knowing she would disappear inside him if he didn't hold on tight.

Afterward, they lay curled in each other's arms, gazing up at the canopy of stars.

"Has anyone ever told you how wonderful you are?" he asked, unashamed of the obviously corny line.

Willie laughed. "Lately, no. It's seems like you're the sole member of the Willie Callen fan club."

"Now, that isn't fair," he said, kissing her cheek. "Even when I think you're the orneriest woman this side of the Mississippi, I adore you."

"I'm not ornery, Joe. I'm assertive. Why is it when a woman is assertive, she's called orn—"

"There you go, Willie. You're being ornery."

She gently bit the hand he had nestled comfortably under her chin. "If it's ornery you want, I'll show you—" She laughed as he silenced her with a kiss.

"We should be getting home," he whispered. "But I don't think I ever want to let go of you."

"Then don't," Willie replied, a serene smile covering her face. He pulled a sleeping bag over them and felt her as she snuggled closer. He sensed the heaviness in his eyes. The stars shimmered overhead, and he heard muted night noises from the valley below. Soon those sounds were accompanied by Willie's soft, steady breathing.

"Good morning, Hannah," Willie said as she entered the office. "It's a gorgeous day, isn't it?"

Hannah looked up from her cup of coffee. She stared openmouthed at Willie.

"G'morning, Sheriff," she managed to blurt out as Willie went past.

Willie stopped and turned around. "Is anything wrong, Hannah?" Willie asked.

Hannah shook her head, then squinted as she looked at Willie. "I was at the debate last night," she said, as if that explained everything.

Willie smiled. "It was a real fiasco, wasn't it?" Without waiting for an answer, she turned and went into her office.

Carl was sitting at his desk. He looked up and grinned from ear to ear when he saw Willie walk in.

Willie stopped and stared at him. "Okay. If you're going to say anything about that disaster of a debate last night, get it over with."

A puzzled look crossed her deputy's face and then he shook his head. "I've already forgotten about that, Willie," he said, still grinning. "And you're right. It was a disaster. But that's not what I want to talk about." He stood up and walked over to her, a report in his hand. "Take a look at this."

She scanned the sheet in front of her. Finally she was grinning like Carl. "Good work." She went to her desk and sat down. "So you finally got hold of Tanner Aviation, the Denver outfit that arranged the helicopter rental for Virgil Jones and Bud Beede last spring in Montana."

Carl nodded. "And the owner, Tanner, said that a couple of months ago someone called to ask about renting a certain kind of helicopter, one called a 'Stealth' model. It was developed for the military, but now it's used by some police forces for surveillance work."

"And they're available commercially?" Willie asked.

Carl nodded again. "For people who are willing to pay the high price tag. Tanner gave the caller a list of three companies in the West where they're available."

"Did the caller identify himself?"

"That's a problem. Tanner said he was given a name he didn't recognize, but he thought the voice was vaguely familiar. When the caller asked about the closest company to southwest Colorado, it triggered Tanner's memory. Tanner thought it sounded like one of the men who'd rented from him before. The men he remembered lived in Cisco."

"But he couldn't be sure who it was?"

Carl shook his head. "Unfortunately, no. Tanner said that since both Bud Beede and Virgil Jones are licensed helicopter pilots, and he'd dealt with both on the phone, he couldn't be sure which it was. But he was pretty certain it was one of them."

"That's not hard evidence. But it's more than we had yesterday." Willie put the report on her desk. "Did Tanner say he would recognize the voice if he heard it again?"

"He said he'd give it a shot." Carl walked back to his desk. "I'm going to check out those three places today. The ones where Tanner said you could get the kind of helicopter we're looking for."

"Good," Willie said. "They would've seen whoever picked up the helicopter. We could get some positive ID."

Willie was still studying the report when Hannah walked in. She poured Willie and Carl a cup of fresh coffee, then stood in front of Willie's desk.

"Thanks, Hannah." The woman didn't move. Willie looked up. "Is there something on your mind?"

"We've got to talk, Sheriff." Her tone was slightly melodramatic, and Carl looked up.

"Sure, Hannah." Willie put the report down. "Sit down."

"I'll be right back," Hannah said as she disappeared into the outer office. She returned with a pile of papers in her hand and sat in front of Willie, still holding the papers in her lap.

"Those are from last night?" Willie asked as she stared at the papers. "All those are phone messages?"

Hannah nodded. "The phone was ringing off the hook. It even started first thing this morning."

"Well, let's see them." Hannah gave the papers to Willie. "Anything I need to get to right away? Or are they all the usual let-me-give-you-a-piece-of-my-mind sort of calls?"

"Look at the top two," Hannah said. "Maybe they make more sense to you than they do to me."

Willie glanced at the messages. "This one is from a Diana Lawrence."

"Yeah," Hannah said. "She said she wanted you to know that her offer was still open. Anytime. She left the number at the bottom."

Without another word, Willie crumpled the paper up and threw it into the wastebasket. Hannah looked surprised but didn't say anything.

"The next one is from 'X'?" Willie looked at Hannah. "What does 'X' mean?"

"Oh. That means it was was anonymous." Hannah paused. "But the caller sounded familiar."

Willie raised her eyebrows. "So this familiar caller wanted to tell me that I should be careful? That's it?"

Hannah stood up, took the paper out of Willie's hand and looked at it. "Oh. I forgot the rest of it. It's supposed to read, 'Tell Willie she should be careful or she may end up deader than Matt Bishop's turkeys.'"

Willie suppressed an urge to laugh. "Matt's turkeys are dead. I don't see how I could get 'deader.'" Out of the corner of her eye, she saw Carl smile. She turned to Hannah. "Who was this 'familiar' voice?"

Hannah cleared her throat. "I don't know if I should say, Sheriff. You know how I feel about telling tales and such—"

"Hannah, for heaven's sake! This isn't some gossip you're giving me. It could be a valuable lead. Who called in this warning?"

Hannah swallowed hard. "I don't want you to take this wrong, because you know how Lucy Wiemer and me haven't seen eye to eye in years, ever since she had me kicked out of the church choir and I—"

"Lucy Wiemer left this message?" Willie looked at Carl, and her deputy shook his head. "Are you sure?"

"Sure as I can be, under the circumstances," Hannah said loudly enough for Joe to hear as he opened the office door.

"What's Hannah so sure of?" he asked as he entered the room.

Willie started to tell Joe that it was none of his business, but Hannah opened her mouth first.

"I was just telling Willie that I think it was Lucy Wiemer who called in that threat last night. Right after the debate."

"What threat was that?" Joe said, the smile having vanished from his face.

"It was nothing, Joe," Willie said. "Hannah's not even sure she got the message right."

Hannah shook her head. "No, Sheriff. I got the message right. I just forgot to write it all down." Hannah waved the piece of paper in front of Joe. "It said to tell Willie that she'd be deader than Matt Bishop's turkeys if she wasn't careful."

"And Lucy Wiemer called that in?"

"Hannah thinks it was Lucy. She isn't sure," Willie added. "Anyway, threats by sixty-five-year-old women that refer to turkeys and me in the same sentence can hardly be taken seriously. Lucy probably wants to warn me that I'd better pay attention to this UFO stuff or the aliens will get mad."

"But this sixty-five-year-old woman has a nasty brother and two even nastier nephews," Joe said.

"Joe's right, Sheriff," Hannah said.

"Hannah, shouldn't you be out front?" Willie looked at the flashing light on the phone. "I think someone wants to get through. I'll call you if I have any questions about these other messages."

Hannah got up and started to walk out.

"Hannah," Willie said, and the older woman turned around. "What you just told me goes no further than this office. I mean that."

"Of course, Sheriff." Hannah hurried out of the office.

Joe walked over to Willie's desk.

"Willie, I don't like this," he started to say, when the phone on her desk rang. She picked it up.

"Okay, Hannah, put him through." Willie covered the mouthpiece with her hand. "It's Homer Beede." Joe sat on the edge of Willie's desk. "What can I do for you, Homer?" Willie was silent for a few minutes. "Homer, calm down. We'll be right out." She hung up, then looked at Joe and Carl.

"Homer said he found the rest of his turkeys dead this morning. He says Bud just discovered them out in his northwest range."

"Isn't that near where he found his birds dead two days ago?"

Willie nodded her head. "He also said that Lucy was up late last night. He said around midnight she saw some bright lights over in that direction. She got him up, and he saw them, too. He said it was the UFO."

"Around midnight?" Joe repeated. "But that's impossible. We were up on Desert Point last night. We would have seen it."

"You two were up on Desert Point?" Carl asked. "But she says it was around midnight that she saw it. What were you doing—?" Carl stopped in mid-sentence when it occurred to him what Willie and Joe might have been doing. He cleared his throat and looked at Willie. "I see."

"Thanks, Joe," Willie said dryly. "Now, why don't we all go look at some dead turkeys?"

# *Chapter 14*

Willie rode out to the Beede place with Carl, while Joe took the newspaper's Blazer. She was grateful that Carl was quiet. Either he didn't want to talk, or he sensed that something was on Willie's mind. "Something" was an understatement. She had a lot of things running through her mind, not the least of which was this case.

She realized that since Homer and his boys were her chief suspects, things would be a lot simpler if their turkey crop had been spared. It would take some pretty fancy reasoning to explain away why the Beedes would destroy their own turkeys just to allay others' suspicions of them. Farmers could get crop insurance, but most of those in San Juan County didn't because the cost was just too high. The Beedes would have to bear the loss of this year's crop just like any other farmer, although that loss would be significantly less for them. Willie remembered that she was still missing one of the major elements of any crime—motive. There had to be a pretty elaborate plan and a motive to put that plan into action, in order for some farmers to rent a high-tech helicopter, disguise it as a UFO, dress up as spacemen and then proceed to kill most of the turkeys in the county. Could the Beedes want their neighbors' land and water rights that badly?

Willie still wondered where Lucy Wiemer and her "dreams" fitted into all this. Was her message to Hannah really a threat or just the ranting of a mentally ill woman? And what part, if any, did Virgil Jones play in this criminal comedy? Joe was right. When Virgil had fled the debate last night, he had looked guilty as sin. But looking guilty and being guilty, she thought, are two different, often unrelated conditions.

Carl sat in the seat beside her. When they were almost at the Beede place, he looked up. "What's on your mind, boss?" Without waiting for an answer, he shook his head. "This is turning out to be one heck of a case. Too bad it happened right before election."

Willie nodded. "It takes something like this to make them forget everything you've done right in the past four years." She sighed. "Oh, well, I can always go back and finish law school. Being sheriff isn't my whole life. What with Ed Mason going into retirement in a few years, Cisco could use another attorney."

Carl looked at her. "I don't mean that you've lost the election already, Willie. Anybody would have to be a fool to vote for Virgil, the way he ran out of the meeting last night. He didn't seem too eager to discuss this UFO situation, either."

"I noticed," Willie said as they pulled onto the dirt road that led to the northeast corner of the Beede place. She followed it for half a mile and then put the Cherokee into four-wheel drive and headed over another mile of rangeland. Finally she noticed Homer's truck, and pulled up next to it.

One look at Homer and she could tell he wasn't in the mood for pleasantries. His usually ruddy face was positively livid. His boys were farther out in the field, examining their dead turkeys. As Willie walked up to Homer, she heard Joe's car coming down the road.

Homer was a large, powerfully built man in his late fifties. He was a widower, and Lucy, his sister, had lived with the family since Lucy's husband had run off almost forty years earlier.

"Morning, Sheriff," he said, his voice unusually clipped. He looked up and saw Joe coming across his field. "What's he doing here?"

Willie looked over her shoulder, as if not quite certain who Homer was referring to. "You mean Joe?" she asked.

"You know who I mean. You were at the debate last night."

"Unfortunately I was." She looked at Joe again as he approached the group. "Dead turkeys are news. Joe has a newspaper. It's that simple." She paused and glanced at Joe again. "Do you want me to ask him to leave?"

"Now, Homer," Joe said, grinning. "Certainly you don't hold last night against me, do you?" Homer didn't answer; he just stared at Joe with two intense, narrowed eyes. "After all the public innuendo you've been dishing out about Willie and me, I thought you could take a little of the same."

"I don't know about any of this innuendo business. I just call 'em as I see 'em." He looked back at his field, littered with the carcasses of several hundred dead turkeys. "And as you can see, it doesn't make sense for you two to think me and my boys are the ones behind this turkey-killing business. Only a fool would kill his own birds."

Willie was about to say something, then bit her lip. *Kill his own birds,* she thought.

"You said over the phone that your sister saw some bright lights in this area last night," Willie said. "Approximately what time did she see these lights?"

"I saw 'em, too." Homer looked down at the ground for a moment. "Let me see now. I'd say Lucy woke me up just before midnight." He nodded his head. "That's right. It was between eleven-thirty and midnight."

"What did these bright lights look like?" Willie took out her notebook and wrote down the time.

"They were bright and pulsating, just like what the rest of the town's been seeing. Lucy says it's just like what she saw in her dream."

"I see." Willie and Joe walked over to the turkeys; Homer followed. Carl was already gathering up some of the carcasses to send to the lab in Denver.

"I don't see why you need those dead birds," Homer told her. "It's pretty obvious to me that they died of the same thing that got Grady Wheeler and Matt Bishop's birds."

"And what do you think that was, Homer?" Willie looked at the him.

"Why, it's like my sister says. It's like Matt and Grady say. It can't be nothing but aliens." He looked at Joe, then back at Willie. "You're just wasting time trying to find someone here to pin the blame on. Any fool can see that what happened here is too strange to be caused by humans." He stepped closer to the sheriff and pointed his finger at her. "Do you know what I'd do if I were you?"

Willie shook her head. "No, Homer. What would you do?"

"I'd call in the National Guard. I'd declare a state of emergency, and then I'd try to get the people out. Lucy says that they're coming for us. She says those that aren't taken are going to get blasted."

"Blasted? Exactly what does your sister mean by the term 'blasted'?" Willie asked.

"She doesn't mean anything by it. It was the term the aliens used." He paused. "I guess they mean they're just gonna come down here and finish everyone off, like they did to the turkeys."

Willie remembered the message Lucy had given Hannah. She looked at Joe. Carl was putting the dead birds in the trunk of her car. "I guess that's all for now, Homer. If I have any more questions, I'll give you a call." She started to walk away, then turned around. "How's Lucy taking all this?"

"Oh, she's sort of tired out by all the excitement."

"Is she home now? I think I'll just drop by and talk to her for a few minutes."

Homer stepped in front of Willie and Joe. "No. It's best not to do that. Not right now."

"Why not?"

"I told you, she's resting. She hardly got any sleep last night. None at all," he said quickly.

"But I'd just like to ask her a few quest—"

"I'll have Doug drive her into town this afternoon," Homer interrupted her. "She'll be ready to talk to you then."

For a moment Willie just stared at him, then she smiled. "I guess I'll have to settle for that, won't I." Willie wondered if Lucy's "prophetic" dreams weren't being helped along with a dose of some drug Homer might be giving her. Why else wasn't Willie able to see her right now?

She turned around and walked to the car. Carl got in, and she slipped into the driver's seat. Joe poked his head through the open window.

"I'll meet you back at the office in about an hour," she said. "I'm going to pay a call on Grady Wheeler on my way back."

"Sounds interesting. I've got to get back to the office. I'll drop by this afternoon." He touched her arm briefly and then was gone.

"Joe seems to be taking a lot of interest in this," Carl observed as Willie drove them over to the Wheeler place. "I can't ever remember you working so close on a case with his brother."

Paul. Willie thought of him for the first time in several days. Joe had so overwhelmingly occupied her thoughts that the old memories of Paul had been tucked away. She remembered how only a few days earlier she'd been constantly comparing him and Joe. Now Joe had become to her a truly separate person. A special person. Paul was still special and would always be, but Joe...

"No, Paul was my best friend, though we never worked together. But then, we've never had a case like this, Carl." Willie turned off the main road. "And I hope we never have one like it again."

"Amen to that," Carl said. He was silent for a moment, but then he looked at Willie. "I know this is none of my business, Willie. But I'm going to bring it up anyway."

Willie turned and looked at him. "What's that, Carl?"

"Well, I've heard you and Joe Kelly have been seeing a lot of each other. There's even talk that it's serious."

"Serious? What do you mean by serious?"

"Some people have seen his car at your place, your car at his place. All night. I guess that's what I mean by serious."

Willie pulled up to the Wheeler place and stopped the car. She turned to Carl. "I'm a thirty-four-year-old single woman. It's nobody's business, including yours, if Joe Kelly and I are 'serious.'" She paused. "It's none of your business as my deputy. But I suppose that as my friend you have the right to ask. Joe and I are seeing each other. I don't know how serious it is." She shrugged. "Sometimes I think he's fascinated with me because I'm different." She laughed. "He's never been involved with a sheriff before."

Carl thought a moment. "You're not worried how all this is going to affect the elections?"

She'd been waiting for that question. "Carl, if the people in this town can't deal with the fact that I'm a human being, and a woman, then it really doesn't matter whether it affects the elections. I'm who I am. And it's time we all accepted that."

Carl looked out the window. "I respect that, Willie. It's just that, well..."

"Well what, Carl?"

"It's just that we've all just gotten used to working with you. It'd be a shame if we had to go and get used to someone else all over again." Willie smiled. "I guess what I'm trying to say is that Wes and LeRoy and I—we don't want you to lose the election."

"Neither do I. But as I said, it isn't the only thing there is."

She opened the car door and got out. She and Carl walked up to the front door of Grady Wheeler's house and knocked. When no one answered, they walked around back and found Grady in his barn. Apparently he was cleaning things up.

"What can I do for you, Sheriff?" Grady said when he saw them. "Since most of my turkeys been killed, I'm reduced to cleaning up around here. Not that it doesn't need it, but after I'm done, then what? It's too late in the year to start turkeys."

"That's true," Willie agreed. "Mind if I ask you a few questions, Grady?" She looked around the barn. Grady shook his head.

"How much of a loss are you going to take from those dead turkeys?"

Grady scratched his head. "A big one."

"How big? Enough to put you under?"

Grady shook his head. "No, no. It'd take more than that. I don't owe nothing on the land. That's been in my family forever, and I haven't had to borrow money on it for years. If nothing happens to the rest of my turkeys, I can cover expenses. But I won't make a profit, either." He looked around. "I'll tell you something, Sheriff. It's a thing like this that makes a man wonder if he *wants* to go on."

"How's that?" Willie leaned against the iron railing inside the barn, adopting a relaxed posture. Carl did the same.

"It just gives a man a mighty funny feeling that there's things beyond the forces of nature he has to deal with." He wiped his forehead with a dark blue bandanna. "I'm not a young man. I really don't have anyone to leave this old place to. My only son's up in Denver. He's got no interest in turkeys." He laughed. "Can't say that I blame him. You know what he said after I told him what happened?"

"What?" Willie asked.

"He told me to take Homer Beede's offer and come up to Denver and live with him." He paused and looked around again. "And I've half a mind to do it."

"Homer made you an offer on your place? When?" Willie could hardly believe it. It looked as though her hunch might be right!

"Oh, he's been trying to buy me out ever since that water thing. A few years ago, I would have never considered it. But I didn't have to deal with aliens then." He shook his head. "Turkeys are bad enough. But aliens and UFOs? It just isn't worth it. What's gonna happen next?"

"Do you know if Beede's made Matt Bishop any offer?"

"Sure. He's been trying to get Bishop's land, too. But Matt's son Ed is working the place. Bishop will never sell out."

"Was Beede's offer fair?"

Grady thought a moment. "At the time it was. But then I don't expect I'll get the same offer now."

"What makes you say that?"

He laughed. "San Juan County's not exactly the best place to be at the moment. Lucy Wiemer's been saying the aliens have chosen us for God only knows what. And now Homer's been hit hard by this thing, too. I heard they got the rest of his birds last night."

"He found his turkeys dead this morning. Did you happen to see anything last night? Any bright lights? Anything unusual?"

"You mean did I see that UFO thing last night?"

"Yeah." Willie smiled. "I guess that's what I mean."

Grady shook his head. "I didn't see anything. But then I went to bed early last night."

Willie looked at Carl. "Can you think of anything else we should ask Grady?"

Carl shook his head.

Willie started to leave, then addressed the old farmer. "But I am wondering about one thing."

"What's that?" Grady asked.

"What would be your reaction if we could find proof that there weren't any aliens, that this whole thing was a hoax—a hoax probably set up to get you to sell your land?"

Grady thought about it for a minute. "Everything seems to be against it, Sheriff. I never thought I'd admit it, but it does look like aliens and UFOs. Too many people have seen 'em." He looked at Willie, suddenly intense. "But if it isn't and somebody's set this up and killed my turkeys, I'd be madder than hell. I'd say you'd better catch 'em before Ed Bishop and I got hold of 'em."

"That's just what we intend to do, Grady." Willie walked toward the barn door. "Thanks, Grady. I appreciate what you've told me."

"Don't wait too long before you catch these guys, aliens or whatever they are. I'm tired of waiting around to see if they're gonna get the rest of my birds."

Willie nodded, and she and Carl left. They were in the car and out on the highway before either spoke.

"It looks bad for the Beedes, doesn't it?" Carl finally said.

"It certainly does. I still can't figure out why they went to all this trouble. How badly can somebody want land?"

"I guess pretty badly," Carl answered.

"But nobody's going to make a million raising turkeys. There are easier ways to make money. Something's still missing."

"Yeah, proof is missing. We have suspects; we have a possible motive. But we don't have any proof. What we need is to catch these 'aliens' in the act."

Willie turned to Carl. "That's exactly what we're going to do."

Willie went back to the office and had a late lunch. Then she took a call from the lab in Denver. She learned that the cylinder cap she and Joe had recovered several nights before contained a concentrated level of a commonly used insecticide whose ingredients she couldn't pronounce. The dose they'd received wasn't strong enough to be toxic to humans unless there was direct, repeated exposure. But obviously it was enough to kill turkeys. The lab technician told Willie that the mixture in the cylinder wasn't available commercially as far as she knew, but it could easily be made up by someone who could mix chemicals. The cylinders were readily obtainable.

All morning Hannah had been fielding calls from reporters and other curiosity seekers. It seemed that ever since Lucy Wiemer's rooftop pronouncement, they were coming out of the woodwork. Everyone wanted to know what the sheriff was going to do when the UFO landed the following Monday. Willie had given up trying to answer these calls without losing her temper. When she called Hannah into her office and solemnly told her it was her responsibility to answer them, the older woman fairly beamed at the idea of her new importance. Heaving a sigh of relief, Willie told her she didn't care what Hannah told anyone, just as long as she told them to stay away.

Willie was sitting in her chair, facing the windows that looked out onto Main Street, when she heard the office door open. She thought it must be Carl or Wes coming back from a late lunch, and she didn't bother turning around. But when whoever it was didn't sit down, she whirled around in her chair. There, standing in her office, was just about the last person she'd expected to see.

"Hello, Virgil," she said, keeping her voice even. "What can I do for you?"

Virgil stared at her nervously for a moment, then looked around. "I think we should have a talk."

"Sure. Sit down." She pointed to the chair in front of her desk.

"I want this to be a private conversation. Just between you and me."

Willie nodded, then picked up her phone. "Hannah, I don't want anyone to come into the office for a while. If Carl or Wes comes back, tell them to get started on those phone calls. They'll know what I mean."

She put the phone down and waited for Virgil to be seated. When he finally did, she waited for him to start talking.

"I guess you wonder why I suddenly walked out of that debate the other night."

"What debate? It was a circus." She smiled. "But I did wonder why you didn't stick around. It looked like things were going your way."

"That's just it. They *were* going my way." He started to cross his legs, then uncrossed them. Willie knew he had something on his mind, and she wasn't going to blow it by rushing him.

"The town is ready to string me up," she told him without bitterness. "In fact, I think that if I don't solve this UFO-turkey case, you'll get the job of sheriff handed to you on a silver platter."

"Maybe. But that's just the point. I don't want to get elected because of this case. I think it's gotten...well, I think it's gotten way out of hand."

"You and me both."

"What I came here to say is that Joe is right. There are two people in this town who are licensed helicopter pilots. And one of them is me." He looked up at her. "But then, I suppose you already knew that."

Willie nodded. "The other one is Bud Beede."

"Yeah, Bud's a good pilot." He stopped and then got up, walked over to the window and looked out. "And it's no secret that I'm good friends with all the Beedes and that they back me for sheriff." He paused again.

"I didn't come here point the finger at anybody. I just came here to tell you I don't have anything to do with this whole UFO thing." He turned around. "And I came to tell you that I'm pulling out of the sheriff's race."

"You're what?" Willie turned around. "Why are you doing that?"

"Let's just say that I feel I'm not really qualified to do the job. I only entered the race because I thought you needed some competition and because..."

"And because?" Willie repeated.

"Because Bud hounded me to do it. And to be perfectly honest, last night showed me I'm not prepared to tackle the job. It takes more than big talk to be a good sheriff."

"If Bud was so interested in the sheriff's race, why didn't he run himself?"

Virgil laughed. "Bud's not exactly the most popular guy in town."

"Neither am I," Willie said.

"But you're respected. People look up to you. Even I have to admit you're one gutsy lady. And Bud...well, Bud's Bud. The die-hard chauvinist and original good ole boy."

"Are you telling me that you let this town vote for you in the primaries and now you're not really interested?"

"I didn't say I wasn't interested. I still think it's a prestigious position. I just came here to tell you that I'm withdrawing from the race and that I don't have anything to do with this UFO and turkey-killing business."

"But you know who does?"

"I didn't say that, Sheriff. I have my own ideas about it all, but just like you, I don't have any hard evidence. And I won't make any accusations until I do." Virgil moved toward the door.

Willie stood up. "You realize, don't you, Virgil, that a serious crime has been committed here. It's a felony. On several counts. Even an accessory before or after the fact could get nailed."

She tapped the desk with a pencil. "You know that coming here doesn't clear you from my list of suspects. Only hard physical evidence against whoever is doing this is going to clear you."

"I'll remember that, Sheriff." Virgil left.

She sat down at her desk. Before she had time to even think about what Virgil's visit had meant, Joe walked in.

"Did you hear the latest?" he asked.

"Latest?" Willie looked up from her desk. "Which latest?"

"Virgil Jones has withdrawn from the sheriff's race. I just saw him coming out of the courthouse, but he didn't want to talk about it." He sat down front of Willie. "He wasn't here to see you, was he?"

"He was." Willie started to shuffle some papers around on her desk. "What he had to say was off the record, strictly confidential."

"Oh, come on, Willie. What did he tell you? Did he say why he withdrew? Did he make a full confession as the Cisco Turkey Killer? What was it?" Joe smiled. "You know I won't leave you alone until I get it out of you."

He paused for a moment, then stood up and walked behind the desk to where she was sitting. She felt his hands on her back, and slowly he lowered his face, letting his lips caress her ear until she could feel the his breath blow against it. Tiny spikes of energy raced along her spine.

"You know, even after I get it out of you I won't leave you alone."

What did that mean? That they would move along in a sort of sensual limbo for the next few years? But what else was she expecting? Promises of forever after? Two divorced people like her and Joe just didn't make that kind of promise. She laughed off her disappointment.

"Is that a threat, Joe?" Just looking into his eyes, she began to feel a familiar hunger. "I've got lots of work to do, so thanks for dropping by with that little bit of news."

"Am I being dismissed?" Joe asked, his eyes feigning hurt.

"You're being dismissed." Willie smiled and looked at her watch. "How about picking me up at my place for dinner at eight? I don't care where you take me, just as long as it doesn't have turkey on the menu. I don't think I can face another dead bird, no matter what shape it's in."

"Eight it is," he said as he stood up. "And remember. I'm a man who doesn't forget a threat."

Willie sat in her bedroom, looking at the image that was reflected in the mirror across the room. It was fifteen minutes to eight, and the woman she saw in the mirror wasn't tired, as she should have been. Instead, there was a faint but unmistakable flush of excitement spreading across her cheeks. For a moment, Willie thought the woman reminded her of someone else, someone younger. Someone in love?

Thought became realization. The Willie Callen she saw in the mirror was in love. Nothing else could explain the sense of elation she had at just seeing Joe. In the past few weeks they had become practically inseparable. As much as Willie wanted to solve this case—and she wanted to badly—she wondered what effect it would have on her relationship with Joe.

Even during the times she was ready to kill him, she had to admit that she would have had a much tougher time handling this case without him. It wasn't just the help in working out the details, the framework for solving the crime. Her deputies could have done that just as well as Joe. It was the emotional support he'd given her that she'd needed most. He'd been around, understanding, accepting her. That acceptance had made her feel like a woman again.

And if she was honest with herself, she had to admit that she wanted more from Joe Kelly than just a sexual friendship. But Willie was also realistic. Not once had Joe even hinted he was contemplating anything more.

Absently, she brushed her hair, trying to find a name for what she wanted from Joe when she heard his knock at her front door. She stood up and smiled. Right now, until she did figure out what she wanted, she was willing to settle for what Joe was prepared to give.

He opened the door, a large pizza box in one hand and a six-pack of beer in the other.

"I thought you'd be too beat to go out," he said, taking the food into the kitchen. She followed him.

"I don't look that bad, do I?" Maybe he was mistaking the first flush of love she'd seen in the mirror for a fever. How romantic! she thought wryly.

He set the food down on the counter, then walked over to her. "You've never looked better." He kissed her briefly, then searched her cupboard until he found some plates. "Actually, I thought I'd spare you the hassle of going out to eat."

"Hassle?" She walked over to the counter and began to nibble on the pizza. "Since when is eating out in Cisco a hassle?"

"It's not the eating out; it's the people," he told her as he put two slices on each plate, then handed her a beer. "Hannah's probably been protecting you from the ugly reality, but this afternoon all I heard about was Lucy Wiemer's predicted UFO visitation next Monday." They sat down at the kitchen table and Joe took a bite of pizza. "But I'm afraid that before the UFO comes to town, we're in for another, very real invasion from members of the press and other shameless curiosity seekers."

Willie popped open her can of beer. "Hannah mentioned that we'd been getting some phone calls, but I've been busy with other things lately." She looked at Joe. "Is it really that bad?"

He nodded. "It's that bad. I have a feeling that Monday will make what went on at the council meeting look like a county fair. Monday is going to be the three-ring circus."

Willie picked up her pizza, then put it down. She'd lost her appetite.

"Cheer up, Willie," Joe told her. "At least whatever happens now, it won't affect the elections. It seems you're going to win the sheriff's race by a landslide."

"That's easy to do, when there's no one running against you." Willie sighed.

Joe shrugged. "I didn't think you'd take it so well," he said. "Maybe I can organize a successful write-in campaign."

Willie's eyes opened wide and then she smiled. "You do, and I'll kick you in your bad knee."

Joe grinned. "That's the spirit, the fighting Willie Callen." He walked over to the counter and helped himself to more pizza. "By the way, how about filling me in on what happened today?" Joe asked casually.

Willie looked up at him. "I'll tell you what Grady told us," she said. "You'll probably find out anyway." She did so, then reminded him that her talk with Virgil Jones was confidential.

Joe was silent for a moment. Then he looked at her. "Well, Virgil's mysteriously dropping out of the election doesn't look too innocent to me. Can you at least tell me whether you think he's in this as deep as the Beedes?"

"So you're pretty sure the Beedes are behind this?"

"I'd be willing to bet my career as Cisco's premier newspaperman on it."

"Until Mike gets back, you're Cisco's *only* newspaperman. But I agree with you. If it isn't the Beedes out there playing alien, I'll be the first to admit I was wrong." She picked up her pizza once more. "What we have to do now is build a case against Homer and sons, get some hard evidence."

"You mean catch the 'aliens' in the act?"

"That would do it."

"Back to my question," Joe said. "Do you think Virgil is involved?"

Willie thought for a moment. The question had been nagging at her all afternoon. Was Virgil in this as deep as his buddies, or was he just a not-so-innocent bystander who thought he'd better try to clear himself?

"My instincts tell me that Virgil knows more than he was willing to reveal to me," Willie said carefully. "But I've always thought Virgil was a lot smarter than those Beede boys. I don't believe he is actively involved. But I think he feels guilty because he knows that his friends the Beedes are."

Joe's blue eyes were alive with anticipation. "So, boss, what's the plan? How are we going to catch this UFO and those pesky aliens?"

# *Chapter 15*

What *was* her plan? Willie wondered. She had a feeling that they'd better move quickly.

"Every time this UFO appears, turkeys get killed," Willie said, thinking out loud. "So the next logical question is, who still has some turkeys left to kill?"

"Grady Wheeler," Joe told her. "Jake and Ina Hauser have some, of course, and so does Royce Jacobs. But Wheeler is the only one who's already had some turkeys killed."

"And Grady told me this afternoon that he was almost ready to sell out to Homer Beede. One more visit from that UFO just might convince him." Willie got up to take another slice of pizza from the box on the counter.

"Okay," Joe said. "Let's assume they're going to attack him a second time to finish his turkeys off, just to give him extra incentive to sell out and make Beede's offer look good. How do we know when it will happen?"

"I think they'll be a little more cautious, since you announced in front of the whole town that the UFO really isn't a UFO but a helicopter that a couple of locals can fly."

Willie came back and sat down at the table. "I don't think they'll risk being as obvious as they have been."

"Or else they'll pick a night when they expect most of the town to be occupied somewhere else."

"Somewhere else?" Willie was about to ask Joe what he meant when she remembered. "Monday night, at five minutes to midnight! The southwest corner of Matt Bishop's farm."

"Exactly," he said. "Now we've found a reason for Lucy Wiemer's ranting and raving the other day. Even if the promised UFO doesn't show up, my guess is that nobody will want to miss the biggest show Cisco's had in years."

"There probably will be some reporters, maybe even some out-of-towners who've heard about it from the press." Willie got up and paced the length of her kitchen, obviously excited. "This afternoon I called Stan Eastman, the sheriff over in Montezuma County, and asked him if we could borrow some of his men. Now I'll arrange to have the whole event covered by Eastman's men. We'll just put in an appearance, and then we'll take a little trip over to the Wheeler place."

Joe got up and walked over to her, stopping her in midstride. "Now, that's what I call a plan." He teased the edge of her ear with his tongue as he wrapped his arms around her shoulders. "Tonight's Friday. It looks like we have some time to fool around before the big event."

Willie laughed. "Just what do you mean by the term, 'fool around'?"

Joe whirled her around in his arms so that she faced him. He lowered his head until his lips were a fraction of an inch away from hers. "It looks like I'm going to have to give you a demonstration." He kissed her then, a slow, easy kiss that told her they had all night.

Willie called all her deputies in at eight the next morning. It was unusual for her to get them together on a Saturday, but she wanted to explain her plan for Monday night and see if they had any suggestions.

She'd called the sheriff over in Fargo County as well as her friend in Montezuma. She wanted to be sure there were enough men to cover Lucy Wiemer's gathering, so that she and her deputies could cover the stakeout at Wheeler's place themselves.

Willie knew everything was under control. It was the first time she'd felt that way since she'd been called out to Grady Wheeler's place a couple of weeks earlier.

She finally knew what had killed the turkeys, how it had been done, who was doing it and why. She hoped it would all come together Monday night. She'd get the evidence she needed by catching the Beede brothers and their father when they came back to finish off Grady's birds.

She couldn't help but smile when she thought of the part Joe had played in helping her get this far with the most difficult case she'd had as sheriff of San Juan County. Willie picked up from her desk the latest edition of the *San Juan Independent*. Joe had really pulled out all the stops in promoting Monday's gathering at the Bishop place. Bold headlines proclaiming the coming event covered the top of the front page of the first section:

Aliens to Return to the Bishop Farm
Local Woman Maintains Contact with Aliens

Willie laughed. Almost everyone in town would be there. Most of the citizens weren't really taking Lucy seriously. They were just using the excuse to have a big party. Willie had heard that several local groups were organizing picnics and games and that most people planned to spend the night in tents or under the stars. It appeared that Monday night's event would rival Cisco's annual Fourth of July celebration.

She and Joe had visited Matt Bishop, who was still in the hospital but making a steady recovery from his heart attack. Before he agreed to let people use his fields as a camp park, Willie and Joe had to give him a promise that the town would clean up after itself. She was careful not to reveal their real plans for the evening; she just asked Matt to go along with the whims of Lucy Wiemer and the town she lived in.

Willie wouldn't have been too concerned if only the folks from Cisco were going to show up. But the story had been carried by several television stations in Denver and throughout the West. Joe had shown her a small article in *America Today*, which meant that the whole event now had national exposure. There was no way of telling how many people would be there. She could only hope that the extra help she'd requested would be enough to keep the anticipated crowd in order.

Joe told Willie that large numbers of people throughout the country were looking specifically for this kind of event. They were even willing to travel great distances to participate in an "alien" visit. Willie only hoped that these eccentrics were a peaceful lot.

She spent Saturday afternoon at the local library doing a bit of research on the whole UFO phenomenon, and was surprised to find out that most of the reported sightings had been made by what appeared to be very ordinary people, no one claiming psychic powers or any previous contact with alien beings.

Most sightings, she read, occurred in fairly deserted, out-of-the-way places, and the only witnesses were usually those people directly involved. Willie knew that the subject of UFOs was usually greeted with laughter and skepticism, so she wasn't surprised that a lot of people chose to keep the sightings to themselves.

This made Willie wonder. For the first time, she seriously considered the possibility that she might have been dealing with a genuine UFO. Although she was certain this particular UFO had very earthly origins, she realized it could have been something that wasn't so easily explained. Willie had always considered herself a very practical person. Now she knew she'd never again look up at a clear night sky without wondering what were the odds on real alien visitors.

She was still buried in books when she felt a gentle nudge at her shoulder. She looked up and found herself staring into two familiar blue eyes.

"Wes told me that I'd find you here," Joe whispered as he sat down beside her, lifting up the cover of the book she was reading. "*UFO Sightings in the Western United States.* You're not changing your mind about this, are you? Am I going to hear the skeptical Willie Callen tell me she thinks we're really dealing with an alien invasion?"

Willie shook her head. "Not this time around." She closed the book. "I just wanted to find out what kind of people we'd be dealing with on Monday."

"And?" Joe asked as they both stood up. "What kind of people will we be dealing with?"

"A mixed lot. Some will be pretty normal, and some will probably be just this side of certifiably crazy." He opened the door for her as they walked out into the early-fall afternoon. "Overall, I think they'll be a rather peaceful group."

"Do you think they'll be disappointed when the UFO doesn't show?"

Willie shrugged. "Most of them would be surprised if one did show. I think the whole point of these things is the chance to participate in the mystery of the unknown."

Joe walked Willie to her Cherokee. When he leaned on the open window after he'd shut the door, she expected him to ask her over to his place for dinner. After all, it was his turn.

"Listen, Willie," he began. "We've been seeing a lot of each other lately."

That's an understatement, Willie thought.

"And we really haven't gotten around to discussing the direction our relationship is taking—"

"So you want to start a discussion right here on Main Street?" Willie interrupted him.

"No, no." Joe shook his head. "What I'm trying to say is that it's something we need to discuss. We're not teenagers. I don't see how we can keep on spending the night at each other's place indefinitely. It's a small town, and I—"

"And you don't want to cause any talk. Is that it? If you're trying to say you don't want to see me tonight, it's okay. There are a million things I've been neglecting. And you're right. It's probably best that we don't see each other all the time, because..." She realized she wasn't sure why it was best that they didn't see each other. Certainly there was no reason she could think of.

"Hold it, Willie. I didn't say that I don't want to see you. I do. Very much." He paused, and Willie knew the "but" was coming. "But..." he started slowly, and she knew she was right. "But I don't really know how I feel about our relationship. I need time to think about it. I need—"

"Go ahead and take all the time you want. If there's one thing that isn't in short supply around here, it's time."

She put the key in the ignition and started the car. "See you around, Joe," she said as she backed out, a little too quickly. Willie wasn't one to hang around and wait for what she knew was inevitable, especially when she didn't want to hear it.

All the way home, Willie wondered what the inevitable was. She knew she was in love with Joe, just as surely as she didn't know whether he felt the same way about her. He was right; they'd never discussed their relationship. It seemed that the turkey case had taken up most of their discussions in the past few weeks.

Now that it looked as though the case was drawing to a close, what would happen next? Was Joe worried that without a case to discuss, they would have very little in common? Willie felt a cold, hard knot twisting in the pit of her stomach as she realized it could be exactly what Joe was thinking.

Willie and Joe arrived shortly after dusk at the southwest corner of Bishop's farm in her Cherokee. Several hours before in her office, she had briefed the law enforcement officers from neighboring counties. It hadn't taken her long to realize that the men wanted to witness the evening's entertainment as well as help her out.

Willie had asked them to be on the lookout for the rowdy drunks and illegal drugs that were an unfortunate reality at public gatherings. But she stressed that she was interested primarily in maintaining the peace, not in patrolling for minor violations or arrests.

She told Joe she wanted to wander through the crowd for a while to get a feeling for the kind of people they were dealing with, and was surprised when he said he wanted to walk around with her.

She hadn't heard from him all day Sunday. Monday he had just stopped by her office to go over the plans for that night's stakeout at Wheeler's place. He was polite but a bit distant. Willie felt that every hour brought her closer to the time when Joe would ask if they could be just "good friends," and wondered what she'd do when he said that. She knew she was in love with him, just as she knew it was useless to try to make him love her.

The size of the crowd amazed her. At least half the people there were unfamiliar. Willie recognized some of them as reporters she'd seen in town the week before. Once again, Cisco had become newsworthy.

"Your headlines worked better than I thought they would," she said to Joe, trying to sound casual and offhand.

"They seem harmless enough," he replied, inclining his head toward a family enjoying an evening picnic of fried chicken and potato salad. All around, parents were relaxing on blankets or lawn chairs, chatting and watching their children run around nearby. "Hardly a group that's plotting a riot."

"They do look like peaceful, law-abiding citizens," Willie agreed. "But what about them?" She directed Joe's attention to a group of six shaggy-looking men and women dressed in black leather and sporting multicolored hair, who were draped over some very large motorcycles. Willie noticed that the ground around them was already littered with empty beer cans.

"Definitely not from Cisco," Joe said, "unless they're the group that bought the Henley place up on Cooper Road. The talk in the diner is that old Henley sold his place to some pretty strange people."

Willie let a look of horror briefly fly across her face, then she managed a very calm "Oh, really?" Maybe they didn't seem so tough, after all. Joe looked at her as she watched them and couldn't maintain his placid expression any longer.

"Just kidding," he said laughing. "Henley sold his place to a retired couple from Milwaukee. Anyway, relax. It looks like they've already attracted the right kind of attention."

Willie turned around and spotted one of the deputies from Fargo County less than twenty feet away, keeping an eye on the group. She couldn't help but feel relieved.

They continued walking through the crowd, amazed at the variety of people who had shown up in the hope of seeing a real UFO.

A young couple dressed like pseudo-Egyptian refugees from a remake of *The Mummy's Curse* had set up a small altar, where they were burning some incense. They'd already drawn a small crowd as they knelt in front of the altar and prayed in some language Willie couldn't identify.

"I wonder what that's all about," Joe said as they stopped to look.

"They're probably reciting something from the Egyptian *Book of the Dead*."

"What makes you say that?" Joe asked.

"It fits," she told him. "I read that part of ancient Egyptian belief deals with the way the soul is transported to the underworld after death. A certain sect of the ancients believed that their dead would return to this earth someday, and current believers are convinced that they'll be returning by spaceship from another planet." She could tell Joe was impressed.

"Did I ever ask you what religion you are?" Joe asked facetiously as they walked away.

Willie laughed.

A larger crowd had gathered at the far end of the field. As they walked closer, they discovered that at its center was Lucy Wiemer. She was seated on a white plastic lawn chair, holding court.

"Behold the psychic prophetess," Joe said. "She's dressed for the part."

Lucy had on a long white gown that Willie suspected was actually a negligee. Over that Lucy wore a gold bathrobe. The effect was more like a woman who'd just gotten out of bed than a spiritual leader.

As Joe and Willie came closer, they saw that Homer and his boys were standing behind Lucy, looking nervous and very preoccupied.

An old man, hunched over and leaning on a cane, was talking to Lucy. Willie and Joe were close enough to hear her final words to the man.

"Don't worry," she said in uncharacteristic soothing tones. "They'll take everyone who comes forward. Everyone." Satisfied, the man moved away at a painfully slow pace. Lucy looked up and saw Willie and Joe.

"You know it's not too late, Sheriff, Joe. I meant what I said. Even though you've doubted me all along, there's still time to repent and get on board."

Willie stared at the woman whom she'd known all her life. She'd never liked Lucy much, and in the past few weeks that passive tolerance had turned to active dislike. But now the old woman seemed so sincere, so openly helpful, that she wondered whether Lucy wasn't a victim of her own fantasy, wanting to believe in something so desperately that she had swallowed her own lies.

"I think we'll take our chances, Mrs. Wiemer," Willie told her. "Besides, Joe and I wouldn't make very good space travelers. We're afraid of heights." She smiled and walked away.

"That was a bit sarcastic, wasn't it?" Joe asked.

"Gathering a group of people with false promises just to get attention is a cheap trick." Willie looked back at Lucy Wiemer.

If Lucy Wiemer was involved in this—and at this point it was impossible to tell whether she was being manipulated and used by Homer—Willie was going to get evidence against her just as she would against the rest of her family.

They walked back to the Cherokee in silence. Willie had a last-minute chat with the Montezuma County sheriff and asked him to be sure that someone kept an eye on the Beede men, noting when and if they left the gathering.

Willie and Joe were halfway out to the Wheeler place when they both turned to each other and started talking. The sudden break in the silence was jarring, and they laughed.

"Sorry," Joe said. "You go first."

"No." Willie shook her head. "I didn't really have anything to say. I was just trying to lighten things up."

"It's that bad?" Joe asked.

Willie turned to him and nodded. "It's that bad. Look, Joe, if you'd rather sit this one out, I'll call you right after it's over. If you're uncomfortable with me, I'll try to understand that, too."

"Are you crazy! I wouldn't miss this for the world," he said. "As for being uncomfortable with you, I'm not. It's just that I have something on my mind, something I want to talk to you about."

Willie held up her hand. "Stop right there. Is this by any chance personal, about you and me?"

"Yes, it's personal."

"Then hold it," Willie said. "I've got enough on my mind without getting any earth-shattering news from you."

"Funny—" Joe commented "—that you should call it earth-shattering, because I think—"

"Let's leave any personal discussions until after tonight. I'm nervous enough as it is."

"Okay, okay. I guess it can wait," Joe said.

It'll have to wait, Willie thought. As far as I'm concerned, it can wait forever.

* * *

They arrived at the Wheeler place just after dark. LeRoy, Carl and Wes were already there. Grady Wheeler had been more than happy to cooperate with Willie when she explained that she thought the aliens would show up tonight to finish off the rest of his turkeys. But she was surprised to see him trailing behind LeRoy.

"What's Grady doing here?" she asked her deputy, then turned to Wheeler. "I thought we'd agreed it was best that you go over to the Bishop place with the rest of the town. This is official business. I can't have a citizen around when we—"

"What's he doing here, then?" Grady interrupted her, and pointed to Joe.

"He's the press. They're allowed to do any fool thing they want to," she told him without missing a beat. Then she turned to LeRoy. "Get him into his truck and out of here. Now."

She started to walk away, but Grady followed her.

"You can't do that to me. This is my place," he told her.

"Look, Grady. You have two choices. Either you leave quietly, or I'll personally handcuff you to a piece of furniture in the house." She stood her ground and glared at him.

"Okay. I'll go, but it's under protest." He trudged over to his truck, got in, then slammed the door.

After the dust had cleared, Joe turned to her. "Was that really necessary?"

"Look, Joe, I won't risk having this blow up in my face because of a stubborn old man like Grady. Do you have any idea how angry he'll be if he catches Homer and his boys over here trying to kill his turkeys?" Willie shook her head. "I'm crazy even to let you in on it, but at least you don't have an emotional investment. Grady's liable to shoot first and ask questions later."

"I see what you mean." Joe ran his fingers through his hair. "It's just that this is a different side of you, one I've caught only a glimpse of before."

"Well, with any luck, after tonight, when things quiet down again, nobody will have to see this side of Willie Callen for a while." Without waiting for an answer, she walked off to join her deputies.

Wheeler had put all his remaining turkeys into some pens near his barn. Willie and her deputies walked around the perimeter of the barn, the pens and the farmhouse, looking for the best places to position themselves.

Joe watched for almost an hour while Willie and her deputies discussed their plans. He was well aware that he was being left out. A few days ago, he would have tried to put himself right in the middle of things. Now he understood why Willie was reluctant to give him too active a role. After all, he was just a local newspaperman, not her deputy.

Willie had Carl conceal two of the sheriff's vehicles in the barn; he parked the other one in a shed on the far side of the house. Joe watched as Willie directed her men into action. Once again he was reminded how different she was from any woman he'd known.

Joe knew that any hope of success depended on blind luck. They had no guarantee that the suspects would actually show up. It was a logical choice, he conceded, but the type of people that would disguise a helicopter as a UFO and then dress as aliens and kill turkeys might somehow defy even the simplest logic.

Joe wished there was something he could do to ensure Willie's success tonight, but he knew he could do no more than what he was already doing. Just being there, by her side, had to be enough. This was her show.

Willie gave out assigned positions, and Joe listened for his. He wasn't surprised when Willie told him he would be in the barn's hayloft with her. The barn had a southeast opening that would serve as an ideal lookout point. The Beedes' farm was to the southeast, and that was the direction Willie expected the helicopter to approach from.

LeRoy would wait inside the darkened farmhouse, and Carl and Wes had positioned themselves out of sight near the barn.

"Everyone understand what they're supposed to do?" Willie asked, checking her watch. "I don't want any guns drawn unless it's absolutely necessary. These people need to be taken into custody, but they don't deserve to get shot. They probably won't even be armed." She looked at her men to make sure they understood her.

"Wes, you go for the pilot. Get him out of the chopper and handcuffed as soon as you can. Carl, LeRoy and I will tackle the other two. Joe here will just observe." She turned to Joe. "I don't want you to get mixed up in this."

She looked at them, and Joe could tell she expected him to protest. He didn't, and she continued.

"Get comfortable. It might be a long wait. But stay alert. And for God's sake, be careful."

Each of her deputies moved to the assigned positions. Joe and Willie walked toward the barn. Sensing the need for a lighter mood between them, Joe ran ahead of her and stood at the bottom of the hayloft ladder. As she approached, he waved his arm with a flourish.

"Enter, my lady. Your chamber awaits."

Willie looked at him, then smiled. "Watch it, knave! This is serious business. I'm not about to get caught by surprise like I did on our last stakeout, if you get my drift." Willie remembered what they'd been doing in the back of the truck on Desert Point. If it hadn't been for the turkeys roosting on the side of the pickup, they might have missed the "UFO" entirely.

Joe followed the narrow beam of Willie's flashlight as she led them up to the hayloft. Willie sat down on one side of the opening, and Joe on the other. It was quiet, and he sensed a tension he could almost reach out and grab on to. Part of it was due to the circumstances, the impatient wait for something to happen, wondering if it would happen at all.

But Joe knew that the other part of it was what lay between him and Willie. It seemed as if every other minute he thought about beginning the discussion he'd mentioned on their way over here. Each time the thought came to him, he swallowed it like a bitter pill. Willie was right; tonight wasn't the time or the place. After this was all over, then he could settle things with her.

Two-and-a-half hours later they were still waiting. They had stopped making any pretense of conversation, and Joe was afraid that Willie had begun to admit defeat.

Trying to lighten her mood, he moved closer to her as she lay on her stomach, watching the sky through the opening in the loft. Joe cupped his broad hand over her left buttock and began a sensuous massage up and down her leg. No reaction.

This calls for sterner stuff, he decided as he raised himself on one elbow and tried to pull the back of her shirt out of her pants. He had managed to get his hand on the soft skin of her lower back when she suddenly turned over and punched him lightly in the stomach.

"I thought I told you no funny stuff on this stakeout," she said quietly.

"I'm not trying to be funny. I'm very serious about this," Joe replied as he worked his hand around to cover her flat stomach.

"You must be oversexed," Willie said, laughing as she flipped back over on her stomach to resume her lookout, trapping Joe's hand underneath her.

Joe started to laugh, too. "You're twisting my arm, you know. The only way for me to get comfortable is to do this," he said as he rolled his body on top of hers, bracing most of his weight with his elbows.

"Help, you're squishing me!" she cried looking over her shoulder at him as he lay on top of her.

But Joe didn't say anything, and he didn't move. He stared out the opening in the loft.

"Joe, I mean it. You're heavy. I can't catch my breath. Get off." But still Joe didn't move.

"Joe, I'm going to get angry, I—"

"Shh . . ." he finally said as he rolled off and knelt beside her in the hay.

"Take a look at that," he said as he pointed out the window.

Far in the distance Willie could make out a ring of pulsating lights moving closer every second.

"Bingo," Joe whispered as Willie sat up.

"Let's hope so," she said as they climbed down the ladder. "It hasn't landed yet. Let's just pray that it's planning to stop here instead of the Bishop place."

Quickly they moved through the darkened barn and out the door to the edge of the pens. Then she heard the whining noises of the craft and reached for Joe's hand, squeezing it briefly before she made her move.

The UFO hovered for a second over the barnyard as if searching for any signs of life. The occupants apparently satisfied that only the turkeys were around, the craft settled down a few hundred feet away from the pens, to the far end of the barn, near where Willie and Joe were waiting.

"This is it, Sheriff," Joe whispered. "Do your stuff."

## Chapter 16

Willie stood crouched behind the back of the barn. She told her deputies not to make their move until the chopper had landed and the two "aliens" had left the vehicle and moved away. Wes was then to approach quickly from behind the helicopter and take the pilot. They hoped this would be accomplished without alerting the other two that anything was wrong.

It seemed to take forever for the "UFO" to land. Willie again marveled at the cleverness of the disguise. She hadn't thought the Beedes had that much of an imagination. The pulsating lights were mesmerizing, and the eerie whine emitted by the ultramodern helicopter reminded her of a science-fiction movie.

Willie felt Joe pressing close behind her as he strained to get a good view of the scene a few hundred yards away. After several anxious minutes, the craft finally settled on the ground. The whining died down. Apparently the pilot had cut the engine while the two "aliens" did their job.

Time moved in slow motion as the men emerged from the grounded chopper. After they got out, they reached in back for the cylinders of toxic spray. Willie could feel the adrenaline surge through her body, and she had to force herself to stay put until the culprits were well inside the turkey pens.

The men were repeating the same procedure Willie and Joe had witnessed a week earlier at the Beede place. Dressed in the clean suits and face protectors worn by chemical workers, they stepped away from their helicopter and walked toward the turkeys. Willie assumed that the pilot had been left behind, but the bright lights made it impossible to see inside the craft. She could hear turkeys begin to stir as the men opened the gate to their pen.

Willie waited until she spotted Wes moving through the darkness, close to the ground and behind the chopper. She held her breath and didn't release it until she saw him pull a figure from the plastic bubble. Apparently the pilot had decided to give up without a fight, because he yelled no warning to the others.

When Wes had the man flat on the ground beside the machine, she knew it was safe to make her move. She motioned for Joe to stay put. Then she turned but had moved only two steps when she heard the blast of a shotgun.

"What the—?" Willie whispered. She saw the figure of a man emerge from a ravine near the barn and rush toward the turkey pens and the "aliens."

"You damn aliens," he was screaming. "I'll make you think twice before you mess with Grady Wheeler." He stopped and leveled his pump-action shotgun in the direction of the pens.

The "aliens" inside the turkey pen hit the ground. Grady fired more shells and then charged forward with a speed that astounded Willie. LeRoy flew out of the farmhouse after him. Willie could see the two men inside the turkey pen crouching low as they moved toward the perimeter.

Grady Wheeler ran into the pen, swearing at the top of his lungs. LeRoy ran in after him, turkeys scattering in every direction. One of the panicked turkeys got caught between LeRoy's legs and tripped him.

No sooner had he hit the ground than Grady turned around and fired his gun over LeRoy's head and at the two men crawling along inside the pen.

"Come on out, you damn vermin! Try to kill my turkeys, will ya!" Grady shouted.

The man had gone crazy. Willie didn't know whether to be grateful or terrified that he was a lousy shot. So far he hadn't hit a thing, but she knew they had to get to him before he did.

Grady continued to yell and shoot as LeRoy inched toward him on hands and knees. Willie crouched against the other side of the pens, moving toward the two men in white. She turned around and saw that LeRoy had finally gotten close enough to grab the old man's legs and bring him down. But as he did, Grady managed to get off one last blast from his shotgun.

Willie heard a loud pop as the bubble covering the helicopter shattered.

"Got the damn thing," Grady whooped as he swung at LeRoy with the butt of the gun, trying to free himself from the struggling deputy. Finally LeRoy succeeded in getting the shotgun out of the old man's hands. He hurled it across the pen, toward the barn.

She saw Carl on the other side of the pen, approaching the two men from the opposite end. With a sudden burst of speed, Willie ran toward the two men. She had her gun drawn, and when she got close enough, she stood up.

"Police. Drop the cylinders," she ordered them. "And stand up. Slowly." She made certain her gun was visible. "Put your hands over your heads and don't make any sudden moves." She saw Carl. "My deputy is right behind you."

The two men looked at each other and then at the crippled helicopter, its lights flashing wildly in the dark.

Willie could tell they were looking for their pilot to help them out, but the lights prevented them from seeing whether he was still inside or had abandoned them when Wheeler's bullet had blasted the bubble.

That's one point in our favor, she thought. Apparently they hadn't yet seen Wes over by the helicopter. She assumed he had the pilot handcuffed by now.

"Come on!" she shouted. "It's all over. Stand up slowly with your arms above your heads."

The two men shrugged and looked at each other, apparently deciding they had no option. They started to do as she ordered.

Out of the corner of her eye, she could see LeRoy and Wheeler. Even though her deputy had managed to get the old man's shotgun away, they were still struggling, rolling across the pen. Wheeler managed to stand up with LeRoy firmly attached to his leg. He kicked at the deputy several times before he hit LeRoy's head, momentarily stunning him. Wheeler grabbed LeRoy's gun from his holster and stood up, shouting at the two men in white.

"I'll show you I can take care of my own," he shouted as he fired LeRoy's .38 in their direction.

Willie felt a stab of pain burn through her right hand, and the gun she held flew out of it. Thinking she must have been grazed by Wheeler's wild shot, she ignored the burning sensation in her hand and searched the ground for her weapon. The two men in front of her had the same idea.

Carl, behind the two men, started to tell them to hold it, when Wheeler fired again. Everyone hit the ground. Willie held herself against the dirt, vaguely aware of a feeling of wetness in her hand. As one of the men approached, she got up into a half-kneeling position. He reached for her shoulders, and she kicked him in the kneecap with all her strength.

The man fell to the ground, clutching at the injured area. She could hear his moans through his helmet. She looked over at the pen just as Joe made a flying tackle on top of Grady Wheeler. The man crumpled to the ground without a sound, sending LeRoy's gun hurtling through the air.

Willie turned around in time to see the other man reach for her gun and get up. Carl was behind him, and she stood her ground. Wes ran toward them from the direction of the helicopter, apparently having decided he was needed. Willie hoped he'd left the pilot helpless. But Wes had no sooner started running across the pen than the pilot yelled a warning to the man holding the gun. He whipped around just in time to catch Carl in the jaw with the butt end of the weapon, knocking him to the ground.

Willie moved quickly and kicked the "alien" in the small of the back, sending him tumbling over Carl, still clutching her gun. She placed her boot squarely on his wrist, pinning his hand to the ground.

Joe and Wes came rushing up beside her. Wes pulled the man off Carl and handcuffed him. Carl got up and walked over to the second man, who was still crouched in pain from Willie's well-aimed kick. Carl hauled him up and secured his hands behind his back.

In the middle of the turkey pen, LeRoy had come to and was bent over a subdued Grady Wheeler. It was only when everyone was accounted for that she stepped forward.

"Before we read them their rights," Willie said to Wes, still panting, "take their helmets off. I want to see who we're talking to."

Joe and her deputies were focused on the two men in white, handcuffed and standing before them. Wes and Carl unfastened the face masks from the suits and took them off. The men offered no resistance, and no one gasped as their faces were revealed.

"Homer and Doug Beede," she said slowly. "I can honestly say that this isn't a surprise." She turned to Wes. "Okay, Wes, now you can read them their rights."

Then she bent over and reached for her gun, which lay where Homer had dropped it. Joe watched her, and as she extended her right hand, she heard him gasp. Then she looked at her hand. It was covered with blood, and for a moment she thought it couldn't belong to her.

"You've been shot!" Joe rushed toward her. Carl moved in behind him.

"It's nothing," she said as she stared her hand. "I can't even feel it." Blood dripped on her gun as she held her hand out.

"Nothing, hell!" Joe said as he reached in his pocket for a handkerchief. "You're bleeding all over the place." Gently he wrapped her hand as Carl bent and picked up her gun.

LeRoy came up to them, the left side of his head already swollen from Wheeler's kick. "Boy," he said. "Who would have thought an old man could have messed things up like that! It's a miracle nobody got sh—" He stopped as he saw Willie.

"Somebody did get shot," Joe said. "I've got to get her to town."

Willie looked down at the already soaked cloth. "I'm okay," she said, this time barely convincing herself.

"Take her in, Joe," Wes said. "We can handle these guys now. We'd just better get them out of here before Wheeler comes to."

Willie felt Joe's arm around her shoulder as he led her toward the Cherokee that Carl had parked in the barn. He opened the passenger side for Willie and she got in. The keys were still in the ignition.

He backed out of the barn, and Willie leaned against the seat, suddenly dizzy. She could feel the blood seeping through her slacks and onto her legs. She tried to compress the wound with her left hand, forcing herself to concentrate on something else.

"Thanks, Joe," she finally said as he pulled onto the main road and headed toward Cisco.

"Why are you thanking me?"

"If you hadn't tackled Wheeler, things could've been a lot worse. That old man went crazy."

"Hell! I should have moved a lot sooner than I did. If I'd been quicker, you wouldn't be bleeding now." He looked over at her. "I know it hurts, but try to squeeze it," he told her. "It might help stop the bleeding."

Willie nodded and turned to look out the window. "It's really a shame," she said, more to herself than to Joe. "As much as I dislike the Beedes, I kept hoping it would turn out to be someone else."

"Like real aliens?" Joe asked.

"Maybe. Anybody but people you've known all your life."

"Greed is a powerful emotion. It's driven men and women to do some pretty insane and stupid things." Joe turned to Willie. "They're lucky nobody really got hurt. It won't go so hard on them."

Willie watched the familiar scenery roll by and closed her eyes. When she heard a siren, she opened her eyes and saw a sheriff's car pass them on the road.

"Apparently Wes called for some backup," Joe said. Willie just nodded and closed her eyes again.

Willie saw the glare of harsh lights through her closed eyelids. She opened her eyes and realized that Joe was carrying her into the emergency room.

"Put me down," she murmured weakly.

"And let you fall over?" Joe answered as a nurse came rushing up.

"It's undignified for the sheriff to be carried anywhere," she told him. "Put me down."

Joe held her tight as he followed the nurse into a brightly lit room. Finally he set her down on a table.

The nurse took her hand and unwrapped the blood-soaked cloth. Willie looked down. Under the bright lights of the examination room, she saw her wound for the first time, a hole in the middle of her hand. Her pants and shirt were covered with blood. She felt the room swim as nausea churned inside her stomach. She looked at Joe and saw him come toward her just before she passed out.

When she woke up, Willie was in a strange bed in a white room. Early-morning light filtered in through the window. One hand was wrapped in bandages, and the other had an IV sticking out of it. A dull pain spread from her arm and swept over her body. She started to move when she noticed Joe asleep in a chair by the door.

He woke up and looked at her. "Good morning," he said, and came over to the bed.

"You've been here all night?" she asked.

"All night? It was only a couple of hours." He shrugged. "I wanted to be here when you woke up."

"What happened?"

"You got shot," he told her.

"I know that," she said. "What did they do to my hand?"

"You had to go into surgery and have some bullet fragments removed. I should leave the rest to the doctor to explain."

She stared at the end of her arm, to the bandages covering her hand. "Is it all still there?" she asked.

"Sure it's all there." Joe smiled. "More or less."

"Less is my guess," she said as a middle-aged nurse came in the room.

"I see you're awake, Sheriff." The woman turned pointedly to Joe. "Which means your friend here has to go. I promised he could stay only until you woke up."

"But now that I'm awake, why can't he stay?" Willie asked, startled by the nurse's logic.

"Because you're going to go back to sleep." She brought out a thermometer and popped it into Willie's mouth before she could answer. "You lost a lot of blood, young lady. The last thing you need is company that'll only stir up what blood we just put back in."

The nurse turned around and steered Joe toward the door. He blew Willie a kiss before he left. True to the nurse's prediction, she fell asleep almost immediately.

Willie spent the next few days in the hospital. The doctor wanted to keep a close watch on how her hand was healing and told her she needed the rest. It was clear from her phone calls and messages that she had turned into Cisco's heroine. People she barely knew were calling her, wishing her congratulations and a speedy recovery. TV stations and newspapers across the state wanted to interview her. She even got a gorgeous bouquet of flowers from Diana Lawrence, who wanted Willie to know that she was still interested in doing the article.

Willie hoped that by the time she was out of the hospital, all this commotion would have died down. The last thing she wanted was this kind of attention.

Joe had added to the fuss by writing two unashamedly glowing front-page articles about Sheriff Willie Callen and her deputies. Willie blushed often, unaccustomed to being the recipient of so much praise.

Her deputies came to visit her, as did Hannah and the mayor and just about everyone else in Cisco. The county district attorney stopped by several times to work with her on the charges he planned to file against the Beedes.

When Willie told the D.A. that she thought Lucy Wiemer had been a victim, manipulated and used by Homer from the beginning, he said his office was going to hold off on any criminal charges against her. He told Willie that he'd have a hard time getting a conviction against a woman her age even if she were a mass murderer, and since her mental state was so questionable, a nursing home might be the best solution for Lucy. Willie was glad to hear that both Matt Bishop and Grady Wheeler were going to press a civil suit against the Beedes to try to collect damages for their dead birds.

The D.A. also questioned Willie about Grady Wheeler and his part in the whole episode. When asked whether she wanted to press charges, Willie hedged, then shook her head.

"I don't want to send Grady Wheeler to jail," she told the D.A. "I just want to whack him over the head a couple of times with that shotgun of his. It might knock some sense into him."

The attorney laughed and told her he'd probably have to charge Grady with something but that he'd recommend probation.

She was surprised when a contrite Grady Wheeler showed up, hat in hand, on the third day of her hospital stay.

"You don't hold that against me, do you?" he asked, pointing to her hand.

"I should," she answered. "You could have killed me or someone else."

"I just went crazy," he said as he stood by her bedside. "I thought about those aliens coming down and killing *my* turkeys, and I couldn't stand it." He wiped his forehead. "It's a good thing I didn't know it was Homer and his boys. It would have made me even crazier."

Willie shook her head. She should've been able to read his anger better and made sure he stayed away. She reached out with her left hand and touched his arm.

"The doctor tells me my hand will take a while to mend, but it should be as good as new. Just be grateful no one really got hurt."

"Thanks, Willie," the old man whispered.

Joe's visits were surprisingly short. When he did come, Willie thought he seemed distracted, preoccupied. Maybe he didn't like hospitals, she thought. Or maybe he was uncomfortable because he wanted to have that personal talk he'd mentioned. Maybe he couldn't bring himself to break the news to her, that he wanted to be "just good friends," while she was still in the hospital. All sorts of reasons and conversations swam around in her head, surfacing and then resubmerging.

On the day before she was to leave, she finally had the energy to confront him. "What's up, Joe?" she asked him.

"What do you mean?" he asked, but Willie knew he was aware of what she meant.

"You know what I mean. I think it's time to have that talk you were so eager to have."

"Talk?"

"The one you wanted to have on our way out to the Wheeler place, the one you said was personal." She looked at his blank stare. "Stop avoiding it, Joe. It's not like you."

"That talk," he finally said. "I've resolved the problem."

"You have?"

"Yes. I've come to a decision," he told her as he walked over to the window and looked out.

Willie waited a few minutes. When it was clear he wasn't going to continue, she did. "Are you going to tell me this decision?" she asked. "Or do I have go guess?"

"Oh, you'll find out," he said as he turned around and faced her. "Just as soon as you're out of the hospital and back to work."

"Why don't you tell me now?" His hedging was making her angry. "I can take it. I'm strong enough."

"I know you'rc strong enough Willie. A little thing like a bullet in your hand can't slow you down. It's just that *I'm* not strong enough, not yet."

Willie knew there was no point in pursuing the issue. She slumped against her pillows and flicked on the TV with the remote control.

Joe came over and kissed her on the forehead. It was a chaste, brotherly kiss. Then he straightened up. "The doctor says you can go home tomorrow. Do you want me to come and get you?"

"If you're busy, I can have Wes or Carl come over," she told him, not looking at his face.

"I'm not busy." He smoothed the sheets on her bed. "See you at three."

He was out the door before she dared look over to where he'd been. Willie felt tears squeeze out of the corners of her eyes and trickle down her cheeks. She buried her face against the pillow. First she'd lost Paul, and that had been difficult enough. But she had a feeling that losing Joe would be much harder.

By the time Joe showed up to take her home the next day, Willie had decided she had done all the crying she was going to do over their relationship. If Joe wanted out, then he wanted out. She knew she'd have to spend the next few years of her life being reminded every time she saw him that she still cared. And in a small town like Cisco, that could happen almost every day.

Joe's mood was light, and he seemed to find delight in trying to cheer her up, to shake her out of the "blues." Could he really be so insensitive? Willie thought. He acts as if he's enjoying every minute of this.

He saw to it that she was settled in back home and then he started to leave. At the door, he stopped and turned around.

"When do you think you'll be going back to work?" he asked.

"As soon as I can," she said, dreading another day spent alone and thinking about Joe and what had changed between them. "I'm going to stop by tomorrow morning and catch up on some paperwork."

"Good," he said. "The newspaper comes out tomorrow morning. I'll see you then." He kissed her and disappeared out the door.

Willie gazed after him. What did he mean by saying "The newspaper comes out tomorrow morning?" It always did. What was different about tomorrow? she wondered.

The next day she was late for work. Getting dressed by herself with an injured hand was harder than she'd imagined. It was almost nine-thirty when she finally parked her car in front of the courthouse.

As she walked in, Hannah beamed at her. "Good morning, Sheriff. How are you feeling?"

Willie looked at her. The woman was positively glowing. "I'm fine, Hannah. I'm feeling much better."

"I can imagine," she said. "And congratulations. I'm so happy for you," she added with a wink.

Willie walked into her office. Had Hannah started drinking? Willie had been gone only a week, and the dispatcher had already congratulated her several times on her having solved the "big case."

As she entered her office, Willie saw her three deputies huddled over her desk. They all turned around when she came in. LeRoy dropped the latest edition of the *San Juan Independent* on her desk.

"Good morning, Carl, Wes." She looked at her deputies. Something was up. "Aren't you staying a little late, LeRoy?"

He shrugged his shoulders. "I just wanted to welcome you back, that's all."

"Thanks."

The men watched her as she approached her desk. "Is anything wrong?" she asked, looking down at her uniform.

"No," Wes answered. "Nothing at all. We just thought—well, we thought congratulations might be in order."

Again the congratulations. Willie suddenly wondered if Joe had written another article about the "Big Bust." She picked up the paper and scanned the front page. No mention of Willie Callen leaped out from the headline.

"What's going on?" she asked, still holding the paper.

Carl shrugged and grinned. "Maybe you should read the paper a little closer. Then you can tell us what's going on."

She turned to the second page and scanned the stories. Then she went on, turning pages and seeing only the usual reports of all the midweek activities of a small town. She'd gotten to the last page and was ready to close the paper, when a picture caught her eye.

It was a photograph she had used for the sheriff's campaign four years earlier. She remembered telling Hannah it was the only picture she'd ever had taken that she really liked. It took a few seconds for her eyes to wander to the caption underneath.

CALLEN/KELLY ENGAGEMENT ANNOUNCED

She stared at the words. It was her name, her picture. How come she didn't know it was her engagement? She read the short article underneath.

Wilhelmina Elizabeth Callen and Joseph Patrick Kelly, both of Cisco, Colorado, announce their engagement.

The marriage will be performed in a private ceremony at the home of the groom on Wednesday, November 5. A small party will follow. The couple plan to reside in Cisco. P.S. Sheriff Willie, I love you. Joe.

Minutes passed before Willie finally looked up from the article. She could feel her blood pressure rising as she rolled up the paper and tucked it under her arm.

"Joe Kelly can't get away with this," she said. "I can't believe he would print something like this and not let me know about—" She stopped and looked up. Her deputies were staring at her. She grabbed her hat from the hook, put it on her head and walked out the door.

"If anyone wants me, Hannah, I'll be across the street." Hannah just smiled and nodded. "Of course you will."

Willie suppressed the urge to scream at her dispatcher as she walked out of the courthouse and across the street.

Debbie smiled as she opened the door to the *San Juan Independent*. "Good morning, Sheriff." She smiled. "I hope your hand is okay."

Willie looked at her. "My hand?" Then she looked down at her still-bandaged right hand. "Oh, my hand. It's better. Thanks. Is Joe in?"

Debbie nodded. "He's in his office."

Willie strode through the small newspaper office and opened the door to Joe's back room.

"Just put the proofs down on the table, Debbie. I'll get to them later," Joe said, not looking up.

"You know I'm not Debbie, you son of a—" Willie stopped in midsentence as he whirled around in his chair.

"Good morning, Willie." He grinned. "I see some things never change."

"What are you talking about?" she asked, aware of the warmth coming at her from his beautiful blue eyes.

"The way you enter my office. You're still the orneriest woman alive when you walk in here." He shrugged. "It must be the smell of the newsprint. Some people really have a reaction to it."

"You know it's not the newsprint, Joe Kelly. It's you."

"Now, that's a different story. I'm flattered."

"Don't be," she said, then walked over to his desk and threw the paper down. She pointed to the offending article. "How could you—?" she stammered. "What do you think—?" She stopped and looked at him, crossing her arms in front of her chest. "Haven't we had this conversation before?"

"That's what I mean. Some things never change." He stood up and wrapped his arms around her still unyielding body.

"Don't you think it's pretty irresponsible to print something like that? Especially when I didn't know anything about it!"

"Are you saying you want to call the whole thing off? Are you trying to tell me you don't want to marry me?" He stood back a bit and feigned shock. "Do you want to break my heart?"

"You could have asked me first." She stared up into his handsome face. The thin scar, his barometer of emotion, had turned crimson. "Why didn't you ask me?"

"I was afraid you'd say no. I was afraid you'd tell me I was crazy for thinking you'd marry an ex-football player who thought he was a newspaperman." His voice was softer, suddenly serious. "Face it. I was just plain scared."

"So you decided to announce it to the whole town before you asked me? That doesn't sound like fear, Joe Kelly. It sounds like you're damned sure of yourself."

"Just a little trick I learned from my football days. It's called strategy." Joe moved in closer and took off her hat, then smoothed her hair away from her face. When he felt her resistance lessen, he bent down slowly until his lips were near hers. "Tell me, did it work?"

Willie uncrossed her arms and let them circle Joe's back. She tilted her head up to his. "Just barely," she answered.

"You're a hard woman to please, Sheriff." He kissed her then, a long, openmouthed kiss, the kind of kiss she had been dreaming about. "But then, I suppose that's just one of your charms," he added before he kissed her again.

* * * * *